DIABHAL

# D|ABHAL

## KATHLEEN KAUFMAN

TURNER PUBLISHING COMPANY

Turner Publishing Company
Nashville, Tennessee
www.turnerpublishing.com

*Diabhal*

This is a work of fiction. All the characters and events portrayed in this book are either products of the author's imagination or are used fictitiously.

Book design: Meg Reid
Cover Design: Francois Vaillancourt

Library of Congress Cataloging-in-Publication Data

Names: Kaufman, Kathleen, author.
Title: Diabhal : a novel / Kathleen Kaufman.
Description: Nashville : Turner Publishing Company, [2019]
Identifiers: LCCN 2019006650 (print) | LCCN 2019009635 (ebook) |
ISBN 9781684423217 (epub) | ISBN 9781684423194 (pbk.)
ISBN 9781684423200  (hardcover)
Subjects: | GSAFD: Occult fiction.
Classification: LCC PS3611.A8284 (ebook) | LCC PS3611.A8284 D53 2019 (print)
DDC 813/.6—dc23

LC record available at https://lccn.loc.gov/2019006650

Printed in the United States of America
19 20 10 9 8 7 6 5 4 3 2 1

*To my husband—my sun, my moon, and all my stars.*

*Coyote is always out there waiting, and Coyote is always hungry...*
NAVAJO PROVERB

*1*

THE SLUAGH APPEARED ON A TUESDAY MORNING.
Grace was quite unaffected at the time. In fact, she was utterly
unaware of their presence for the hour it took to set the dough
to rising. She had half hung the wash before her eye set to twitch-
ing and her lips became numb. By midafternoon, her speech was
slurring and her eyes had crossed. Boyd hadn't known what to do.
For all his suspicions, he hesitated to call the elders. It could, after
all, be a case of the flu; or perhaps the grain had gone to rot, and
the ergot was causing her to mutter and her head to twitch in tiny
spasms. No need to set the elders to worrying over something that
could be cured with a night's rest. When the children arrived home
from school, their backpacks in hand, he sent them to their rooms
to finish their homework. Later he heated a can of soup from the
cupboard and sliced them both a slab of yesterday's bread. He put
them to bed and told them Momma had a fever and they shouldn't
go say good night for they might catch it as well.

Boyd sat up with his wife until the sun rose. By that time, she
was pacing the floor in uneven steps and speaking in a tongue he

did not recognize. Her eyes flitted from side to side before settling back to staring at a fixed point on her nose. She wouldn't take any water or food, waving it away and cringing as though the mere scent of the canned soup was poison. By sunrise, Boyd knew it was far bigger than ergot or influenza. The faint scent of ash emanated from her skin, and her sour breath held a hint of sulfur. Locking her in the bedroom, he readied the children to go to school. "Momma still has that fever," he told them. His girl, Ceit, fixed a long, unreadable gaze upon him as he spoke.

"You should call the Matrarc," she said simply.

Boyd knew in that instant that she wasn't fooled. He clumsily packed their lunches, unaccustomed to the task. Ceit took charge of getting her little brother to brush his teeth and to wear matching socks. By a quarter to eight, they were both out the door on the way to the bus stop. Boyd sat down at the dark wood dining table and buried his head in his hands. He should call the elders; he could feel it in his heart. He should follow Ceit's directive and call the Matrarc. But in the end his courage failed, and he phoned Grace's mother, who, while not yet the matriarch, was the one who would best be able to explain the situation to the elders.

Hoping she had somehow recovered in the hour or so that Boyd had spent getting the children ready for school, he crossed to the bedroom door and turned the handle. Grace was standing at the window staring at a point in the distance, her eyes uncrossed, focused straight and sharp at the horizon where the hills met the sky.

"They're coming," she said clearly, not looking at Boyd. Her voice was rough from disuse and lack of water.

"Who?" Boyd asked, not sure he wanted the answer.

"The Rabharta," she replied, turning from the window to regard him fully. "They're coming. They're coming. They're coming."

There was no urgency or alarm in her voice, yet it sent a wave of chill down Boyd's spine.

"Darlin', you need to take some water, some food. You need rest," he mumbled through his suddenly thickened tongue and tangled words.

Grace shook her head and turned once again to stare out the window.

"I need to see the Matrarc. But not here—by the stones." Her voice was level and definite. It was all Boyd could do to nod, even though his gesture went entirely unseen.

*2*

NO SOONER HAD BOYD PHONED MÁTHAIR SHONA
than she was at the door, a handful of fresh sage in her cloth bag.

"Na Trí Naomh," Máthair Shona said quietly as Grace sat on
the edge of the bed and stared up at her with bloodshot eyes. "We
need to call the Daoine Sìth. But not at the stones. She cannot be
out in the air."

Thus commenced the procession of elders to the small flat, with
its barren yard and leaky sinks. Boyd felt a pain in the pit of his
stomach each time the doorbell rang and another of the Society's
great revered and respected entered through the rusted screen
door and stepped onto the worn carpet. It was entirely irrational,
and yet he felt the sting of projects long neglected as the Ceannairí
sat on the sofa with the ripped cloth and set their water glasses
on the chipped and worn side table. He'd never felt his inadequa-
cies more than he did as the elders congregated in the secondhand
family room, staring at the cheap prints in flimsy frames that hung
on the walls.

"What is the condition of the girl?" asked Mór Ainsley as she sat on her throne—a giveaway Barcalounger, found on the corner a few streets over soon after Grace and Boyd had moved into this flat. They had wrestled it through their door, and Grace had wiped it down with pungent white vinegar. They had delighted at their find, the centerpiece of the family room. It was older than the children; Ceit had come soon after the Barcalounger's arrival, and Alan a bit after that. All in all, the worn leather chair had sat in the tiny flat for over ten years, grooves worn into the floor from its carved wooden legs.

Mór Ainsley sat in it as though it were woven of the finest golden thread, as was her way. The simplest cotton tunic looked to be made of the finest silk when it lay next to her ivory skin, her wrinkles running rivulets and paths that stretched to the ancient times. She was the Matrarc. As there were none who could step into the role, she kept on living; and though her age showed itself in the deep rivulets surrounding her eyes, she was as sharp and fierce as she had been in her youth.

Mór Ainsley waited for a reply. "I asked," she repeated slowly, "what is the condition of the girl?"

Boyd stepped forward. "She won't eat or drink since yesterday. She stares out the window. 'They're coming.' Asked who, and..." He trailed off, not sure how to continue.

"Who is coming?" Mór Anisley asked in a measured tone.

"The Rabharta," Boyd said quietly, knowing the words could never be taken back. "She says the Rabharta are coming, and she wants to go to the stones."

The room was silent for a moment, and then the quiet clucking of tongues rose from the silver-haired women who filled the room.

"Quiet," Mór Ainsley commanded in a near-silent whisper. Immediately the air hung in stasis, waiting for permission from the

Matrarc to circulate.

"She cannot go to the stones," Máthair Shona said as she dropped to her knees on the threadbare carpet, the bond connecting her and her ailing daughter compelling her to override the Matrarc's command. "She cannot. The dark ones will find her there. We cannot protect her at the stones if they have already touched her mind."

"Silence, love," Mór Ainsley said softly, raising a hand and shushing her daughter. "Have a sit," she stated with well-worn authority. "I need to see the girl. Can she come to me?"

Boyd nodded, though unsure if that was true. Grace had not objected to her confinement in the bedroom, nor had she tried to leave it. Would she willingly breach the boundaries to meet the elders here, in her own family room?

As he knocked quietly on the door, Boyd's heart jumped in his chest. The collection of ancient women behind him regarded him expectantly. The woman within the room was his entire heart. Her hair was golden-red, the color of sunrise and the best parts of the sunset. When she looked up at him—her face a mottle of cream and freckle—and smiled, that was all it took to lock Boyd's heart up in hers. They had been children together and matched early. He did not remember their first conversation nor the first time he heard her name, which suited her as spring suits the newborn dove. He only remembered the feeling of eternity, the newly fraught notion that his life was no longer his own; everything from this point on was for the glory of the woman in front of him. He had been playing with the idea of leaving, striking out on his own. It would have meant the end of all things here. He would have entered the outside entirely alone. But the courtship had changed all that. One full moon cycle was all they were given to determine if the match was right to be settled. Boyd had known on the first night as they walked beside the nighttime ocean, the waves rolling back into blackness. Everything had always been about her, and all the time spent without her had been readying him for that moment. He knew that at nineteen, and he knew that now as he stood outside her door, waiting to lead her to salvation or slaughter—he knew not which.

The hospital was a short distance away, the Society kept a car that sat largely unused locked in a garage at the end of the cul-de-sac, and Boyd could drive. He could get her there before noon. If he handed her off to the wrinkled faces and arthritic hands that waited in the family room, what would become of her? If he drove her to the hospital and handed her off to psychiatry and the inevitable injections of drugs, what would become of her? In that moment, Boyd stood between two equally terrible impasses. He understood Ulysses and the call of the sirens, and at the same time he heard the unyielding surge of the sea. He knew that either decision was likely to, in equal parts, break his already fragile heart and save the core of his soul. He looked back at Mór Ainsley, her silver eyes boring into his. She nodded, and he was left without decision. Boyd entered the room.

Grace was staring out the window at the horizon.

"Are we going to the stones?" she asked, her voice a low rumble.

"Mór Ainsley wants to talk first. Will you come to the other room, love?" Boyd asked gently. "Will you take some tea?"

"I'd like some tea," Grace said softly. "But the Ceannairí are wasting time. I need to get to the stones." At that, she turned to face him, her face worn from the night but her eyes shining. "I'm not myself," she said in an oddly even tone.

"No," Boyd responded, his voice cracking a bit.

"The children…" she said quietly, looking down.

Boyd dropped to meet her knees. He took her thin hands in his. "No worry, love. I told them you have a fever and are contagious.

They're fine, love, fine," he said with too much enthusiasm.

"I'm not myself," Grace repeated, her eyes focused on the grain of the wood floor.

"No matter, love. We'll fix that." Boyd stroked her hands. He stood up and leaned forward so his forehead touched the top of her head, which smelled of ash and sulfur.

"Get me to the stones," she said so quietly that Boyd had to strain to hear the whisper.

3

THE ELDERS WERE STILL SEATED IN THE FAMILY ROOM when the children arrived home from school. Ceit nodded at Mór Ainsley and allowed Máthair Shona to wrap her up in kisses and hugs, all the while her pale eyes impassive, staring at the circle of ancient women. Alan, as usual, stood back, taking stock of the situation. He was like his father, and Boyd had always known that, especially in times of crisis, it was the women who were in charge. Once released, Ceit took her brother to the next room. She would watch over him as the elders reached their decision. Boyd knew she didn't even need to be asked—ten years old and as wise as the Matrarc already. Mór Ainsley had always favored the girl. Even though in her quiet way her favor was barely perceptible, Boyd knew she was watching his pale-eyed daughter with the perpetual furrow in her brow.

Inside the bedroom, Grace continued to pace the floors. Still she refused water and food, and she ignored the tea. It was going on twenty-four hours now. Her lips were cracked and dry and her hair dull, hanging in a lank clump down her back. Boyd went back and forth between rooms. The Matrarc would not go to her, and Grace would not budge from the bedroom. Boyd understood the game they were playing. Grace was holding true to what she had said: she would talk to them at the stones. Mór Ainsley had drawn a line in the sand: she would not budge until the young woman came to her, knelt before her, and asked for healing. Neither was going to acquiesce. Boyd watched with increasing anxiety as his wife's steps became uneven and her breath ragged. She stood at the window, staring at the horizon.

"They're coming. They're coming. They're coming." She murmured over and over. Back and forth she paced, her bare feet barely leaving the floor as the weary pace became a determined shuffle. Boyd brought a fresh glass of water and sat on the edge of the bed, the weight of the expectation waiting outside the room on the worn furniture boring a hole in his skull.

"Please, love, come see the elders. Maybe then they'll take you to the stones. Maybe then you can find a way to take a drink, eat a little something."

She stared at him, her eyes catching the setting sun. Her lips parted slightly as though she were about to speak and then closed, the words quickly swallowed. Her gaze once again fixed on the horizon.

"They're coming. They're coming. They're coming." she spoke softly and rhythmically.

In the family room, a stir of movement startled Boyd. He rose and opened the door. The elders were leaving. They were standing and gathering their things. Empty teacups lay scattered on the low end table. Boyd cast a look back at Grace and then hurried through the doorway.

"Wait," he pleaded. "You cannot leave her in this state." He tried to catch Máthair Shona's eyes and failed. "What are we to do?"

"Your wife has been kissed by the Sluagh." Mór Ainsley spoke quietly. "I cannot negotiate with them. She must come to me. Until she can, whatever magic I possess is useless against them." At that, she took a step forward and Boyd stepped aside, useless to try to persuade them to stay.

"Stop." A thin but strong voice pierced the air. "Stop."

The elders turned at the sound, but Boyd knew the source before the lot of them. Ceit was standing in the doorway to the kitchen, her hair released from her long braids. She stood fixed in position, her pale eyes emanating a light that held no earthly source.

"If you leave, the Sluagh will take her before the sun rises in the sky," Ceit said firmly. "Her soul will become fodder for the dark, and they will rise back against the lot of us, taking the weakest in their wake. Which one of us will it be? I feel it won't be me... but maybe you." She pointed at an elderly woman on the periphery of the group, who took a step back at the girl's words. "Or you." Ceit pointed again and again. "Or perhaps you."

"Young one, you are crossing a line," Mór Ainsley growled, her eyes reflecting the fire from Ceit's. "You cannot speak so."

"I can, and I will," Ceit responded, her voice so low that Boyd had to strain to hear. His heart beat against the prison of his ribs. He knew this was no matter he could intervene in. Even at ten, his daughter was more heir to this line than he would ever be. If ever anyone could challenge the authority of the Matrarc, it was she.

"We're going to the stones," Ceit said with an adult firmness in her young voice. "We will go alone, or you can go and provide the protection from the Dé ocus Andé. Otherwise, we watch her wither until she dies of the thirst or the madness itself takes her whole." With that, Ceit turned and walked back into the kitchen, her small frame silhouetted in the harsh overhead light.

The group of elders paused in the doorway. Mór Ainsley's face was pale, but she did not appear angry.

"The child is right." She looked to Boyd, never quite meeting his gaze, as was her way with men. "Bring Grace to the stones in one hour's time. We will cleanse the area and prepare the deamhandíbirt."

4

CEIT LED THE PROCESSION. ALAN WALKED BEHIND THE
women, holding Boyd's hand. Grace walked on her own, strength-
ened by the decision to go to the stones.

Ceit had known since she arrived home yesterday. The story
about a fever might have fooled Alan but it hadn't her, not for
a minute. She had smelled the ash as soon as she opened the
door. She had lain on her bed, and her mind permeated the wall
between their bedrooms and connected to her mother's brain. It
was cavernous and dark, as though the poison of the Sluagh had
wormed secret passages through the fleshy matter. Voices pinged
off the sides and swirled, and Ceit had strained to hear the words
they spoke. She knew the dangers of staying too long in such a
place as this. She knew the Matrarc had once been able to do these
things and now she was blocked. Ceit also knew that no one but
she knew this—and that Mór Ainsley knew she was wise to the
façade.

The veil hid them for the most part from the late-night

beachgoers and teenagers who walked the Venice Beach board-walk. Ceit felt the veil's familiar weight hovering over them. *The elders move so damn slow*, she thought. Ceit suppressed her frustration. It was not productive here, and she needed their help in this. Behind her, her mother stumbled, and Máthair Shona steadied her. Her grandmother was strong but had never been a leader. Her mother hadn't been either. She was content with her life. She'd talked about having another baby, and Ceit had sighed at the thought. Babies and fitted sheets and soup from cans—that was the life her mother sought.

Ceit had her first vision before she was old enough to start school. She hadn't told anyone, but Mór Ainsley had known. The stain of it had permeated her luan.

The old woman had walked up to her and stared down. "You're no longer a child," she said simply. Ceit had known at that moment that, indeed, she was not a child despite the body she was forced to inhabit. The vision itself had been fearful; the first often were, Mór Ainsley told her later. She had seen the forest from the fairy stories, not the scant green to be seen in the city. No, this had been the old forest, filled with terrors. The dark ones had crawled from the treetops and down the ancient trunks to the mossy ground. They surged toward her and reached out their fingers—composed of fires long left dead—to wrap around her ankles and legs. Ceit looked to the sky and had heard the tongue in her ears.

"Tha iad a' tighinn."

They were the same words her mother had been muttering since yesterday. But the cord was not so finely wound as it was with Ceit. Her mother existed in a world of instant oatmeal and laundry detergent. Ceit did not harbor ill will toward her despite her myopic view of the world. It was not her fault her eyes did not see. Ceit had long since ceased to be a child and now walked the line between what others saw and what she knew herself to be.

She saw the fearful trepidation in her father's face at times. He knew even more, perhaps, than her mother did. Men had never held much of a place in their Society, but he managed his status with as much dignity as could be expected. He sometimes talked about moving their little family from the cul-de-sac, even though Ceit knew it would never happen. Her mother would never go, and the elders would never permit it.

They approached the spot where Mór Ainsley would need to lift the veil and allow them entrance. It was a skill Ceit would not hold until her official day of reckoning, which would never come as long as the Matrarc drew breath. The stones were dark in the light of the new moon. All the noise and activity of the beach was far behind them—whether by magic or honest distance, Ceit did not know.

She turned to face the elders. Her mother stopped abruptly and stumbled forward. Ceit took her hand and steadied her.

"It's time," Ceit said simply, and Mór Ainsley nodded.

With a simple gesture of her arms, Mór Ainsley murmured the ancient words. The stars grew nearer and brighter. The moon widened and became the full moon of the old world. The stones were no longer the sharp beach rocks filled with rats and possums; instead, the smooth white stones of the old world shone in the newly lit night.

"Let us begin," Mór Ainsley said softly.

The others gathered round in a circle. Boyd and Alan stood to the side. They were not welcome in this and knew their place. Ceit could feel the energy snapping at her heels. Grace seemed to feel it as well. She knelt in the center of the circle, her face fixed at the night sky.

"We call to the gods of the old and new." Mór Ainsley raised her voice. Around the circle, the elders murmured to themselves, the old prayers floating up to join the stars. For her part, Ceit stood silent. This wasn't what she was here for. She felt the pull of the dark sea behind her, and she suppressed an urge to laugh aloud. The ridiculous old women with their chants and prayers could not stand against the tide that was swiftly coming to shore. It would be far too late for them when the time came. Soon she would not need the Matrarc to lift the veil for her. Soon it would shudder in her very presence.

In the center of the circle, her mother curled into a ball, the Sluagh winding their way around her wrists and fingers. They were playing with her, taking their time, as Ceit knew they would. She wished her mother no harm, but sometimes harm wasn't a thing that could be avoided. The time was coming—not tonight, but soon. Behind her, the sea rose from its confines and towered overhead, a wave frozen in perpetual stasis. It was the call of the old women that caused it to behave so. The sea still believed them to be in charge. Ceit would allow them to live in that reality for a time. A reckoning was coming, and swift at that. She caught Alan's eye from the edge of the circle. The little boy's face was pale and his eyes wide. He had never been privy to the old ceremonies, and he was now only because it was their mother at the center.

*Enough,* thought Ceit with a sudden bout of impatience. With a will that overpowered the chanting of the elders, Ceit summoned the night ocean to rear back and rise. A wave rose and surged, taunting the elders huddled on the sand. With the wave of her hand, Ceit pulled it forward and then dropped it with a crash back into the sea. The chanting stopped abruptly. Mór Ainsley stared, unblinking, at Ceit. Fear passed across her face for a brief moment.

In the center of the circle, Grace Robertson moaned and writhed in the sand. The edges of the Sluagh wound their way up her legs, around her ankles. A trickle of oily blackness leaked from her mouth. Ceit braced herself as her mother convulsed and shook, then lay still. The elders whispered to themselves, charms and curses, whatever they thought would keep the darkness at bay.

In one fluid movement, Grace rose from the beach and stood tall, turning in a slow circle and locking her eyes on each of the old women who knelt before her. The irises of her iridescent eyes expanded to fill the expanse of her eye sockets. As she turned, two night-black holes took the place of her naturally pale eyes. She stopped moving when her eyes met Ceit's. In a low growl of a voice that was foreign to Grace Robertson, foreign to any living thing in this plane, she spoke.

"Careful how you enter this world, daughter." The thing that had been her mother smiled, showing a row of finely sharpened teeth. "You know less than you believe. You can live in sweet and blissful ignorance, like those around you, for all eternity if you wish." The creature at the center of the circle paused, and a forked tongue the color of ivory flicked out to lick its lips. "If you awaken, you bring me with you—you bring so many with you—and we will nurture you till you take back what is yours." The forked tongue darted in rapid circles around what had become a slit-like opening in the center of a flaccid and deformed face. "You will bring the old to the new and end the hunger of the darkness. You will bring the everlasting life to those worthy enough to demand it. Or you can go back to sleep and follow these old fools home, sleep in your bed, and remember this as a dream." The skin began to slide from the bone, and the sharpened teeth dropped one by one. Missing lips from which to speak, the sound of the voice circled in the sharp ocean air. "We will wait until you are ready to decide, daughter."

Ceit blinked, and the nightmare creature was gone. Her mother stood at the center of the circle, staring at Ceit with her sea-pale eyes, her mouth curled in a soft smile. With a start, Ceit realized this was all the elders had seen. They had not seen the Sluagh or heard them speak. They did not see them now as they lurked beneath her mother's skin. They did not know she was already dead, her soul devoured. They saw only this shell, which held a deceptive peace.

Mór Ainsley stood with obvious effort, her ancient joints fighting the gravity of the sand and night. "We need to take her home. We need to prepare. The Sluagh have a strong hold."

"It's too late," Ceit whispered.

Mór Ainsley shot her a look. The remains of a wave rolled beneath them, soaking their heavy wool skirts. "You see too much, child," she said simply.

"I feel better," said the thing that had been Grace Robertson. It smiled, and Ceit shuddered.

"Tha iad a' tighinn," Ceit murmured, and the elders stared at her, their faces impassive.

"Yes, my girl. Yes, they are," Mór Ainsley whispered.

5

CEIT SAT IN THE BARCALOUNGER, HER PALE EYES FIXED on the door to her mother's room. Mór Ainsley had been in there with three of the elders for over an hour. The others milled about the living room, fussing with the teapot and grumbling under their breath about the state of things. Her father and Alan had been banished to Máthair Shona's flat, two doors down. They had not objected to their removal, as this was not a place for men. Her father had packed Alan's toothbrush and pajamas into his battered backpack and cast worried glances at the bedroom door. Ceit had felt a wave of sympathy for him. He loved her mother, as much as anyone loved anyone in this life. Ceit did not know what or who the creature in the bedroom was. She did know that, at least for now, her mother was nowhere near. Perhaps she was still lurking inside, but the Sluagh that had risen at the stones had sapped Grace Robertson of life. The spirits had released her mother's body for the time being, leaving her a cowering shell. Only the Matrarc could bring her back, and Ceit doubted the old woman still held the power to do so. Ceit also knew that her father could not comprehend this on any level. He understood things in the way that all men in the Society understood—from the periphery.

He wasn't really her father, not in the ways that mattered in their world. The mná of the Society stood outside such confines. Ceit was fatherless. The blood that ran in her veins belonged to a line that ran the length of the ancient world.

The Sluagh were a dangerous dark; they attracted other night creatures with them. The Rabharta were a shy sort, not likely to lurk about on their own, but Ceit could smell them around the perimeters of the house. They weren't the only ones either. The Fuath called from the water that lay a few short blocks from the cul-de-sac. They would not leave the protection of the ocean, but when Ceit closed her eyes, she could see them snapping at the edge of waves and creeping as far as they dared onto land before they retreated with the tide. With a flick of her finger she attempted to turn on the overhead light. Instead it flickered, and the room stayed dark. Ceit silently cursed and tried again, focusing her energy into the task. The light overhead sputtered, and then with a pop the bulb cracked and died. The elders who wandered the room clucked their tongues. They thought her a child. Ceit did not care what they thought of her—impetuous, precocious were the most common terms, but she had heard them all.

The door to the bedroom opened. An elder named Ailsa, whose gray hair spun madly from her tight-wound bun, stood wild-eyed in the frame.

"We need water, boiled—but touch no silver to its surface. Do you have a wooden spoon, child?"

Ceit nodded and stood.

"Stir it three times once it begins to boil, and then bring it forth." Máthair Ailsa's voice was weary, and Ceit noted the bags under her elderly eyes.

In the kitchen, Ceit cast glances at the elders who tried to help her with the pot and water. They stepped back as though an electric shock had passed from her finger to theirs and then retreated to the living room. Ceit proceeded on her own, using the step stool to pull down the pot and fill it with water. The wooden spoon wouldn't save her mother, but the Matrarc was prepping for a show, and Ceit understood the need for such theatrics. Ceit could hear the Rabharta at the glass, their nails tapping the panes. They wouldn't dare enter while such a fuss was being raised. Ceit set the burner to high and turned to face the darkened window.

"Níl fáilte romhat anseo," she whispered. The ragged nails of the Rabharta pulled back, and they retreated to the darkness. They would return in time. Ceit knew it was not the old woman in the next room who would make them take their leave. She stared at the pot and the blue flame that licked the bottommost edges of its surface. The Rabharta were not the villains the elders thought them to be. They were like most things in this life—a tangle of interpretation and apprehension, an unknowable darkness that by its very nature was feared. Ceit removed the glass lid of the pot and watched as the miniscule bubbles struggled to the surface of the water. With her mother's wooden spoon, she delivered three very deliberate stirs in the direction of the waning moon.

It wasn't until she entered the great room that the clucks of the elders reminded her she hadn't worn oven mitts. Her bare fingers held the pot of boiling water, but they felt no heat. Ceit cast an annoyed glance about the room, and the chickens fell silent. At the door, she closed her eyes, willing them to hear her presence. Máthair Ailsa opened the door and reached for the water, grimacing under the heat. Ceit could see her mother lying on the bed, her hands pulled up to her neck and her face twisted in a grimace. The Sluagh slunk around the edges of the room, the Matrarc keeping them at bay for the moment. But Ceit knew it was an uneasy truce.

Her mother was weak; they would find her again if the elders did not expel the spirits from the house. The Rabharta waited outside the window, looking for a way in. Ceit locked eyes with Mór Ainsley, who seemed to have aged years in the hours spent in the room.

"Keep out, girl," she growled. "This is no place for you."

"You'll need me before the night is through," Ceit said simply, and then closed the door, leaving her mother whimpering on the bed. The little girl with the pale eyes returned to the Barcalounger and resumed her post.

6

"THE ELDERS WILL NEVER LET HER GO," BEN SAID softly. "You can call for a doctor to come here, but the old fecks will never let him in. They'll have been at it all night. Your best shot is to wait till morning."

Boyd slumped over the table, his face drawn. Alan had fallen asleep finally, his eyes red from crying. Boyd hadn't known how to comfort him. There were no words for what was happening to his mother. Alan had been scared out of his wits by the scene at the beach. The old women chanting and carrying on, and Grace, there in the middle of the lot. He hardly recognized his daughter any longer; she was as a stranger to him. Never a normal child—if there was such a thing in this place—she had now turned as one of the old ones, hidden in her child's body.

Boyd longed to get his family out of this place. They could move anywhere, even just across town for all he cared, and start over. He had carpentry skills, and he knew if given instruction he could learn more. He could carve out a life for his family away from this madness. He had talked to Grace about it a fortnight before she grew so ill, and she had quietly nodded.

"They'll try to stop us," she had murmured.

Boyd had taken her hands and looked in her unfathomable eyes. "Then we pack what we can carry, and we leave at night. I have a bit of money, enough to get us a room until I get a job. We can start over."

He had spent the whole of the next day hopeful, mentally packing his bags. The children would be fine. They knew the outside world. They attended the local school, a concession the old women had had to make after Child Protective Services had started asking questions. The whole lot of them attracted attention, and it would attract a heap more to try to bar them leaving.

But Grace had gotten sick, and all was lost. She looked as though she were already dead. A wave of premature grief overwhelmed Boyd and forced him to lean farther onto the kitchen table and swallow a sob.

"If you try it tonight," Ben was saying, "if you barge in there, I'd bet you a buck you'll never see Grace again. They'll remove you altogether. Best to wait till sunup, then we'll go get her and take the kids."

"And what of Ceit?" Boyd asked in a rough voice. "I guarantee you Ceit won't go. She's bought the line of this place hook and sinker. Jesus, you should have seen her. She's as much them as the old ones are."

"We can come back for her," Ben said fervently. "It's not like they'll hurt her. They all act like she's the next Matrarc."

Boyd nodded. "Okay," he said firmly, although his voice still shook. "In the morning, I'll bring a doctor to her if I can't get her out."

7

"TÉIGH LE SÍOCHÁIN AGUS LE GRÁ."

The chant continued as a low murmur that escaped from under the door of her mother's bedroom. At some point after midnight, as the elders lay dozing on the worn furniture, the phone rang. Her father's voice was strained, his tone agitated. He had been told not to contact the house, nothing that might serve as an interruption, but a pipe band could have marched through the flat for all the old ones in the next room were aware.

"I think I have to call someone," he said quietly. "I've been sitting on it, and your Uncle Ben agrees. We need to call a doctor. It's late now, but I'm thinking first thing in the morning. She'll be all right until morning? Right? Is she sleeping?"

Ceit sighed. Her mother had been subject to the old ones' infernal chanting for hours now. If she was sleeping, it was out of spite and perhaps boredom.

"No," Ceit said simply. "The Matrarc is trying to draw out the Sluagh. She believes if she does it before the sunrise, the Rabharta will be kept at bay."

Her father was silent for a long moment. "Ceit, my girl, I'm coming by in the morning, no matter what they've told me. Your uncle and I will be there. We'll all go together, all right? We'll take your mother to a real doctor, not the elders, and then we'll see what needs done. I know what a racket it will raise, but I can't sit back and do nothing."

Ceit nodded without speaking. The blackflies were beating themselves to death against the hall light. They had been collecting there all evening, the scent of unwashed skin and sulfur attracting them from across the veil. By morning the cloud would be so thick, she'd need to bat them outside with the hickory wood broom.

"Bring the doctor here. She cannot be moved," Ceit said. "But know the root cause of the illness has little to do with medicine. I'll take care of the elders."

"Love you, my girl," her father said sadly.

"As I do you," Ceit replied before hanging up.

She crossed back through the great room and set another pot of water to boil. They hadn't asked, but she knew they would shortly. At the window, there was a faint tap, tap, tap.

"Téigh le síocháin agus le grá."

The chant continued from the next room. The tapping matched its rhythm.

"You're not wanted here," Ceit said firmly as little bubbles rose in the pot.

Tap, tap, tap.

"You'd do well to crawl back into your hole. The elders won't have it." Ceit reached for the wooden spoon and, with three deliberate strokes, spun the boiling water into a cyclone.

"Girl!" Máthair Ailsa cried from the doorway.

Ceit appeared with the pot of boiling water, and the old woman looked taken aback. Her face had turned an ashen shade. Her wiry silver hair shot out of her bun in disrupted bursts.

"I'll take it in myself, thank you," Ceit said, shoving past the old woman, who started to object and then flopped her hands uselessly. The elders were huddled over the bed, her mother's form still except for bits of spittle that flew from her mouth.

"Téigh le síocháin agus le grá."

The infernal chanting was low and demanding. The room stank of urine and ash. Mór Ainsley looked up from her post, her eyes dark coals and her face sticky with her efforts. The room was ice cold, yet the old women's bodies had created a rank sort of humidity that hung over the occupants like a fog.

"Get out of here, girl," Mór Ainsley whispered, her voice cracking with the effort.

"I won't," Ceit insisted, taking careful steps with the pot of water as she crossed the room. She set it down on the night table next to the bed, shoving aside the empty vessel she had brought them earlier. Her mother's face was the perfect milky white of the full moon. Her eyes were open wide and stared fixedly at the ceiling. She was wearing her nightdress from the old country. It had once been ivory but now was stained black in places and torn in others. *She would be upset about that*, Ceit thought absently as she looked down at her. Her mother prized the nightdress and washed it by hand, hanging it on the line instead of feeding it to the elderly dryer that regularly singed their clothes.

Without being told, Ceit dipped a finger in the boiling water and ran it down her mother's forehead. "Múscail anois," she murmured, and her mother stopped her silent struggle and lay still.

"Listen, cailín," the Matrarc growled. "This is far beyond your sight."

"It's beyond yours, old woman," Ceit spat. She crossed to the window and examined the threshold of white heather and salt that lined the sill.

"You think this will keep the Rabharta out?" She turned to meet the eyes of the elders, who stopped their chanting and stared at her as though her red-gold hair had formed into horns and hooves. "Salt and heather—as though the Rabharta were Kelpies or the Blue Men?" With one broad stroke, she swept the tangled branches and salt off the sill and onto the floor. "No," Ceit said firmly. "You'll kill her, you will. We were shown the path at the stones, and you are playing here with fairy stories and chants as though it were 'Ridere of Riddles.'"

The elders pulled back as though Ceit had raised a fist to their very flesh.

"Fine then," Mór Ainsley said in even tones. "Let us begin Rite na Fola."

*8*

THE ELDERS HAD BACKED AWAY AND WERE LINING the wall of the bedroom. Only Ceit, Máthair Shona, and Mór Ainsley knelt by the bedside. Rite na Fola demanded the immediate bloodline of the afflicted; everyone else was useless to them in this time. The stones had shown them this path as clear as day, and Ceit still shook with frustration that Mór Ainsley had wasted so much time with the old remedies. The boiling water and the salt—children's stories for children's monsters. She wasn't surprised her grandmother hadn't intervened. Máthair Shona was a weak-minded woman, never to be the Matrarc, just as her own mother never would be either. If she'd stayed rooted on the chair in the next room, they'd have drowned her mother before dawn and the Rabharta would have marched in and picked off the weakest of the bunch with no more than a stir in the stale air. *Fools.*

Ceit swallowed her anger as the women knelt by the bedside, locking eyes with one another. Mór Ainsley would need to lead the ritual. Her place was still at the head of the family, however numbered her days might be. The dagger had been brought from the old country, its blade as sharp as it had been back in the days of the Earls of Atholl. The cuts would need to be precise and measured. Too much and the Sluagh would lap at it ceaselessly, falling into a drunken haze; too little and the iron-scented bait would fail to attract its prey. Ceit closed her eyes. She could feel the Sluagh clustering at the edge of the darkness, waiting in anticipation. They were ready to reclaim one of their own. They had been patient, and the long hours had grown their appetite.

Her mother's eyes focused, and she stared around her wildly.

"They're coming," she rasped. "They're coming."

"Yes, love, and we're here to take care of that now," Mór Ainsley whispered.

To her side, Máthair Shona wept, her tears rolling down her face in silent waves. Only Ceit was stone-faced, determined.

"It's time to begin," she intoned in a steady voice.

*9*

THE WAIL OF THE SIREN AND THE FLASHING LIGHTS
drew the old women's faces from the scene on the bed and to the
window. Mór Ainsley grimaced.

"It's her fool husband," she muttered. "Can someone take care
of this before the damnable taobh amuigh ruin everything?"

Máthair Ailsa slipped from the room. Ceit knew she was calling
Uncle Ben. Her father was past listening to reason, but Uncle Ben
had always been fast to anger and even quicker to fear. It would
take one strongly worded threat from the old woman and he would
do what was necessary to get rid of the outsiders.

Ceit sighed, the tension in the room holding fast as they waited
for the commotion outside to die away. Why hadn't her father
done what he said he would do? The morning would be different.
The old women would be asleep, and the imminent danger past.
One way or another the Sluagh would be in retreat from the light
of day. They could bring a doctor to her mother, and no one would
raise an eyebrow. But now, it was a disaster.

A moment passed, and then Máthair Ailsa returned and nodded

at the Matrarc. Ceit regarded her mother's still form on the bed. She looked as though she were sleeping. The Rabharta had fled, albeit temporarily, from the lights and the wail of the siren. For a moment, everything looked to be still.

Mór Ainsley met Ceit's eyes and stared hard at her, a slight furrow to her brow.

"It's not over, girl. You do know that, yes?" she said softly.

Ceit nodded. Already she could hear the tapping of the Rabharta's claws on the glass window pane.

"It's not," she said simply.

At that, her mother opened her eyes and locked them on Ceit. She pushed herself up and shook her arms out in front of her. Ceit looked to the Matrarc, but Mór Ainsley was staring questioningly at her granddaughter. Ceit smelled the burn of organ meat, and she felt her stomach turn to ice.

"My girl, my girl, my girl," the thing that had been her mother murmured in a voice that was achingly familiar. "Ailie Bain o' the glen, bonnie lassie, winsome lassie…" the creature sang in her mother's voice. Ceit was filled with a sudden and terrible rage.

"Shut it," she said firmly. "You're not my mother. I can see you."

The monster before her lifted the corners of its mouth ever so slightly, just enough for the ivory fork of a tongue to dart out and back in.

"Prap's not, prap's not…Ailie Bain o' the glen, Wha' could help but lo'e her…"

At that, the creature opened its lips, and from the emptiness inside a flood of ash erupted forth. Ceit cried out and was knocked to the floor, the ash invading her nose, mouth, eyes. She felt like she was drowning. She felt hands on her face, scraping the ash from her nose and mouth. She heard Mór Ainsley as though from a great distance, muttering in the old language. She heard a terrible giggle emanate from the thing that had been her mother. Finally, Ceit stopped choking and sat up, the elders lifting her and continuing to pull the sticky ash from her face.

On the bed, her mother began convulsing and fell back to the pillows. Her eyes rolled back into her head, and a thin line of blood leaked from her ear. Ceit's heart felt as though it would beat out of her chest. Instinctually, she dipped her ash-sodden finger into the pot of once-boiled water at the bedside. As white foam began to form at the corners of her mother's mouth, Ceit drew a long line of water from her mother's forehead to her chin. Instantly the convulsions stopped; the Sluagh had released their grip on her, for the time being. She curled into a ball on the bed, moaning nonsensically.

Ceit reached her hand into the water and then drew it down her own face, wiping the ash from her skin.

"We must continue with the Rite na Fola," she said softly. The Matrarc gave a silent nod.

10

BOYD PACED THE FLOOR AS THE AMBULANCE PULLED into the empty driveway. *Of course it came here,* he thought numbly. *I called from here. It came to the address.* He kept repeating the facts in his head, but it hardly made it any more real. Ben was talking to someone on the phone, he face pale as sea foam.

"Sir? Hello? Is anyone inside?" The voice on the other side of the door was strong, persistent.

Boyd opened the door and let the night air rush over him.

"Sir? We received a distress call. The details were unclear. Are you in danger, sir? Is someone injured?" The paramedic couldn't be over twenty years old, a baby with no idea of what he'd stumbled into.

Boyd started to speak. "It's my wife. She's not—"

He was cut off by Ben barging past him toward the paramedics. "I'm so sorry, officers. It's my brother who called you. He's not thinking right."

The paramedic narrowed his gaze and looked past Boyd and Ben into the living room. "Is there someone here who needs medical attention?"

Ben shot Boyd a look of pure terror. "No, sirs, and we apologize for making you come out all this way. My brother, he's out of his head. I think he hit the drugs. We were smoking a joint, and it hit him the wrong way, if you know what I mean."

Boyd was stunned. He stared at Ben and then at the parmedics. "No, no… it's not that. I'm fine. I called. It's my wife—"

"Who ran off and left you today, and thus we're here, right?" Ben interjected.

The paramedic quickly glanced at the others standing behind him and then turned back to face them. "We'd like to examine you—both of you," he said.

Boyd could tell that Ben's half-composed story was not convincing. "My wife needs help. She's sick." Boyd tried to explain but found his tongue tripping over itself in its exhaustion. Ben slammed the door shut in the stunned parmedics' faces. They immediately began banging loudly on the surface.

Ben turned to Boyd with a fever in his eyes. "For god's sake, just trust me. They'll fucking kill her if we don't get rid of this."

Boyd shook his head, confused. "But you were the one who said we should barge in, take her ourselves."

"I know what I said, and you have to trust me that we can't do this right now," Ben said urgently.

Boyd nodded numbly and opened the door. He consented to getting a light in his eyes and his blood pressure taken before the paramedics told him to drink lots of water and maybe have a bite to eat.

Later, as the two brothers sat on the sofa together, Boyd stared at a fleck of chipped paint of the wall opposite him.

"I don't care what you say—I'm calling again when light breaks." Boyd's voice was soft but firm. He ony hoped morning wouldn't come too late.

## 11

"RITE NA FOLA IS A SACRED RITE OF OUR PEOPLE," intoned Mór Ainsley. "It is to be conducted only in the most dire of circumstances, and only the Matrarc can lead it."

The old women huddled along the wall of the bedroom, listening raptly. Ceit knew that despite their collective age, most had never seen Rite na Fola performed. She certainly hadn't, only read of it in the ancient books Mór Ainsley had brought with her from Cork when she was young.

"We use the sacred athame brought from the old country, blessed in the fairy rings of our ancestors."

The Matrarc held a small bronze-and-steel dagger aloft, making a show of displaying it to her audience. Ceit sighed with impatience, but she knew the theatrics were part of the ritual. The telling was as much for the spirit realm as it was for the living. It was a warning of sorts, a chance for the Sluagh to leave of their own accord.

"Only the direct blood of the cursed is allowed in the inner circle." The Matrarc motioned to Ceit and Máthair Shona, and the rest of the old women who filled the room pressed themselves closer to the wall. "We will draw the Sluagh and their coward companions the Rabharta to us through the blood and then drive them out. The Rabharta will flee first, and we keep the window open to allow them to go back to the darkness." The Matrarc motioned to the open window from which the autumn Santa Anas whipped in and set the remnants of the white heather and salt on the windowsill to stirring in the air.

"The Sluagh will lust for the spilled blood of the cursed and her kin. When they have gathered, I will cast them out before they drain our Grace of her life entirely. If we fail and the Sluagh take her final breath, then her soul will wander with the restless dead for eternity." She raised the athame over her head dramatically, and Ceit withheld her frustration. She had seen the Sluagh speaking through her mother at the stones and doubted there was anyone left to save. However, the Matrarc sensed that her mother was still present, so Ceit tried to swallow her doubt.

"Téigh le síocháin agus le grá."

The elders chanted the phrase in hushed voices; the effect was of a thousand whispers dancing in the wind that tore through the space. The first hairline cut was to be made over the area of the spleen. The old books talked of the humours, which Ceit knew to be nonsense, but nonetheless the tradition was part of the magic. Mór Ainsley held the dagger with a steady hand and ran it gently over Grace's pale skin. A ribbon of bright blood immediately rose to the surface and began to trail down her waist. Máthair Shona took the dagger and ran another hairline split the length of the liver. The sticky crimson seeped to the edges and ran freely. Throughout, Grace lay still, her eyes wild, looking from side to side. She muttered words that had no place in mortal ears. Ceit was the only one who heard. The others saw her lips move and heard nothing other than the low scraping of the Sluagh as they skulked through the shadows of the room.

The dagger was gingerly passed to Ceit, who held its bronze-and-steel weight in her small hand. It had always been this way; she had held the dagger in the ancient times as she did today, her form changed but the memory intact. Feeling the draw of the Rabharta as they peered trepidaciously through the open window, she raised it over her mother's exposed center. Letting the blade guide itself, she allowed it to graze the skin until the blood rose to the line. Her mother gasped and continued her unearthly murmuring. The Sluagh waited with still breath from the shadows. Most of the elders had left the room, joining the others outside the door. Those who remained held their useless twigs of white heather and murmured their inconsequential words.

"Téigh le síocháin agus le grá."

The Matrarc nodded, and Ceit handed her the dagger. Mór Ainsley pulled it down her own palm and laid her bloodied hand on the black-red gore rising from the first cut. They continued in a circle until three hands and four generations of blood inter-mingled. Mór Ainsley nodded again at Ceit, and they began the summoning—low words, barely audible, in a language long since extinct that predated even the Gaelic of the ancient world. No, these words belonged to the fae folk and were spoken by human-kind only when the need was most dire.

Ceit closed her eyes and felt the air beginning to stir. The forces from the edges of the room began to lift. Soon the Sluagh would leap to the center, hungry for the spilled blood, careless in their lust. In that moment, Mór Ainsley would have the window she needed to plunge the dagger into the center of the blackness and disperse the demons into the night. The blood would then be mixed with the coarse black earth of the garden and sprinkled in a circle around the house until the Rabharta and all the night creatures grew tired of their game and left the house alone. If they succeeded in driving out the Sluagh and chasing off the vermin, her mother would return to them and all would be as well as it could be for a time. That is, Ceit shuddered, if there was anything left of her mother that could return.

The slow scraping of claws across the wooden floor set Ceit's hair to rise on the back of her neck. Next to her, Máthair Shona stumbled over the ancient chant and then regained her pace. The Matrarc raised the dagger high over her head, her eyes wide, the pale hue catching the glow from the bedside candle, dancing in the shadows. Ceit could feel her mother's skin growing clammy and knew that she did not have much time left. The Rabharta were watching from the shadows. They would take their cue from the stronger evil. They would wait until the Sluagh were satiated and then unite to drink the last drops of her mother's blood and call Grace Robertson's spirit into the never-ending night.

The Sluagh pushed their way into the circle. Every touch of their rotting and desecrated flesh made Ceit shudder with disgust and something as close to fear as she had ever felt. Just as they were about to make their plunge, and just as Mór Ainsley was to drive the dagger into the center of their darkness, the Matrarc ceased to chant and locked eyes with Ceit. In that instant, Ceit knew it was too late. Grace had been but a distraction. The Sluagh claimed the blood they desired. Storm clouds rolled through Mór Ainsley's eyes, and she lunged toward Ceit, the dagger high in her hand, her mind already rotted through with the haunted imagining of the restless dead. Máthair Shona screamed and fell back. Ceit reached out and grabbed the ancient blade with her bare hand, not feeling the cut of her flesh nor the free-flowing blood that spilled over her mother's still form.

"Ar ais go dtí an dorchadas," she whispered, her voice a steady flow that filled the room. The remaining elders screeched and ran out the door, which then hung open, the light from the next room an unwelcome force. The Sluagh dove for the freshly spilled blood. It was too much; the Sluagh would consume it and her mother. The Rabharta arrived to join in the feast. Ceit had seen this moment in dreams for as long as she remembered. Wrenching the dagger from the old woman's hand, she grasped it with both hands, ignoring the fresh flow of blood from her palm. She plunged it downward straight into the tangle of souls that fed on the living. With an inhuman cry that sounded of the spring lambs and all things that die in terror, the Rabharta fled to the shadows and out the cracks and breaks in the wooden house, back into the night.

On the bed, her mother lurched, the dagger sticking out of her stomach, her own blood mixing with her daughter's. Grace Robertson's eyes opened wide, and her lips pulled back in a strangled grimace. The ivory forked tongue escaped between her pale lips and scanned the air.

"Be careful how you enter this world, daughter," the thing whispered. "Are you ready to welcome your true self? Are you ready to open? This one is ours already, but we are so hungrrrryyyy…" The last syllable became a schreeching wail, one that pierced Ceit's ears and made her lose her balance for the intensity of the sound. Grace's pale eyes, so much like Ceit's, fixed on Mór Ainsley. The Matrarc started rotating in slow, deliberate circles, her eyes rolled back so only the stained sclera showed. She was muttering, the Sluagh feasting on her even as they came and went freely from every pore of what had once been Grace Robertson. Ceit doubted there was even a scrap remaining of her mother in the decaying form on the bed. The Sluagh had used her as a path to the one they truly desired. The darkness was circling in Mór Ainsley, ready for a final assault.

Ceit locked eyes with the old woman. With a power that

had long lain dormant, with scarely a breath to reconsider what she must do, Ceit reached far into the darkness and tried to pull the retreating forms of the Rabharta from the edges of the night. She felt her power waver and her invisible grasp slip. She needed their noise and chaos right now. She needed the Sluagh to look away for a moment, just a moment, and she could free her great-grandmother from the grasp of the Sluagh as they lapped the blood from her veins. But the terrified and cowardly Rabharta screamed their way into the night, escaping Ceit's grip and fleeing to the farthest corners of the darkness. The old woman's lips parted in a cry of rage and delight. She lunged at Ceit, the Sluagh controlling her dying brain. The Sluagh would devour her entirely in a moment's time, and Mór Ainsley's soul would be locked in step with them for eternity. Ceit looked around the room frantically. She needed to interrupt their feast.

The Matrarc shook as though a bolt of electricity had run its length through her elderly body. Ceit fell back, desperately grabbing the still-lit candle from the bedside. The old woman leaped toward Ceit, her lips moving silently, the Sluagh coursing through her already stiffening flesh. Ceit plunged the flame into her chest. The Matrarc lunged back in shock and pain. Ceit collapsed to the floor. It had been the interruption she needed. She saw the old woman suddenly snap out of the spell the ancient evil had cast upon her, convulse, and clutch her chest. The Sluagh, expelled from her form, emitted from their many mouths a roar of anger and frustration that shook the walls. On the bed, her mother's eyes rolled back in her head and she shuddered. In shock, Ceit watched her great-grandmother draw her final breath, her body free from the cursed Sluagh, her soul free from the restless dead. The Santa Ana winds rocked the tiny bedroom, and the Sluagh were swept out in a rage. Ceit's mother lay dying, blood hemorrhaging from the wound in her gut. Her great-grandmother was still, her open eyes locked on the heavens.

"Call the hospital," Ceit said to Máthair Shona.

*12*

CEIT WAS BROUGHT BACK TO THE TINY FLAT IN THE
cul-de-sac one last time after "the incident," as everyone referred to
it. She was to collect her things—one bagful, they had told her. Ceit
hadn't needed one bag. She was ready to leave behind the rough
wool dresses and solid shoes. She packed a few books, including a
book of fairy stories with crumbling pages that her mother used to
read to her at night when she was very young, and a delicate gold
chain on which hung a golden crescent moon. Strictly speaking, it
was her mother's, but Ceit knew she would never claim anything
in the house as hers ever again. She took a soft knit cardigan from
her mother's closet and the bronze pocket watch and chain that
her father had kept on his waistcoat. Again, Ceit knew the item
would go to waste. The child protection officer charged with the
unsavory task of supervising the process stood in the hall.

"Don't you want to pack your clothes?" she asked in a voice
mixed with confusion and wariness.

Ceit took a breath and turned her eyes to the stern woman

standing in her hallway. Looking up, her lip quivering just enough to be noticed, she widened her eyes just a bit and said in a soft voice, loud enough to hear but soft enough to make the officer in the navy-blue pantsuit and ill-fitting sturdy shoes take a step forward, "All those things...they remind me." Ceit took a calculated pause and started again. "I just want to be a normal girl."

The officer's masklike face twitched. She wasn't supposed to indulge the girl—get in and out and don't let the child manipulate the situation. Though only a ten-year-old girl, she was a person of interest in her own grandmother's death and the attempted murder of her mother. Ceit could read these thoughts like a banner in the sky as they rolled across the woman's mind. *Get her in and out and don't listen to any of her stories,* the ice-faced officer thought desperately. *Get out before noon, get her back to the group home, go back to the station, never see her again.* Ceit gave a small smile, not too much or it would look as calculated as it truly was. *No one in her entire family wanted this one,* the officer practically screamed in her thoughts.

As they had pulled up, ancient eyes from the cul-de-sac had peeked from blinds and then slammed them shut. The officer couldn't possibly have known, but Ceit knew they were sprinkling salt around the perimeters of their houses as she stood there. White heather wreaths hung on every door. The officer hadn't taken note, but Ceit had. The elders who had been in the room on the night of the incident were being investigated for their roles in Grace Robertson's injuries and Ainsley Robertson's death. Some were back in their homes under heavy watch and parole.

"Please, is there a way I can get some clothes like other kids have?" Ceit said softly, allowing her lip to quiver and a tear to form in her eye. It was a bit much even for her, but it was either the theatrics or else they stand in this damnable hallway for the next hour.

"Yeah, okay. I guess I can see your point. I'll bring it up to your caseworker, kid," the officer said, her voice softer than it had been all day.

Ceit grabbed a rag doll with a missing eye off her bed before closing the door behind her. She had never played with dolls— never played at all to be honest—but this had been her mother's, all the way from the old country, passed on to her from Máthair Shona. It held the residual power of her family, and that was always useful. The effect, as she stepped into the hallway ready to leave, was of a very young girl with pathetic little, carrying a tattered doll. The stern child protection officer's veneer cracked, and she took Ceit by her free hand to lead her to the car out front.

"Jesus, kid, it's like a whole other world here." She breathed the words as she held open the door.

"It is indeed," Ceit responded simply.

Ceit did not mind the Open Arms Home for Children. The other girls were a bit older and as such left her be. She shared a dormitory-style room but had been given the farthest bunk, against the wall, next to the window. There was a bed above hers, but the occupant paid her no attention, and the others avoided her when they could. They had heard her story; they knew why she was there. Ceit stayed to herself, ate as little as she could at mealtimes, and kept to her bunk, reading the fairy stories over and over and listening to the other girls' thoughts. It wasn't a thing she was always able to do; even the slightest guard could keep Ceit from another's mind. These girls, however, left behind and unheard as they were, practically screamed their every thought. *They worry about such mundane things*, Ceit thought. One girl had a crush on a male counselor who worked in the boys' wing of the home. She fixed her hair and pinched her pale cheeks, as though he would ever notice her. They were allowed a bit of television every night, but Ceit ignored it. She'd never had a television in her house, and the swirling drama inside the heads around her provided much more entertainment.

The Rabharta tapped on the window at night. Ceit was tempted to throw open the glass and let them in. They had run from her when she needed them, and now they hung about as though asking forgiveness. Ceit had no patience for it. The chaos they could cause would be entertaining at least. But she remembered her lost grip on their darkness on the night of the incident, and she doubted her ability to control this force. She cursed her small frame. She needed more years training with the Matrarc, and that chance had been destroyed. She was alone here, and apart from what equated to parlor tricks, she was powerless.

The other girls already thought her odd even though there was no way they could know how easy it was to read their thoughts or predict their actions. One night, a girl with cocoa skin and great dark eyes sat on the end of Ceit's bed. Ceit looked up at her calmly and smiled. The girl was nervous. She had lost the bet. The others had been talking about Ceit when she couldn't hear, and this girl, with her rough, unkempt hair and crooked teeth, had been nominated to ask the question. Ceit knew she was coming, of course. She had heard all their secret giggles and whispers. The rumors were she had killed her own grandmother or alternately that her grandmother had tried to kill her. Some girls had heard that she had stabbed her mother. Others thought the scars that lined her hands from the ancient dagger (currently sitting in the evidence lockup at the local police station) were evidence that she had stopped her grandmother from stabbing her.

"Hi," the girl said nervously. "I'm . . . I'm Desiree. Um, I haven't really talked to you before," Desiree stuttered. Ceit did nothing to set her at ease; her discomfort was delicious.

"I, um, I...just the other girls and I were wondering..." She trailed off.

"Did I kill my grandmother? Try to kill my mother?" Ceit asked bluntly, making sure to keep her voice level and tinged with little-girl sweetness. She reached to her side and grabbed the rag doll, holding it to her chest. The effect was exactly as she wanted. Desiree cringed, her face contorting with silent reaction.

"Why wouldn't any of my family take me? I must be guilty, right? But if I am, why didn't they do anything? Why am I here instead of in juvie? Or maybe I should be tried as an adult, if I killed someone and tried to kill another. I should be in jail, right? Will I try to kill you next, or them?" Ceit pointed at the peeking faces of the girls who huddled on a bed at the far end of the dormitory. Ceit cast a sympathetic look at Desiree, who acted like she wanted to flee and never return.

"Look, I'm sorry. It's just, we're...you're so quiet, and we...Jesus, I shouldn't have said anything. Never mind, okay?" Desiree popped up, hitting her head on the bunk over Ceit's.

"No, I want to tell you. Come closer." Ceit leaned forward. Desiree sat back down, her whole body shaking. Ceit leaned in and whispered in the girl's ear. "My grandmother was killed by demons, like Freddy Krueger. They are out there, right now in the night, waiting for you to fall asleep." Ceit leaned back and motioned to the window with her chin. "Right now, look closer..."

Desiree's face twisted with an urge to vomit or scream. "Fuck off! That's, that's...Jesus, bullshit." Her lip quivered slightly, betraying her angry tone.

"It's okay. As long as you don't go outside, they'll never find you. Now go tell your friends what I told you. And leave Jesus out of it—he has no part in this."

Desiree stumbled backward and ran out of the room. Ceit

leaned back and grinned, picking up the book of fairy stories. Truthfully, it was bullshit; the Rabharta had no interest in Desiree or her giggling friends. But Ceit knew it was better they fear her and keep their distance than know the truth. That would really terrify them.

13

PROGRESS REPORT, TEN WEEK
Subject: Ceit Marie Robertson
DOB: 10/15/1975

Ceit Marie Robertson was enrolled in the Open Arms Home for Children ten weeks prior and has been in residence since that time. In addition, C. Robertson has been enrolled and is attending Carthay Center Elementary School, fourth grade. Her academics are quite advanced. Her reading level tested post–high school level and mathematics was far beyond the elementary-grade level. She is bilingual, her second language being Irish Gaelic, which was reported to be widely used in her family group.

Academically, C. Robertson is progressing well. The concerns among her counselors and teachers have been social in nature. The other girls at Open Arms Home have reported a degree of trepidation toward her, and as such, the child is isolated. In school, she is much the same. Group projects and activities are a particular struggle.

She is receiving therapy sessions from Dr. Todd Harrington, who specializes in child psychology. Physically, her wounds healed, and her scars are minimal. Emotionally and socially, it is impossible to tell how her past upbringing will continue to affect her. Dr. Harrington's report follows.

At this point, it is recommended that C. Robertson stay in the custody of the Open Arms Home and the petition for custody made by her father, Mr. Boyd Robertson, be denied on the grounds that B. Robertson is still an active witness in the impending trials and his living situation is unstable. This matter is due to be rereviewed pending changes in B. Robertson's status.

*14*

AFTER HER CONVERSATION WITH DESIREE, THE OTHER girls avoided Ceit entirely. Ceit enjoyed the relative power that came with being a pariah. She enjoyed the worried looks the counselor cast her way. She enjoyed the sessions with Dr. Harrington, and she made sure to bring the rag doll to every session. Its mere presence was enough for him to immediately soften his voice and talk to her as one damaged, one who had been ever so terribly abused and was too stupid to know the extent of it. It was, of course, basely offensive on many levels, but entertaining on so many others.

In truth, Ceit's childhood had been rather mundane. By and large, the Society—no matter how they had been painted in the newspapers since the Matrarc's passing—valued quietude and peace beyond anything else. It was the root cause for the near-total isolation that they practiced. Ceit had read the papers; she knew that the city was investigating. Did they have weapons? Was child abuse going on? Some sort of perverse child pornography ring? Or were they dealing drugs? She smiled at the thought of any of the elders ever venturing near a drug dealer or looking at anything so scandalous as pornography. No, they were a quiet lot. The thing that made them exceptional and strange was far beyond the grasp of those who led such queries.

Dr. Harrington tried to get her to talk about the incident. When she would not, he tried to get her to speak of her everyday life in the Society. How was school? Ceit had told him about her elementary school class and the Christmas pageant where she had played a sheep in her class's depiction of Christmas in Australia. The doctor had looked surprised, and Ceit had suspected her thick case file had neglected to mention that she and Alan had attended Westminster Avenue School, close to their house. No, the good doctor had assumed that she and the other children of the cul-de-sac were shut-ins. There weren't many children in the cul-de-sac, and she knew the elders had been skeptical of allowing access to public school. Nonetheless, Ceit and Alan had left every day to go to school and returned in all the usual ways, by bus and foot. The elders shopped at the market. Occasionally, her mother and father took her and Alan to movies. The reality of the Society was so much duller than Dr. Harrington's vision. It seemed a shame to disillusion him. So instead of focusing on the creeping regularity of their lives, she focused on all the things that set her apart—like the dresses made from wool imported from the old country.

"Why were you made to dress in such a way?" the doctor had asked.

Ceit had shrugged. She liked her new KangaROOS sneakers with the pockets and her denim pants. Her T-shirt had PAC-MAN on the front. Although she had never played the game, she enjoyed the image of the little circle devouring everything in its path. But why the rough woolen dresses? In a very patient voice, Ceit explained that the elders believed that they needed to maintain a connection to their bloodline, and that was done by maintaining the old ways. The dresses were but one way.

"What else?" the doctor probed.

Ceit sighed. It was everything, but nothing to the eye. The way they addressed each other, the meals they ate, the bread that was made from the same yeast that had been brought from the old country a hundred years prior, or so the story went. Ceit had always doubted the veracity of that particular story. But at the same time, if anything was to last a hundred years, it would be the rot of a dying world.

How had her parents met? Her father? Was he a good man? The doctor's questions went on and on. When Ceit tired of answering, she'd pull the rag doll to her chest and blink tears to her pale eyes. Instantly, Dr. Harrington would cease his inquisition and offer her a tissue, maybe a candy from the jar on his desk. "Would you like to draw a bit?" he would ask. Ceit would offer a small, sad nod and sit at the child's table in the center of the room while Dr. Harrington made notes on a pad of paper.

One day, perhaps, she would tell him exactly what the core of the Society was—had been, really. It would crumble now that the Matrarc had passed and they had cast her out. She was next in line, and they all knew it. Without her, the Society would fade from the earth, a forgotten oddity, a story told to the new homeowners who would buy up the dilapidated houses as the occupants died off. The houses—flats as the Society referred to them, as though they were still in Cork—would be bulldozed and replaced with modern structures with tall glass windows and balconies on the roof to allow views of the ocean. The Society was dying, and the old magic that ran in their blood would die with them. Ceit smiled at the thought and drew a row of neat houses with white fences, red flowers in the windows. One day she might tell the doctor exactly what had caused Mór Ainsley to try to drive the ancient dagger into her heart, but not today. Today she drew a child's picture, a prop in the same way the damnable doll was, a distraction, a way to bide her time. Without the drag of the Society, the world was open to her, and her power was growing.

*15*

SESSION NOTES: 01/05/1986

Subject: Ceit Marie Robertson (hereafter referred to as CR)

Doctor in Session: Dr. Todd Harrington (hereafter referred to as TH)

*The following is the official transcript of the recorded session on the date noted above.*

TH: What would you like to talk about today, Ceit?

CR: I had a nightmare last night.

TH: Can you tell me about it?

CR: (indistinct rustling) I don't really remember, but I was home and Mother was there. She was scared.

TH: Do you know why she was scared, Ceit?

CR: Don't know. Grandmum and Great-Grandmum were there too, but they didn't see me.

TH: Ceit, do you remember the night your mother was hurt? The night your Great-Grandmum died?

CR: How do you know my dream was about that?

TH: I didn't say it was. Do you think that is what your dream was about, Ceit?

CR: I don't want to talk about my dream anymore.

TH: All right, Ceit. Do you want to talk about the night your mother was hurt?

CR: I don't remember.

TH: That's fine, Ceit. That's what we're here to work on. How far before that night can you remember?

CR: I don't want to talk about that.

TH: Okay, Ceit, let's start with something else.

CR: I'd like to draw now.

Session Ended

Notes:

*We have recorded sessions in which the subject, Ceit Robertson, described the incident that led to Ainsley Robertson's death and Grace Robertson's injuries in clear detail. She alternately claims to have no memory of the incident. It is not known why she is either unable or unwilling to discuss it in regular sessions. Post-traumatic stress may be to blame, coupled with the shock of leaving her family and community. Continued treatment is recommended.*

*16*

ON A PARTICULAR TUESDAY MORNING TOWARD THE
end of January, Ceit's class was filed into the tiny library and was
made to sit cross-legged on the rough carpet. Ceit, as usual, sat by
herself in the back row. She was wearing a T-shirt that had a rainbow unicorn on the front and sandals on her feet that showed off
her toes. Ceit was glad to be rid of the rough woolen dresses and
sturdy shoes. They had always been far too hot. Even the elders
would admit it during the summer, and they would occasionally
allow the children to run about in their undershirts.

Ceit wondered what was befalling the Society now. She tried
to find out from Dr. Harrington, but he avoided her questions in a
way that said she, a child, couldn't possibly be interested in all that.
But she was, and Ceit would find out.

On the night of the incident—so soon after Samhain—as
her mother lay bleeding, the utterly useless Máthair Shona had
stretched herself across the body of her daughter and wept. Ceit
had walked into the next room to discover the elders shrieking and

muttering curses. Though her blood flowed from her hands, she had not grown light-headed. Her pale eyes full of fire, she stared down the room. The useless old women shrank back. It had been the wretched Máthair Ailsa who took her by the shoulders and stared her down with her withered eyes. Ceit had known then that she was out. As a child, she was helpless to fight the room of scared old women. Máthair Shona would follow her pack and refuse to accept taking over her care. Her father had never been a part of them, not really. None of the men were. He had been tolerated for her mother's sake. Ceit had known that was the first moment of her otherness.

"Beidh meas ann," Ceit had said. At that, she'd walked out to the front stoop and waited for the shrill whine of the ambulance.

But here she sat on the rough, worn library carpet while her teacher—another old woman with skin as tough as the carpet on which she sat—adjusted the television set. A space shuttle was launching today. On it was a teacher with curly brown hair. Ceit's class had written the teacher letters to take into space, but that had been long before Ceit had joined them. Ceit knew what she would've written, although she doubted it would have done much good. She had seen this play out in her dream the night before.

In her dream, she was walking down a long metal corridor. She was to press a particular button. Outside the metal walls, the icy blackness of space awaited. As she approached a hulking steel-gray door, Ceit lifted her hand in front of her face and waved it back and forth, the image leaving blood trails in the air. She pressed a large panel with multicolored lights, and the door receded. Inside was a chamber, devoid of anything barring cold metal walls. In the dream, Ceit's hands bled freely, as though they had just been cut, the iron-black substance clawing its way out of her skin and circling her in a sort of dance. Ceit turned and spun as the great metal door closed behind her, sealing her in her own tomb.

Ceit hadn't known what it meant, but now she did. She could taste the fear of the seven souls as they waited, strapped inside their tomb. They would feel everything, know everything. Their stomachs would drop as they plunged back to the earth. Bile would rise from their guts. They would claw at their restraints, desperate to escape their fate. It made the blood rush to Ceit's head, and she felt a wave of light-headedness. As the announcer on the television prattled on and the children around her shifted in anticipation, Ceit raised her hand.

"I need to use the restroom," she said.

"Good lord, child, you'll miss the whole thing. Can it wait?" the old woman at the front muttered with impatience.

Ceit shook her head.

"All right then."

Ceit rose to her feet just as the shuttle launched into the sky. A milky-white wave overtook her vision. Her heart raced, threatening to escape from her chest. She reached for something, anything to steady herself, and found only air. She knew she was falling. The blood from her hands floated into the sky around her, and she twirled as it formed dark-iron ribbons in the space. Around her the steel walls grew smaller as her tomb shrank and heaved. She felt the stab of panic as the seven souls in their sealed mausoleum became suddenly, deathly aware that they would all die. As she fell, she heard the gasps of the other children, the shriek of her old-woman teacher, and the concrete impact of her head hitting the worn gray carpet.

Incomprehensible words surrounded her, the hot breath of the other children in her face, the touch of their sticky fingers as they pawed at her, trying to rouse her.

"Back up, everyone, back up." A muffled sound filtered through the overwhelming din. Silence and then, "Jesus. Jesus." And all the fingers and breath receded from Ceit's still form in a rush. Ceit knew it had happened, even though she lay blind and immoble on the floor. The orange-fire blast from the shuttle had filled the screen. The sound of soft wails filled the room.

"Get them out, back to the classroom. I'll get the nurse for this one." The orders emitting from another adult voice sounded as though they were a thousand miles away. There was the clammer of footsteps and doors slamming, and then Ceit lay still on the worn gray carpet, alone with the seven souls in their metal tomb as they plummeted to their fates.

*17*

CEIT WAS SITTING IN THE FRONT ROOM, READING A paperback V. C. Andrews novel. The counselor had tried to take it away earlier. It wasn't for her, she'd said; Ceit was too young. But after Ceit had fixed an icy stare at her, the woman shuffled off, muttering about the older girls leaving their things about.

Ceit didn't care a bit about the age appropriateness. She liked this silly story. A girl with the improbable name of Heaven was living in the Ozark Mountains, complete with an outdoor privy. Heaven was walking her myriad of brothers and sisters down a mountainside to school when Ceit was interrupted by the doorbell ringing. Ordinarily, answering the door was strictly reserved for staff. The girls were not to answer nor invite anyone into the home. Ceit looked around. Seeing no one, she carefully folded the corner of her novel and set it aside.

Ceit stood staring at the young man in his crisp white button-up shirt, the outline of an undershirt barely visible. He had pens in his pocket and a dark backpack strapped to his back. His hair was neatly combed—too neatly for Ceit's taste—deliberate, as though he had spent a great deal of time figuring out exactly what impression he wanted to make that day. He held a book with no title on the spine, but Ceit knew exactly what it was. Before he even opened his mouth, she knew he was a missionary. There was a temple down the street. She had often heard various counselors talking to the young men who rang the bell while holding books and wearing backpacks. They were not to come around here, they'd said. Take us off your list, they had demanded. Still they came. In a house full of so many lost girls, there were far too many opportunities for salvation.

"Hello there, young lady!" the man said in a falsely chipper voice.

Ceit stared at him and nodded toward the book.

"Book of God?" she asked flatly.

The young man looked taken aback. "In a manner of speaking, yes, it is, miss. My name is Elder Nathan, and I would love to talk to you about the Church of Jesus Christ of Latter-day Saints."

Ceit considered the request. Her paperback novel was just getting good. Heaven was beginning to flirt with her own brother, which Ceit found in equal measure revolting and intriguing. Still, Nathan looked fun, and it had been so long since she had had any fun. Since she'd fainted at school, the counselors were treating her as though she were made of glass. Her teacher with the leathery skin had requested she be moved to the other fifth-grade class. No explanation had been offered to the group home, and in lieu of a parent who actually cared, her caseworker had simply acquiesced. So Ceit had found herself in a new room full of suspicious eyes. She sat in the corner and half-listened to all the lessons she already knew. She grew a sprout from a bean in a cup. She wrote paragraphs with nicely phrased hook sentences. She did her long division without a calculator. Ceit was biding her time. But Nathan looked fun, and his book was sure to be nearly as intriguing as V. C. Andrews.

"Sure. C'mon in," Ceit said brightly.

Nathan looked shocked. He stuttered a bit and then entered through the open door. Ceit motioned to the messy arrangement of sofas and chairs that made up the front room. Nathan sat down, and Ceit sat across from, considering her approach.

"Well, thank you for the invitation. I love getting a chance to talk to folks about the word of God in our world and the work the church is doing in his name." Nathan set his backpack down and pulled out a brochure full of children's illustrations.

"Do you talk to your God?" Ceit asked pointedly.

To his credit, Nathan didn't skip a beat. "Every night, young lady. Every night I speak to God in my prayers, and my actions all across the day are a testament to his word."

Ceit smiled. "The counselors here have told you not to come to this house, haven't they?" She glanced over her shoulder to the hall. "Why do you still come?"

Nathan paused and winked. "Well, I had a feeling that you might just open the door today, and I had a special something I wanted to talk to you about—just you."

Ceit felt the hairs on the back of her neck stand up. "You're not really a missionary, are you?"

"Young lady, you are as sharp as you are lovely," Nathan said with a grin that showed a mouth full of perfectly white teeth. "We've been looking for you and worrying after you. A great many of our congregation have been sending their best wishes your way."

"And what congregation would that be?" Ceit asked, intrigued.

"Oh, I think you know," Nathan said in a singsong voice that perfectly matched his pristine exterior. "You were to be the

Matrarc of your people. Waste of your talents, if I do say so myself. Your people will suffer for casting you out as they did, but that is not our concern. No, best thing that could have happened, really. You know that they say—whenever a door shuts, somewhere a window opens."

Ceit regarded the young man cautiously. He smelled metallic and also like dirt. "Isn't the expression 'Whenever God shuts a door...'?" she asked with an ironic smirk.

Nathan laughed, a trilling sound with a canned artificiality to it. "Oh, let's leave God out of it, shall we? Why is that one always getting all the credit? No, Ceit, I'm here to guide you, offer you a new family, as it is. You've been drifting, have you not?"

Ceit nodded, suspicious. "Who are you?"

The young man smiled and pointed to the plastic name tag on his crisp white shirt. "I'm Nathan, a young man on my mission here in the big city. I come from a tiny little dot of a town right outside Saint Paul, and isn't this just the most exciting thing?"

"Is he still in there? Nathan, that is," Ceit asked, a smile playing on her lips. "Or are you like the wasps that overtake the honeybees?"

"Oh, young Nathan is fine," the young man said with another wink. "He'll come to standing on the sidewalk outside and wonder where the time went, and didn't he just have the oddest day." The young man who was not Nathan leaned in and whispered, "I came to deliver a message and make your acquaintance. We are all most glad to know you are in good health. Your new family is waiting—a family who will never cast you out. You are the daughter of a new world and the light that was promised us for a thousand years. You just have to decide when it's time to give up all this"— Nathan rolled his eyes back and forth in an exaggerated and comical manner—"and wake up. You can't spend your life scaring your bunkmate and teasing the psychologists. Waste of your talents, to be sure." The young man looked up, listening. "Your counselor is coming, and I will be sent to the sidewalk with a few stern words very shortly. We'll send another soon, and as we can, we will take you to meet your new brethren. We are so very glad to make your acquaintance, Miss Ceit Robertson."

On cue, the counselor entered the room and immediately began bawling at the young man who was not Nathan. He apologized through a perfect smile and offered her the brightly illustrated brochure that talked of heaven and hell and all things between.

"It's certainly been a pleasure, and I hope you have a blessed day." He waved at Ceit and disappeared out the door.

Ceit endured a seemingly endless diatribe about the dangers of letting strangers in the door and how she was never to answer the bell but rather to go get an adult. Ceit nodded and turned back to her book. Heaven could not afford the school lunch, and her younger sister was sick with hunger pangs. Ceit smiled at the possibilities of the afternoon.

*18*

Subject: Ceit Marie Robertson (hereafter referred to as CR)
Doctor in Session: Dr. Todd Harrington (hereafter referred to as TH)


TH: Good afternoon, Ceit. And how are you today?

CR: Well, thank you. You'll be wanting to talk about my father, I suspect.

TH: Do you want to talk about your father?

(indistinct rustling)

CR: They told me I'll be seeing him. Visits, they said.

TH: How do you feel about that, Ceit?

CR: I think it's fine. But I can't live with him?

TH: Not right now. How much have your counselors told you about your father's situation?

CR: He's not in trouble. The courts said he wasn't at fault. Why can't I live with him?

TH: It's a bit more complicated than that, I'm afraid. Your father has petitioned the court for visitation, but given everything that's happened, neither you nor your brother will be living with him quite yet.

CR: Alan is with Grandmum.

TH: Actually, no. According to my paperwork, Alan is staying with your mother's cousin, Aoife Robertson. Do you want to talk about that?

CR: Why I'm not there? Why I'm in the home?

TH: How do you feel about the home?

CR: I like the home fine, but I don't understand why I can't live with my father or with Aoife. My father has requested I live with him, has he not?

TH: Yes, he has. You and your brother. But the court feels that for now, anyhow, you both are best where you are, just until your father's situation is more stable.

CR: He wasn't responsible for what happened to Mother or Great-Grandmum. He wasn't even at the house.

TH: No, he wasn't there. You are quite right. But the courts are still trying to understand why he didn't do more to alert the authorities to what was happening to your mother and to you too. You understand that we all know you weren't responsible, right?

CR: You don't believe that.

TH: Of course I do.

CR: No, you don't. You think I'm unsettling, and you scratch in your notes that I might have a deviant personality. You wonder if I manipulated my grandmum into saying I was innocent. You get the gooseflesh on your neck when I talk sometimes, and you don't quite know why. You think that I might just be responsible for the whole affair, and the whole of you wishes you'd never been assigned this case. You've been drinking too much outside of work. It won't lead to anything good. You can already feel yourself slipping back into those old habits. Can't you?

*The recorded session ends abruptly here. More is audible but indiscernible. Dr. Todd Harrington declined to assist with the transcript of this recording, and this was the last session between the minor child Ceit Marie Robertson and Dr. Todd Harrington. Upon further analysis by the board, Ceit Robertson will be moved to a living facility where she can receive more emotional and psychological support. Visits with the minor child's father, Mr. Boyd Robertson, will be permitted under supervision of state guardians.*

*19*

THE KNOCKING AT THE DOOR INTERRUPTED CEIT'S
packing. There wasn't much to pack: a few changes of clothes
courtesy of the state, the silly V. C. Andrews paperback novel that
she'd grown to rather enjoy, the book of fairy stories, her parents'
jewelry that she'd taken from the house, and the rag doll. That,
along with a green toothbrush and the shoes on her feet, was all
she had. The knocking persisted, and Ceit knew it was meant for
her. Never answer the door, the counselors had told her. But she
was being moved anyhow, rehomed for her own good, they had
said—but she had known better. She'd lost her temper with the
good doctor. It was a fault, she knew. It would have been better to
just let him prattle on in his way. Now she was to be transferred
to home where they "can better help you with your emotional
issues." That was how the counselor had phrased it, but she had
seen the seething pool of fear and loathing underneath her words.
They were all quite glad she was being moved. She made them all
uncomfortable.

The girls in the dormitory were frightened of her. Now that Ceit was leaving, they had started whispering stories to each other about times she'd looked their way and they'd tripped for no reason or the dinner wherein she'd made a girl choke on her food, requiring the counselor to grab the girl around her chest and force the bite back up on the floor. It was all nonsense, of course. Ceit didn't care to expend the required energy to trip a silly girl or to get a bite of pork chop stuck in someone's throat. If they knew how little she thought of them, they'd be insulted. Most people were entirely wrapped up in the idea that others gave enough of a damn to wish them harm, when in fact, chances were that they didn't think of them at all. The greatest evil to be faced is not malice, but the simple act of being disregarded.

The knocking persisted, and Ceit suspected that she was the only one to hear it, at least for the next few moments. The one that had visited before had promised to come back, and she suspected that on the other side of the wooden door was another unsuspecting missionary or the like. It concerned her, but she did not find the attention frightening. Mór Ainsley had always told her that she would attract attention out in the world. It was one of the chief reasons that the Society was as sequestered as they were. Mór Ainsley had been no different, and from her stories, the one who came before her had also been a beacon of sorts. Her mother and Máthair Shona had not entirely understood. They had gone through their lives ordinary, invisible. But Ceit knew.

She also knew that if the Sluagh had never appeared, if her mother had never been attacked and all had gone on in an everyday manner for years to come, she would have eventually been pulled from school and kept in the care of the elders. Even before the incident, she had started attracting attention. One day, a middle-aged woman had followed her home from the bus stop. The woman had exited the bus with Ceit and Alan, even though Ceit had suspected that it was not her stop. The woman had followed her as if in a daze, stumbling over curbs and cracks in the sidewalk until they reached the cul-de-sac. Then she had just stood there, her face blank and her body swaying back and forth slightly.

She'd stayed there until nightfall. Mór Ainsley had clucked and waved her hand. The woman had suddenly shaken off the haze in which she had existed for several hours. In a confused manner, she turned in circles, entirely unsure of where she was or how she got there. The poor thing was near tears when Ceit's mother had gone out and walked her back to the bus stop, telling her she must have gotten turned around. That was the difference between her mother and the rest of the lot that lived on Sinder Avenue— the other women were content to let the poor sap stand there at the corner lost for an eternity. The men, few and far between in the cul-de-sac, knew better than to defy the elders. Only her mother had defied them, soothed the poor thing, leaving her with a foggy invented memory of a pleasant afternoon.

They had all known, of course, why the woman had really been there. She had enough of a sense of the way things were to pick up on Ceit's energy, even young as she was. It was intoxicating, and the woman had been drunk in a sense, helpless to do anything but follow. Mór Ainsley had explained to Ceit that as she grew, this sort of thing would happen more and more, and she would need to learn to stifle her presence when she was out in the world. Ceit hadn't really known what she meant at the time, but now she did. She suspected the one who stood on the other side of the door and the one who had visited her earlier in the guise of the young man from outside Saint Paul were drunk in the same manner as the woman on the bus and, as such, were not to be trusted.

For those outside the current, Ceit was frightening, unpleasant, unsettling. For those whose souls were somehow locked into the rhythm that ran beneath the waking consciousness, she was a candle in the darkness. Ceit didn't entirely trust the one who had visited her earlier but was being left with little choice. The new home they were moving her to was a lockdown facility. She had heard the other girls whispering about it when they were convinced that Ceit couldn't hear. She would be under intense supervision. They kept the grounds guarded, and she would be allowed out only on the bus to and from school. There were mandatory therapy sessions, and her visits with her father would be heavily supervised. Ceit knew it was the workings of the good doctor that had led to this. It was funny—you never knew what would make a person snap. She had seen other things in his past, of course. He did not guard his mind well. Dr. Todd Harrington had mistakenly believed, as so many others did, that his thoughts and reactions were his own.

Ceit stood on the other side of the door, staring at the wood. She could leave it alone, go on with her life as it would be for a time, go to her therapy sessions, smile sweetly, and stay quiet and contrite. She could do well in her classes and visit with her father and play the game they had lain before her until it was determined that she was not disturbed or dangerous. Then what? She would go live with her father once again? She suspected not. He may not be in legal straits, but there was a reason the courts were agreeing only to visitations. Ceit suspected it had to do with his psychological being. Dad had grown up in the Society, and entering the regular world was bound to be a shock. Ceit wondered if the reality of it hadn't driven him mad.

He used to talk about leaving. Ceit wasn't supposed to hear, but in their tiny flat with its paper-thin walls, everyone heard everything. She had known even back then there was no actual danger of them leaving. The Society had a way of convincing those within its fold that it was the only reprieve from the folly of the world. *Ironic*, Ceit thought darkly. *The madness they sought to hide from hunted them down and ate them one by one.* No, the cul-de-sac on Sinder Avenue was not like anywhere else.

She suspected that in the best-case scenario, she would live out the next eight years in a series of homes that were not her own. She had a choice to make: she could play into the way of the powers that locked her in this system or trust in the current that flowed beneath their waking lives.

With a breath, she opened the door.

## 20

"HELLO THERE," THE YOUNG MAN SAID BRIGHTLY. IT was not the same one as last time, but the crisp white shirt and neat, stainless cuffs and backpack were identical. I'd love to talk to you about the word of our Lord," he said with a wide smile.

"You'd do well to learn their lines if you are going to borrow their bodies," Ceit said flatly.

The young man smiled at her, nodded, and chuckled. "I suppose so, but you'll be the only door I'm knocking on today. Besides, I'm close as the dickens, aren't I?"

Ceit nodded. "I guess. What do you need?"

"Won't take but a minute of your time, and I'll send this young man right back out to his doorbells." The figure leaned in, and Ceit could see the vacant expression in the man's eyes. He would wake later in a daze, not remembering anything, and whatever force was speaking through him would likely forget to set him right.

"We heard you're moving," the young man said. "It so happens that we are in a position to help you. We have one of our own at

MacLaren Children's Center. Goes by the name Annbeth. Never fear, this is advantageous. Soon you will be with your people."

"Suppose you're not my people," Ceit said calmly. "Suppose I don't want to be with you."

"Oh, child," the young man said. "You have been through so very much. You'll see when you reach MacLaren—you will need a friend."

"Who are you?" she asked, an edge to her voice. "Why use this prop to speak to me? Why not just show yourself?"

"Soon enough, child," the young man said. "We would stand out far too much in this neighborhood. You have enough attention drawn to you as is. No, this hapless soul that we've simply borrowed for a time draws no attention whatsoever. It's best that way." The young man stopped, listening. "Your keepers are coming, and that is our cue to be on our way. Good luck on your move, my daughter. Wait for Annbeth. She will guide you through the storm."

With that, the young man turned and walked back to the sidewalk. Ceit closed the door just as a counselor entered the room.

"I heard voices. Someone at the door?" she asked cautiously.

Ceit shook her head and went back to her bed to finish packing. Later, she looked out the front window to see the young man standing in place, still confused. Quiet as night, she slipped out the front and approached him. He looked at her with fear, lost as he was.

"I don't know how I got here," he said in a small voice, vastly different from the tone that had come from him earlier.

"You visited our house," Ceit said softly and in a cadence meant to create a rhythm. "You talked to us of your God. You should come back tomorrow. Tell your church to come to this house all the time. They love to talk to you here."

The young man nodded and smiled.

"Go back now. They'll be wondering where you got to."

As the young man walked back down the sidewalk, Ceit smiled. She was due to leave in an hour. The missionaries would take months to dissuade. It was her last gift to the Open Arms Home for Children.

*21*

Subject: Ceit Marie Robertson

*The following are notes from the minor child's state-supervised visit with her father, Boyd Robertson. Dictated by A. Aburlach, Social Services, El Monte, CA*

The visitation began at 3:45 p.m. on 04/15/1986, in the children's visitation conference room at MacLaren Hall Children's Center. The minor child, Ceit Robertson, has been in residence since 04/01/1986. The conversation between the subjects was not recorded, but the video transcript is available upon request of doctors and certified staff. Let the record show that Mr. Boyd Robertson was found not guilty of conspiracy to conceal a crime for his participation in the incident that occurred against his wife, Mrs. Grace Robertson. Mr. Robertson has been in intensive psychiatric care. The state of his wife's health and the resounding impact of his life in a cult-like environment have rendered him temporarily unable to properly care for his minor children. His requests for custody of Alan Robertson and Ceit Robertson have at this time been denied with intent to be revisited as his counseling and therapy progress is assessed and Mr. Robertson's overall health improves.

The visit was uneventful, leaving little to be noted. Conversation was limited. The two played a board game, neither displaying notable reaction or emotion. Further visitations are recommended with the need for supervision to be determined.

*22*

ANNBETH WAS A STOUT, DARKISH WOMAN WITH HAIR over her top lip. Ceit liked her immediately. She spoke plainly, and the other girls made fun of her, calling her dyke and butch. Ceit didn't care a bit about that. Annbeth had met Ceit on her first day at MacLaren, barking at the security officers that she would show her to the dormitory and to let her be. She wasn't hiding behind a missionary's body. She was who she was in every sense of the word. She led Ceit to a corner bed in a long room full of cots. She warned her to keep her things locked up, that the older girls would try to steal the jewelry, and Ceit had smiled at her. Woe betide the ones who stole from her. Annbeth had smiled back. She understood what Ceit was capable of.

Annbeth walked her to and from the common room and sat with her over a Scrabble board, a prop that gave them a chance to talk. Ceit soon learned she did not need her voice to talk to Annbeth; the two were able to connect their thoughts in a manner that made frank discussion much easier.

*"Why did the others contact me in such a way?"* Ceit asked silently, spelling out APPARENT and marking the score.

*"They're young and as such like theatrics. It was not the first occasion they've had to play with the missionaries."* Annbeth's thoughts sailed back at Ceit as she added EAR to Ceit's T.

*"How long will I be here?"* Ceit asked. She hated MacLaren. It was a dark place. She was in a hall for girls between ten and twelve, and even at that, there were nightly fights. Girls cried themselves to sleep and showed up with bruises inflicted by all manner of horror in the morning. The halls for the older girls were far worse. Ceit had to walk past them to go to the dining hall. They stank of foulness and were so crowded the cots flowed over into the hallway. Empty-eyed girls sat against the cinder block walls, watching Ceit and Annbeth pass.

"Not long," Annbeth responded out loud, and smiled.

Ceit knew they had a plan, and she hoped it moved quickly. She had been awoken the night before last by sobbing. In her mind's eye, Ceit had seen a girl from Sr. Girls' hall sitting in the institutional darkness, hugging her knees. Ceit had slipped from her bed to find her. She discovered the girl rocking back and forth in the hallway, wearing tattered sweatpants and a torn shirt. Someone had touched her; someone had hurt her. Ceit had sat next to her, knowing full well the girl had no awareness of her insight. Ceit had laid her small hands on either side of the girl's head and, with her lips pursed together, blown a forgetting wind into the girl's mind. It was the only kindness she could give her when there was no justice to be had. The girl had stood, her mind cleared. She was confused at her torn shirt, and she looked to Ceit with fear in her eyes.

"You were walking in your sleep. You fell and tore your shirt," Ceit had whispered. "Go back to bed now." The girl had nodded.

*"I don't like this place."* Ceit's thoughts sailed across the Scrabble board to Annbeth as she added UST to Annbeth's R.

"*Nor do I*," Annbeth thought back. "*It is full of the worst of our lot—those who speak of the light and are full of the darkness. But you must bide your time.*"

Ceit's mind sat silent for the rest of the hour. She knew that the therapy sessions she went to twice weekly held her in this place. She'd resisted the urge to dive into the good doctor's head the way she had with Dr. Todd Harrington. It would lead only to more time behind these walls. School held no reprieve. The teachers knew which children had come from MacLaren and treated them accordingly. They had not been told why Ceit was in MacLaren, only that she was disturbed and not to provoke her. Ceit was seated in the back of the classroom and never addressed; she sat forgotten. She would shuffle back to the bus as soon as the bell rang. As much as she dreaded the walls of Jr. Girls, she couldn't stand the reproachful gaze of the teachers at school.

Later that night, Ceit hugged her rag doll and stared at the ceiling. The elders on Sinder Avenue floated by in her head. She had maintained her sense of humor when at Open Arms, but now that was entirely lost. They would pay for what they had done to her. They would pay for the lies they fed her mother and for the fear in her father's eyes when he looked at her. She would not be here long. And when she rejoined the world, there would be a reckoning.

23

SESSION NOTES: 06/15/1986

Subject: Ceit Marie Robertson (hereafter referred to as CR)

Doctor in Session: Dr. Leanne Morrison (hereafter referred to as LM)

*The following transcript marks the first session with Dr. Morrison and the minor child.*

LM: Are you comfortable, Ceit?

(indistinct rustling)

CR: Yes.

LM: I'd like to talk to you about how you are settling in at MacLaren Hall. Do you like it here?

CR: Does anyone like it here?

LM: Are you being treated well?

CR: Not particularly. The bread at last week's breakfast had mold spots. When I complained, I was sent back to my dorm.

LM: What would be another way you could have handled that situation, Ceit?

CR: Eat the mold, I suppose. Is that the right answer?

(indistinct rustling)

LM: Ceit, I'd like to ask you what some words mean. You tell me what you think, okay?

CR: It's not as though I have a choice.

LM: You do have a choice, Ceit. You can choose not to answer. But I do hope you will help me understand you a bit better. Can I ask you about some words that came from some of the original reports, so we can better understand what happened to your mother and great-grandmother?

CR: Go ahead.

LM: Thank you, Ceit. Let's start with a word you referenced when you first talked to the social workers. What are the Sluagh?

CR: They are the souls of the dead, those who have been wicked in their waking lives. They walk the earth looking for other sinners.

LM: Do you believe the Sluagh are real, Ceit?

CR: It matters not what I believe.

LM: Did your mother believe in the Sluagh?

CR: Yes. They had her in their grip, though my mother was not a sinner, nor was she wicked. She was weak-spirited, and the Sluagh attack the weak ones the same as the wicked.

LM: You have called your great-grandmother the Matrarc. What does that mean, Ceit?

CR: Matriarch. She was the head of the Society.

LM: Would your grandmother have been the next Matrarc?

CR: No. Nor my mother. As I said, they were weak-spirited. I was next in line. It is why they have shunned me and cast me out. It is why I am in MacLaren Hall while my kin are home in their beds.

LM: There was a phrase you repeated when you first arrived: "Tha iad a' tighinn." What does that phrase mean?

CR: You're not saying it right.

LM: I am sorry for that. Perhaps you can help me? I understand you spoke Gaelic in your home, is that right?

CR: Yes, we did. It means "They are coming."

LM: Both you and your father stated that your mother repeated this phrase over and over before the incident occurred. Who are "they," Ceit?

CR: The dark ones—the ones who follow the Sluagh. The Rabharta.

LM: What are the Rabharta?

CR: A cowardly sort of creature. They follow in the wake of the Sluagh, eat at the leftover bits. They are scavengers.

LM: So the Rabharta are a sort of bird?

CR: (inaudible sound) Hardly. They are to be feared far more than a bird. They can rip your mind from your body as sure as you breathe.

LM: Are these monsters, Ceit? Like in stories?

CR: Monsters, yes, and they are in stories, but not the fairy stories you tell children. They are in the stories that are passed on from line to line. They are stories that are told to keep the darkness at bay.

LM: Ceit, I'm not understanding. Do you believe these stories to be real?

CR: (inaudible sounds) You do not believe them to be so, but that does not make them false.

LM: I'm trying to understand, Ceit. Is there one word you could use to translate Rabharta?

CR: Madness.

(indistinct rustling)

*This marks the end of the recorded session. This also marks the last session with the minor child, Ceit Robertson, and Dr. Leanne*

*Morrison. The minor child will be under the care of a new physician, to be determined. It is recommended at this time that the minor child stay in residence at MacLaren Hall until a suitable foster home can be determined.*

24

BOYD READIED HIS LUNCH. HE WORKED AT THE HOME
Depot, a brand-new store in town. The managers said it was the
wave of the future. Everyday people would be building their
own decks, installing their own floors. Boyd worked in the back,
unloading lumber, driving a forklift, and moving heavy pallets
around. It was good work, solid work. He made enough to afford
his apartment. Every day he worked to make it ready for his family
to return to him. It would happen anytime, the social workers said.
He needed to establish his income, needed to have a suitable living
space, needed to complete the counseling. Anytime, they said. It
would happen.

On Saturday mornings he drove his used Honda that his social
worker had helped him find to his wife's cousin's apartment in
Torrance and picked up Alan for his mandated six hours of visitation. He was allowed to take Alan anywhere as long as he was
back at Aoife's white-walled, brown-carpeted apartment by the
appointed time. They went to the beach sometimes, Torrance or

sometimes Malaga Cove, far from the crazy bats from the cul-de-sac and the damnable pile of rocks called the stones. He bought Alan hot dogs, and they drew designs on the sidewalk in chalk. He was relieved that Alan was far from Sinder Avenue. Aoife had left the Society years ago. Alan had no memory of her, but she was kind and sympathetic to Boyd. She had stubbornly refused to take custody of Ceit, and Boyd knew better than to press the issue. It was the lingering influence of the Society. They had fed Aoife lies about Ceit from the day she was born. The lot of them refused to see his girl as a child. But Aoife had agreed to help as much as she could, and for that Boyd had to be grateful. Máthair Shona and Boyd were facing consequences for their involvement in Grace's injury. Ainsley's passing had been officially labeled a heart attack, but Boyd shivered to think of how that had come about.

On Sunday mornings he drove to El Monte and entered the prison-like structure that held his daughter. He was not allowed to see her alone. The social worker had thrown a lot of words at him. She was undergoing therapy as well, they said. She was traumatized and not adjusting well to life outside the cult, they said. Boyd had exploded at that. She wasn't damaged. The girl had gone to a normal public school. Sinder Avenue wasn't a prison, but now she was being locked in a cage. Still, the visits were stilted, quiet. Ceit was polite. She followed every rule, and he did not recognize a hair on her head.

It was worse in the afternoons when he drove to the residential hospital and sat with his wife. She moaned and stared at the ceiling. She would either not recognize him or she would scream his name in fear. The doctors had no explanations. The physical wound had, for the most part, healed. There was no obvious permanent damage.

In the beginning, they had asked him a million questions. What was the nature of the belief that she was possessed? What was the tradition regarding it? Boyd had no answers. The men were never part of the real work of the Society.

At night, Boyd sat alone in his apartment. He fussed with the odds and ends he picked up at yard sales and thrift markets for the children's room. He folded and refolded the extra set of bed sheets. He stared at the black-and-white television set he had found at a garage sale. He didn't know what the Sluagh truly were or if demons were real. He did know that a force beyond his understanding had torn his family away from him, and if there was such a thing as the hell the elders spoke of, he was in it.

*25*

ANNBETH WAS CROSS. SHE HAD REFUSED TO SPEAK TO Ceit for a full week. Even her thoughts had been silent. When she did speak, she growled, her voice full of frustration and contempt.

*"You want to stay here forever, do you?"* she silently hissed over the Scrabble board as the other girls milled around the common room.

Annbeth's thoughts hit Ceit hard, knocking her back in her seat.

*"You need to cooperate, Ceit. Your last doctor left MacLaren altogether. She recommended you for the secure observation ward. Thank your stars, child, they thought it an overreaction."*

Ceit responded out loud, "I didn't do anything. I just answered her questions."

Annbeth slammed a Y to the end of MOLD and caught Ceit's pale eyes in a hard stare. *"You know what you did,"* she answered silently. *"I heard the good doctor started having nightmares the evening after your last session. She's on medical leave. Did you know that? Hearing voices, scratches at the window, and you know nothing about that?"*

Ceit suppressed a smile and sent her response silently back to Annbeth while adding ELT to the M. *"It was she who asked about the Rabharta, and she who didn't believe what I told her. I did nothing. The uafáis do not care to be mocked, and the doctor scratched in her notepad that I had a vivid imagination. They didn't include that in the report, did they?"*

Annbeth considered the words and finally reached across the board to add a simple O to the T.

Out loud, she said softly, "We are working on getting a home lined up for you. Someone connected to us. There will be, of course, a bit of a process. We want you out of Los Angeles. We think that is best for now. Your father will agree. You need to find your center, and we are everywhere."

Ceit nodded. She had resigned herself to the truth that she would likely never be placed with her father after the last visit. He looked at her with fear.

"Ceit, my girl," he had whispered, but he pulled back slightly when she reached out to take his hand.

They had played a board game while the social worker or whatever she was sat in the corner and took notes and pretended to be invisible. Her father had told her that Alan was well, staying with their aunt Aoife—who was not actually an aunt but a cousin, and who was smart enough to have avoided any involvement in the entire incident on Sinder Avenue. Ceit didn't remember her entirely. She had left the cul-de-sac years before.

"Why am I not there as well?" Ceit had asked.

Her father had sat silent, an unrolled dice in his hands. "You need to understand, my girl," he said, looking into her eyes, pleading with her to understand. "You're too much for them right now. The people here think you need a little extra attention. And Auntie Aoife isn't prepared to take in two children. My situation will change. As soon as this clears up, I will have both of you back. Your mother will get better, and we will leave this place, go up north, where it snows. Do you want to see the snow, my girl?"

Ceit had known then that she would never leave with her father, just as she had known that her aunt Aoife's inability to take her in had nothing to do with space. It was an unsettling truth that both of them discerned but neither was willing to acknowledge. Her father's tie to the Society was broken. Her mother lay silently staring at the wall of the hospital, her brain wiped of its function and her heart dead, eaten by the Sluagh. And while her father still held his heart safe, it was his nerve that had been destroyed. He would never stand up to the Society. And for him to take Ceit back in, no matter where they moved, it would be a small war—one he was incapable of fighting.

Ceit nodded at Annbeth as she cleared away the Scrabble board. She would do her best to remain quiet, unnoticeable, and then maybe she would be free from this place.

*26*

THE SUMMER PASSED, AND CEIT FELL INTO A RHYTHM.
She held hands with the other girls when they were taken on day
trips to the pier or to a matinee movie. She ate her handful of
popcorn one piece at a time while Daniel LaRusso packed his bags
for Japan on an impossible trip with Mr. Miyagi. She sipped warm
sodas and sat in the scant shade of the Jr. Girls' activity yard while
the others played kickball. She became invisible.

She was assigned a new psychologist. This one, Dr. Leo Dorner,
did not ask her what the Gaelic words meant or if she remembered
the events of the day of the incident. No, Dr. Dorner showed her
objects and asked her if they reminded her of anything. They never
did, but Ceit knew that was not what the doctor wanted to hear.
She told the good doctor that the handkerchief reminded her of
Máthair Shona and how Grandmum used to bake cookies. A lie
to be sure, but it was what Grandmums were supposed to do. The
painting that was no more than a blob of red paint with a streak
of black down the center was a sunrise, she told Dr. Dorner. It
was the moment right when the night was leaving, and the day

began. Another lie, but Dr. Dorner had smiled through his bristly mustache and noted her reaction.

Ceit did see something in the painting, but not something she could talk about and still hope to leave MacLaren Hall. The painting wasn't a sunrise—it was a death. The blood spilled wide on either side of a great divide. The world split into two and those left in the middle forced to take sides. That was what Ceit saw. She heard the screams of those who had decided early where they stood and were now slowly realizing that they were on the wrong side of death. There was no afterlife for them. They were doomed to eternal judgment, a forever of waiting to see what decisions their dead god made for or against their favor.

Ceit had not said any of this, of course. But she retracted her bitterness about the dead god. Mór Ainsley had taught her that all the gods were dead, only some were further gone than others. The problem was not the lack of a living god but rather the convoluted concept of what *dead* really meant.

"Our bodies are a perfect state of chaos," the old woman had told Ceit in a soft voice. "We are ruled by no god or man. We are a function of the universe, the stars, the darkness that stretches above the light. In that place, we wield a degree of power. It grows stronger the more you realize how incongruent the teachings of man are with the vastness of the dark."

The red paint with the black stripe was the closest incarnation of that lesson Ceit had ever seen. She asked Dr. Dorner if she might hang the painting on the wall next to her bed. He had laughed and said of course. He chuckled and told her it was "found art" from a garage sale. Ceit had smiled and quietly seethed. He was experimenting on her, finding trash and seeing what she would say.

Still, the red-and-black painting was hung on a small hook over her pillow. The other girls looked at her curiously and never asked. They never asked anything about her, and her valuables—the jewelry, the fairy stories, her doll, and the paperback novel—were never touched. She knew it was not just her own negotiation of the dark that kept them from her things. They respected her. They saw she could lead them home if they only allowed it to happen.

Ceit had chores and tasks to be completed throughout the day. She was assigned to help the adults with the babies in the nursery. She was to give the youngest baths in the plastic tub, shake powder over their bottoms, and then fasten on diapers. She was then to hand the screaming infants off to the teens from Sr. Girls' hall who took them to their cribs, fed them formula from bottles, and waited for them to sleep. It taught her responsibility, the adults said. Ceit suspected it was less about responsibility and more about allowing the adults to watch *Days of Our Lives* on the small black-and-white television in the nurse's office. As the infants were transferred to their teen nannies, Ceit would linger in the doorway. Anna won't marry Tony, and the one-eyed man has sworn to kill Bo. Ceit wished someone would kill Bo. She found his utter conviction that he must save all the women who come into contact with him entirely intolerable. She thought he was a bit like Tom in her paperback novel, *Heaven*.

After the babies had been fed, Ceit sometimes stayed in the nursery and read to them from *Heaven*. It was just like *Days of Our Lives* but without the incessant caterwauling from the heavily made-up soap women. No one cried in *Heaven*—not when Granny died, not when Our Jane spat up her food, her intestines rejecting the scant nutrition that Heaven provided. Ceit felt bad for Sarah and tried to explain to the fussy babies that she was simply trapped and that the concept of good and evil was far more gray than black.

The other nursery workers paid Ceit no mind; they were happy to leave her with the unhappy, abandoned infants and go on about their business. Ceit read to the babies about Logan and school lunches of tuna sandwiches and milk. She knew that so many outside these walls felt her to be the blackness that they feared, and she smiled at the idea. She was not Patch, who wanted Bo dead only so he might bed Hope. She was not Pa, who lusted after his own daughter and lived in the memory of a girl from the big city.

It was not morality that kept Ceit above this sort of depravity; it was an understanding of chaos, the senseless beating of her atoms against the senseless beating of the fabric of the universe. The undying, unrelenting chaotic beat of it all somehow careened its way to order. It was when you denied your true nature that the darkness overcame you. Stefano rejected his path and lived in constant turmoil. Ceit accepted the inevitability that right and good did not exist—there only *was*. She whispered these truths to the infants as well, as they grew drowsy. They quieted immediately. Ceit spread her arms, sending the hope that they grew to prove the ones who had left them here wrong. She spoke the ancient words and blew a soft breath over their sleeping forms that they might rise above the darkness and find their way in the chaos of being.

*27*

SCHOOL STARTED AGAIN IN THE FALL WITHOUT MUCH fanfare. Ceit climbed into the van with the other Jr. hall girls, and they were shuttled to LeGore Elementary. Ceit sat in the back of the room and did the work that was passed to her. She rarely spoke and ate her cafeteria lunch by herself at a table in the corner. The other girls from Mac were wary of her and stayed away. The children from normal families who were driven to school or rode the yellow bus were even more distant.

Annbeth had warned her to lay low, and so she did. Once a week she sat down with Dr. Dorner in his cellblock-like office at MacLaren Hall. Ceit answered his questions in a small voice, the type of voice she imagined Annbeth would want her to use, the sort of voice that would not scare away yet another psychologist and lead to yet another questionable mark on her record.

She turned eleven, and there was a sad sheet cake in the cafeteria for all the girls with birthdays in October. Ceit listened to the subdued singing and scraped all the icing off her square of cake, mashing it down with her plastic fork until she was allowed to leave the party. Alan drew her a birthday card, bright crayon images of balloons and his name in his blockish child's script. Ceit knew he must have asked his school to mail it for him. She admired his bravery. Even as little as he was, he was more man than their father, who dared not rise against the Society.

She still visited with her father from time to time, always in the artificially cheery family room and always with the social worker sitting in the stiff chair in the corner, taking notes and trying to appear unobtrusive. Her father never asked her about Mac. He talked about how they would go up north, up the coast, settle in together when all this was squared away.

Dr. Dorner sat with Ceit in his sunless cell of an office and explained everything in words that Ceit could tell were carefully chosen.

"The trials are finally over," he said slowly. "Do you understand about the charges?"

Ceit nodded. "Because of the Matrarc's death, and what happened to my mother."

Dr. Dorner nodded. "The courts had to decide if it was all an accident or if it was someone's fault. Do you understand that?"

Ceit nodded again. "What about me?" she asked. "I didn't have a trial."

Dr. Dorner was quiet as he weighed his words. "No," he said slowly, "you did not." He leaned forward, wrinkling his caramel-colored suit jacket. "The court decided that you were not at fault and so there was no need for a trial."

Ceit stared at the doctor impassively. "You think I was at fault?"

To his credit, Dr. Dorner did not flinch or even blink at the question. "No, I do not," he said calmly. "I think that the adults in the room were the ones who were responsible, and I agree with the court that you did nothing wrong."

Ceit nodded. "So what happened to them all? That's what you wanted to tell me today, isn't it?"

Dr. Dorner took a deep breath and paused. "Yes, it is." He started listing the elders who had stood at the periphery of the room and watched and wailed. Ceit grimaced to hear their names. *Mess of feckin' cowards, they are.* All the elders who had been in the room had been charged, along with some of the others who had lingered outside. "They were found not guilty of knowingly causing harm to your mother but guilty of a thing called obstruction." Dr. Dorner narrowed his eyes. "Do you know that that is, Ceit?"

Ceit absently ran her finger in circles on his steel desk. "Getting in the way."

"Yes," Dr. Dorner replied, obviously relieved. "They were not sent to jail, but rather they will be under parole for a year or so. Your grandmother is another story."

"What of her?" Ceit asked. "They've explained this to me before. She plead guilty and took a deal. She's in prison."

"No, they decided against that. I think the court recognized your grandmother is not dangerous. She will be on what they call house arrest for a time."

Máthair Shona had traded information for a reduced sentence and was therefore at odds with the Society. Ceit's own shunning made her angry, but she suspected that her grandmother was utterly devastated. The old woman had never known another life. But the old women of Sinder Avenue were fickle, and Ceit suspected with her remaining on the cul-de-sac, they would soon enough invite Máthair Shona back into the fold.

The doctor sighed and leaned back. "I don't know how much of this I should explain to you, Ceit. You seem to understand all of it. But my fear is that somewhere in all this you will start to feel as though you were guilty too, and that is not what I want you to think."

Ceit looked up from the desk and locked her pale eyes on his. "I did what I did. I had no choice in the matter. There was no good outcome. My mother was already lost, and the Sluagh had turned to Mór Ainsley. She'd have killed us all, and her soul would have been lost. I don't expect you to understand except to say that my grandmother was no more guilty than the elders that stood and watched."

The doctor considered this for a long moment. "I'm afraid there's very little left to be done, Ceit. Whatever really happened that night is likely known to only you and your grandmother. The adults in that room had a responsibility to protect you, and they did not do that. Whatever it is you did to protect yourself and your mother, you did because you were not being protected. Do you understand that?" His voice was heated, but not in anger.

As Ceit stared unblinking at his face, she realized that this man really believed her to be innocent. She laughed out loud then, a barking sort of cough. The absurdity of it all.

*The good doctor would do well to not look too closely for blame in any of this,* Ceit thought, her mood dark as she walked back to the Jr. Girls' hall. Blame was not what the elders or the doctor—or the court, for that matter—should be concerning themselves with. No, blame was but a word—an empty way to absolve oneself of guilt.

# 28

BOYD SAT NERVOUSLY ON THE STIFF SECONDHAND SOFA in the living room of his tiny apartment. Alan would be arriving any minute. The officials from the state of California had deemed Boyd's progress in therapy to be adequate, his living space acceptable, and his job and income stable enough to warrant restoring custody. He had finished assembling the bunk beds in the second bedroom that morning, and clean sheets lined both mattresses. Boyd had a dresser and a small desk with a mismatched wooden chair furnishing the room. He had wondered if he should hang posters or decorate in some way, but he came to the conclusion that he didn't know what his son would like. It had been over a year since his little boy had lived with him, and as much time as they spent together on the visits, there was much he did not know about his child.

There would be follow-up visits, and Boyd was to continue his individual therapy in addition to family sessions with Alan. It had been strongly recommended that he try to limit his dealings with the cul-de-sac inhabitants, but Boyd hadn't needed a warning. He had no mind to set eyes on those people ever again. Because of them, his wife lay as one dead in the long-term facility, her mind wiped. She seemed to have no memory of him or Alan. When Ceit's name was mentioned, she appeared visibly upset, and so he had stopped talking to her of the girl.

Boyd felt a hole in his very being that could never heal stemming from that terrible night. His Grace, with her red-gold hair and eyes that shone of moonlight, was gone forever. The frame that lay in the hospital bed was not her. She was treated for bedsores and fed through a tube when she refused to eat. She absently sang nonsensical songs and spoke in rhyme when she spoke at all. Boyd had started visiting less and less. The nurses did not seem surprised, and he found the scab that formed over his splintered heart began creeping inch by inch toward entirety.

He had a fridge full of fresh vegetables and fruit, and the cupboards were stocked. He had macaroni and cheese to make for dinner tonight. It used to be Alan's favorite. Boyd wondered if it still was; he had no way of knowing. Aoife had been relieved that her goodwill duty was over. She had been kind to Alan, if not a bit distant. Boyd could not blame her. She was still a young woman, and she had been raising someone else's child for over a year now. She had packed his school lunches and met with his teachers, taken him back and forth from his appointments and spent endless hours in court hearings. She had done her time. At their last meeting, when the judge had granted Boyd his renewed custody, she had leaned in and kissed Boyd's cheek and locked eyes with him for a long moment.

"Time isn't quite what we understand it to be," she had said quietly. "The boy will forget the bulk of this. Give him some new memories."

Aoife had been right, of course. Boyd planned on doing just that. He did not know what to tell the boy of his sister. The court-appointed therapist had talked Boyd through this, suggesting that he allow Alan to write her letters, maybe even arrange for a visit. She told Boyd to be honest with Alan and explain that Ceit needed extra help right now and that was why she was not sleeping in the other bunk bed.

It was a lie. Boyd shook with the shame of it, but he had asked that Ceit be left where she was. The social workers had been concerned but had followed his request. "She needs more help than I can give," he had said. "I'm not prepared to take her in yet." He hadn't offered the reason, and they hadn't pressed. His girl had been in MacLaren Hall for a long spell. She had spent her last birthday there. Now the winter holidays were approaching fast, and she would still stay there for a time to come. If he thought on it too much, Boyd knew he'd go as mad as his poor wife.

It wasn't supposed to be this way. Some weeks earlier, the approval from the social services people was just about to be granted. Boyd had been home, repainting his shabby kitchen with a bucket of pale-lemon paint that his boss at the Home Depot had gifted to him along with a set of brushes and tarps. "A welcome home present for the family," the man had said. Boyd had blinked back tears at the kindness of the gift. He had been lining the corners with the clean, crisp paint, thinking about his children and how they'd react to the space he was creating for them, when the doorbell rang.

Through the peephole, he had seen a young man in a crisp white shirt and with a backpack strapped to his back holding a thick black book in his hands. Boyd had grimaced. He had nothing against Mormons. They were a harmless lot in his eyes. There was a temple not too far away, and this wasn't the first knock on his door. He opened the door a crack and offered a strained smile.

"I'm sorry, not intereste—"

But the young man cut him off.

"Oh yes you are, Boyd Robertson. You are most certainly interested in what I have come to share with you." The young man flashed a grin full of perfect teeth and nodded slowly.

"How do you know my name?" Boyd stuttered.

"You know, it'd be easier if you let me in, and I can share the good news with you—the word of the Lord, so to speak," the young man with a name tag that read "Hello! My Name is Elder Dallin" pinned to his crisp white shirt said sunnily.

Boyd shook his head. "I'm quite busy," he said curtly, all the hairs on his arms standing at attention.

Elder Dallin pressed a hand against the door, preventing Boyd from closing it. "But, Brother Boyd, we need to discuss our mutual friend—your young daughter, Ceit."

Boyd felt his apprehension rising to anger. "Don't you talk about my girl! You have no idea wha—"

"What she's been through? Who she is?" Elder Dallin said with a practiced and sympathetic turn of his lips. "But we do. I confess to not quite being myself in this"—the young man gestured to his torso—"this costume, if you will, but I bring important news of young Ceit that you most certainly would like to hear. I mean you no harm."

Boyd nodded numbly and opened the door. Elder Dallin nodded his head and entered, pausing to look around the apartment.

"Ah yes, fixing up the place, I see. This will be a fine place for children—well, one child. Your son is due home soon, yes?" The young man turned to Boyd, whose blood was pulsing in his ears.

"In a few weeks, both the children should be home." Boyd was tired of these games. He felt his impatience growing. "Look, did those old bats in Venice send you? Is that why you know so much about my family? Or did you just read all the stories in the newspaper? Love watching someone else's tragedy? Who the hell are you?"

"Who the hell, indeed." Elder Dallin chuckled. "No need for such emotion, Boyd. I was not sent by the old women on Sinder Avenue, nor am I some sort of ghoul who has been stalking you through the news. No, my interest runs much deeper than all that."

"What the fucking hell are you talking about?" Boyd growled, tired of the Mormon's double-talk.

"I'll get right to it," Elder Dallin said, and his demeanor changed. The plastic, sunny expression changed to an almost menacing look. His eyes narrowed and darkened. Boyd felt ice form in his veins. "I am part of an ancient order, much older than your Society, more powerful than those 'old bats,' as you put it. Young Dallin here is on loan. We sometimes repurpose the more susceptible among you for our purposes, like delivering a warning."

Boyd's head was swimming. He felt his feet frozen to the ground. "But that's not possible," he muttered.

"Not possible?" The thing that was not Elder Dallin laughed. "You watched your wife being eaten alive by demons in your own home, and *this* is not possible?" The young man's lips twitched. He was visibly annoyed. "You are not to bring Ceit here."

"What are you talki—" Boyd burst out in dismay.

"You leave Ceit where she is," Elder Dallin interrupted, his voice suddenly steel. "Ceit is in the care of our organization. We have one of ours looking after her. You know—you've always known—that she is no ordinary girl. Your dear cousin would not take her. No one would take her. In your heart of hearts, you don't want her either, do you?"

Boyd felt as though the wind had been knocked out of him. It was true. In his most secret and shameful thoughts, he dreaded bringing Ceit home—her pale eyes watching everything, her odd ways, and her manner of knowing everything before he ever said it. He would be damned for admitting it, but the girl unsettled him, scared him.

"Don't be so hard on yourself," the young man intoned. "She is not of this world entirely. One foot in and one out, so they say. It's why the old women treated her as they did. They never took her for just a little girl, did they?"

Boyd shook his head miserably.

"You leave Ceit where she is. And when they ask you—and they will ask you soon enough—you are to sign over your custody to the ones who will request it. They will take her to us, and we will help her reach her, um... full potential, so to speak." The Mormon's voice was deadly still, and Boyd felt his hands shaking.

"What if I refuse?" he asked, his courage waning.

"Then it would be a shame for there to be no choice. A mother incapacitated. A father passed to the wonders of our Lord's heavenly kingdom prematurely. Your son would miss you greatly. He is supposed to be home soon. Your daughter will not care." Elder Dallin leaned in until he was an inch from Boyd's face. His breath smelled of ash, and Boyd was immediately spun back to those terrible nights spent caring for Grace, the sour scent of sulfur sticking to the air.

Boyd nodded. His skin tingled as though it sat separate from his body. "You mean to hurt her?" he asked, barely audible.

Elder Dallin leaned back and laughed, a hearty sound from his gut, the plastic smile and congeniality regained. "Hurt her? Good lord, no. We plan on helping her to become the best she can be. She will be a queen among us, every need taken care of. She will want for nothing. A life of luxury and hero worship. She's a celebrity among us, you see, so the worst pain she will ever know is the unending adoration of those who love and worship her. Can you give her that?"

Boyd nodded his head. None of this seemed real, and yet he felt a weight lift from his shoulders.

"Good, that's settled." Elder Dallin turned to the door, pausing to look around at the apartment once more. "A nice place for a child. You should get a dog. A good dog can help a child forget almost anything." With that, the visitor had trotted out the door and down the front steps.

Sometime later, Boyd had looked out to see Elder Dallin walking up and down the sidewalk, an expression of childlike confusion on his face. He was muttering to himself and checking a foldout map. Boyd knew this was not the same person who had knocked on his door. He had little understanding of such things, but he had grown up in the Society and knew that some things were not to be understood.

That had been weeks ago. He had told the social worker to leave Ceit where she was. He had worked to prepare for Alan, his uncomplicated, loving little boy. They would build new memories together and try to forget that they had left Ceit behind, try to forget that Grace lay in a bed as though she were already dead and buried. They would build a new world, just the two of them, a place rooted firmly in the concrete and mortar of reality, no magic and no threats.

The doorbell rang, and Boyd rose, straightened his slacks, and crossed to welcome his son home.

*29*

ON A LONG NIGHT IN DECEMBER, AS THE WINTER RAIN poured down outside and the wind whipped around the edges of MacLaren Hall, Ceit dreamed of her great-grandmother. Mór Ainsley was sitting in the great Barcalounger that had been the centerpiece of their home before everything had broken. She sat and stared out the front window, her eyes unblinking. Ceit approached her. In the bedroom, she could hear muffled sounds—someone crying, the low chant of the elders. Her steps were beyond her control as they brought her closer and closer to Mór Ainsley, who sat still as night with her fixed gaze. As Ceit reached the arm of the chair, the old woman's head whipped to the side.

"You're a fool," Mór Ainsley said simply, her voice annoyed and rusty from disuse.

Ceit did not respond. Her words were stuck in her throat.

"All that potential, and you go and trust a band of showboat magicians. We'd have done better to sell you to a circus early on, make a pretty dollar off you. But I thought you had more sense.

Never can tell." Mór Ainsley turned back to stare out the window.

Ceit struggled to make a sound. She screamed at the top of her voice, but the resulting noise was nothing more than a croaky whisper.

"Who?" she gasped.

"Who do you think, girl?" Mór Ainsley snorted. "Your father was born a fool and has proven himself nothing to be surprised by. Your mother was a pretty little girl, and her mind was a simple one as well. Your grandmother was blind to all that we were. But you—you were special. You came to this world with a great path in front of you, and there you sit, locked up as a bird in a cage, listening to amadán."

Ceit choked on her own voice.

"Save it, girl," Mór Ainsley snapped, and then pivoted in the chair to face Ceit fully.

"I'm not here to hear your nonsense. I'm here to tell you to wake up. I saw the teachtaire that had hold of your mother that last night. I saw it at the stones, and I know what it told you. The Sluagh and the Rabharta are but the vultures following a much greater darkness. You are the reason your mother's soul was leached from her body. They are looking for you. And here you are, putting all your trust in the bréagadóirs. They show you a few tricks, and you follow them like a peasant."

"What do I do?" Ceit managed in a mangled gasp.

"Wake up, girl," Mór Ainsley said firmly. "You heard the teachtaire at the stones. You must decide if you are a carnival act, a novelty, an aisteach, or if you are worth the suffering your presence brings." The old woman regarded her coldly. "Wake up."

With that, Ceit had flown from her bed and woke on the floor, scrambling at the cold concrete. The girl in the next bunk stirred and looked over.

"Jesus, freak, go back to bed," she muttered, and rolled over.

Ceit lay back down and stared at the ceiling, her body shaking. The dream was as vivid as her bed or the walls or the rain that beat down outside. Mór Ainsley was dead. Ceit had killed her, and no one seemed to care. She was damned, if one believed in that sort of thing. She felt a deeper and more unsettling stab of discontent settle in her gut. She knew what the dream spoke of; it was warning her about Annbeth and the entity she represented. Annbeth would not speak of the group. When Ceit had pressed her for information, she avoided her questions, telling her that it would become clear in time. Ceit closed her eyes. It was past time to find out exactly who Annbeth was and what was capable of speaking through the poor missionaries and other susceptibles.

She was alone here at Mac. She knew that. Her brother had gone home to her father's new apartment this past week. She would not be joining them. Her father had refused to take custody of her. Dr. Dorner had told her all this gently, as though the news would break her, but Ceit had already known. She had known for some time she would never live with her father again, or anywhere outside of this institution, unless she listened to the Matrarc and woke up.

*30*

SESSION NOTES: 01/17/1987

Subject: Ceit Marie Robertson (hereafter referred to as CR)

Doctor in Session: Dr. Leo Dorner (hereafter referred to as LD)

*File notes: CR has been in protective custody of MacLaren for ten months. It has been decided in conjunction with her father, Boyd Robertson, and the caseworkers at Child Protective Services that the minor child, CR, stay in the custody of MacLaren Hall indefinitely or until suitable foster care can be found. This session follows an incident (outlined in the disciplinary reports available in Section 2b of the case file).*

LD: How are you feeling today, Ceit?

CR: (inaudible noise) Fine.

LD: Would you like to discuss what happened on Friday?

CR: You have your notes.

LD: I'd like to hear it from you.

CR: I'm sure you would. You want to know if I'm sorry?

LD: Are you?

CR: Not particularly. I wasn't at fault.

LD: Are you upset about the custody issues with your father?

CR: (inaudible noises) I never expected to go home with my father. I know full well that I will be here until I turn eighteen or I escape on my own. No one wants to take me into their home. So do I care if you have some notes on a file? Or that someone had to clean up a mess? Or that someone's feelings were hurt? No. I'm not sorry.

LD: Ceit, we want to help you—

CR: (loud noise) You want another posting. You want to pass this case off to another so you can take that job in Gardena you were offered.

LD: (inaudible noises) I don't know how you can know that. Was the staff talking about tha—

CR: No, no one was talking about it. I just know. Just like I know that when you go home at night, you lay in your bed and let your mind wander. You wonder what I'll look like in five years, maybe even less. You wonder...

LD: That is utterly untrue. If you are trying to get a reaction from me, then—

CR: I'm getting one, aren't I? But it is true, isn't it? You wonder what my hair smells like and why I don't sound like any eleven-year-old you've ever treated. You think there's something wrong with me and that it isn't exactly scary. In fact it's rather—

End of Session

*Dr. Leo Dorner has been removed from the case at his request following this session. Another therapist is to be assigned.*

## 31

CEIT KNEW IT WASN'T GOING TO GO WELL FOR HEAVEN at Farthingale Manor. It never goes well for unwanted girls in places where men hold all the power. Ceit curled up in the common room and read *Dark Angel*, a gift from Annbeth for the holidays—her only gift, in fact. Since her dream, some time ago now, she had been extra cautious of Annbeth. But she remained Ceit's only ally in this place, so even if she was the wrong path, it was the only lifeline Ceit had. She followed all the rules. She went to school, she did the chores at Mac, she turned off her light at the assigned time, she tried to get along with her new therapist.

Annbeth had been cross after Dr. Dorner left, and Ceit hadn't cared much. She hadn't said anything that wasn't true, and he had been getting tiresome anyhow. She was tired of identifying garbage he found on the side of the road or in the giveaway bins and telling him how it made her feel. She was tired of all of it.

The incident he'd been pressing her to talk about had started because of an older girl with a lisp and a strawberry mark across her face. She was named Melanie, and she had tried to fight

Ceit three times already. Ceit had a perverse enjoyment of the anger the attempts brought Melanie, the red rising in her skin so the two halves finally matched. Melanie could have stopped it at any point, but she chose not to. It had been easy to duck from the common room or tell Annbeth so Melanie would end up with detention and extra chores. This had, of course, only made Melanie angrier. Ceit should have been more careful.

It had started when Ceit found her lockbox smashed and the items inside it gone. She had known immediately. Ceit was still in the Jr. Girls hall. Melanie was in Sr. Girls' and had had to sneak into the other ward to pull this off. Ceit had felt the air tingling around her as she walked down the hall to Sr. Girls. Once there, she found Melanie and her eejit friends sitting on their beds, giggling.

"You lose something, little girl?" Melanie had called out.

Ceit hadn't answered. Instead, she reached toward the glass of the window the group sat next to. Using a force that had lain dormant in her for months, she pulled back on the night air and sent razor-sharp shards of glass flying into the room. They hit the band of shocked girls full force. Ceit had been trying to crack the glass, but her concentration had slipped. Slightly shaken at what she'd done, she had crossed to Melanie's nightstand, narrowly avoiding the screaming, bloody girls as they fled past her into the hall. Inside was her mother's crescent moon necklace and her father's pocket watch, the book of fairy stories, and her V. C. Andrews books. It wasn't much, but it wasn't to be touched by the likes of Melanie.

Later Ceit found out that Melanie had had to be transferred to the Greater El Monte Community Hospital, where they tried to save her eye and eventually failed. Ceit was frustrated but not particularly sorry. The girls all swore that Ceit had broken the window and thrown the glass at them. Ceit had laughed and said she was on the opposite side of the room, far from the window, so how could she have done such a thing? There was no truth to be found. The authorities included a file in her disciplinary records. Melanie and her friends stopped trying to fight Ceit.

Surprisingly, Annbeth had not been angry. She had nodded slowly when the incident was recounted to her and then said they were near the time when Ceit would leave Mac. She knew she wouldn't leave here with Annbeth's people either, not if her dream was to be believed. But it was a better fantasy than most in this place, so she did what she could not to encourage more looks of fear from the other girls. She read her book and did her homework... and waited.

*32*

HEAVEN IS A FOOL TO GET INVOLVED WITH TROY, BUT
Logan is much worse. On the television in the nurse's lounge, Ceit
watched Kayla on *Days of Our Lives*. Kayla has been captured by
Professor Schenkel, and Ceit fought back giggles as Carrie cried
and wailed about space aliens. Time passed.

Soon enough the school semester was over. Ceit was due
to go to junior high next year, *If next year is spent at this place*,
she thought wryly. Ceit received a half dozen letters from Alan
throughout the spring, and nothing from her father. The return
address for the letters was Alan's school in Torrance, so Ceit sent
her replies there instead of the apartment. She sent her letters from
her own school, slipping them in the outgoing mail in the school
office. It was supposed to be for official school business only, but
they never checked closely. Ceit suspected Alan was employing
the same trick. She wasn't sure how the letters reached her little
brother; perhaps a sympathetic counselor saw the name and held
them for him. For Ceit's part, they appeared every so often during
weekly mail call.

Alan wrote that their father was sad and that he slept too much. He wrote that he missed her and wished he could come see her, but everyone told him it was not a good idea. He asked Ceit why it was not a good idea. Ceit kept all the letters under her pillow. The little boy was always the one with the guts when it came to the men in her family.

As Ceit eased into yet another summer at Mac, she readied herself. She had stayed out of trouble since the glass incident. Melanie still had a bandage over her eye, and Ceit had taken to calling her Patch. Her face would grow red, but she never raised a fist against Ceit again. No one could prove how the glass had broken, and no one believed that Ceit had been capable of smashing a window with her bare hands and cutting the girls. So the matter was largely ignored and forgotten except by those who had been there.

One muggy day in June, Annbeth appeared at the door to the Jr. Girls' dormitory. "You have a visitor," she said, her voice reflecting her confusion.

"Huh." Ceit put down *Dark Angel*. She had read it three times already and was just at the bit where Troy tries to kill himself because he thinks Heaven abandoned him.

"A woman who says she's your cousin," Annbeth said flatly.

"I thought you knew everything about me," Ceit said with a smirk as she walked down the hall with Annbeth.

"I don't know who this is," Annbeth said, casting her a sideways glance. "Do you want me to stay?"

Ceit felt her annoyance ripple through her expression. "No, I don't want you to stay. I'm not a child."

"No. You're not," Annbeth said curtly. "But this isn't any of our people, and your family hasn't turned up in months."

It was true. The visits with her father had abruptly ended after

Alan was released back to him. No explanation. Her current therapist, a Dr. Sonia Katz, was all about getting her to talk about the pain it must be causing. Ceit had little to say on the subject. It wasn't unexpected. In fact, it was a bit of a relief, although it would have been nice to see Alan.

The visitation room was a grim place. Ceit suspected that it was modeled after the visiting halls in prison, which seemed to be the design scheme for the entire damnable place. Rows of folding tables and metal chairs. A corner with a cheap couch and armchair, a bleakly hopeful sun-colored rug in the center. Posters hung from the wall, faded from age. They held optimistic messages like "The Best You Is You Right Now." Ceit wondered about the logic of that statement. If you were a wretched person, it was a bit of a death sentence.

Inside the room sat a young woman, somewhere around thirty years old, perhaps a bit younger. Her hair was light brown with a streak of amber. Her eyes were pale, and she looked a bit like Ceit remembered her mother looking before the world had fallen apart. She rose when Ceit approached. Annbeth paused at the doorway and then disappeared. Ceit was sure she was listening in, and it sent a wave of frustration through her.

"Hello, Ceit. Do you remember me?" the woman asked.

Ceit shook her head. "Not entirely. You look as though I knew you once, a long time back."

"I'm Aoife Robertson." The woman extended a hand. Ceit stared at it and kept her own to her side as she sat down.

"Of course. You took my brother in for a time," Ceit said politely.

Aoife nodded. "I did." She paused. "Look, it's weird for me to be here, I know that. I owe you an explanation."

"No, you don't." Ceit stopped her. "You took care of Alan, and I appreciate that."

Aoife nodded. "I couldn't take you."

"No?" Ceit asked, narrowing her eyes. She was curious why, after all this time, this woman felt she needed to explain something that felt a million years away.

"I was going to," Aoife stuttered. "Your mother, she was my cousin. She helped me get away from the Society." She smiled at Ceit's surprised expression. "You didn't know that, did you?" Ceit shook her head. "Your mother never let on to what was really going on in her head, but there was much she didn't agree with."

Ceit gave a small nod. That was true. Her mother led a simple life, but it was like the surface of the sea. The older Ceit grew, the more she saw that it was more complicated than she had thought when she lived on Sinder Avenue.

"She lied for me. She told the elders, Mór Ainsley, that she didn't know where I was. She sent me money when I first set out, helped me." She paused. "I remember you. You were always the favorite of the old ones, even when you were a baby."

Ceit considered this. "Why stay in LA? Why take Alan in at all if you were trying not to be found?"

"The elders stopped looking for me long ago. I was never of much concern to them. Look, Ceit..." She leaned in, obviously conscious that she could be overheard. "I have to leave Los Angeles. I have to get away, and they cannot find me," Aoife said softly.

"Who?" Ceit whispered.

"I had a dream," Aoife said quickly and softly so that Ceit had to turn her ear to hear the words. "I know how that sounds, but you and I know that dreams are never just that. I had a dream. The Matrarc was there, and she was warning me. I couldn't hear her. It was like the sound was off. She spoke and spoke, and I saw your face—not like it was in my memories, a tiny little girl, but you as you are now. I saw you here."

Ceit nodded. "You didn't take me in before because you feared me."

Aoife shook her head violently. "No, it wasn't that. Not you. I wanted to take you and your brother in both. I was warned not to. A man showed up at my door, one of those missionaries, you know. He forced his way into my apartment and told me that I was to leave you here. He spoke in a voice not his own. He knew things about me that no one knew. I wasn't afraid of you but of what would follow him if I disobeyed."

"So, what of this dream?" Ceit asked. Her head was buzzing. Annbeth's people had kept her in this godforsaken place and made it sound as though she had no choice.

"Even though I could not hear, the Matrarc was telling me to come get you, telling me you were in danger." Aoife spoke all in one breath, her face pale.

"So you're here to get me," Ceit said flatly, knowing it was not the truth.

Aoife's face looked pained. "I can't. I came to warn you to get out no matter what. Get away from whoever wants you here. I can't do it. They'll kill me, I know they will. I woke up the next morning and that same damn missionary was standing on my steps. He's been there, in front of my house, every day. I wouldn't be surprised if he followed me here. I called the police, and they said to call the damn Mormon temple. I can't. I'm leaving, and I can't say where I'm going." Aoife leaned in toward Ceit's ear and whispered, "Don't let them take you. Get out as soon as you can. The one who walked you here is not to be trusted. The Matrarc showed me her face."

With that, Aoife stood and nodded at Ceit. "I have to go," she said too loudly, for the benefit of Annbeth, who was listening on the other side of the wall. "I'll visit again soon, cousin."

Ceit nodded and caught Aoife's hand as she turned.

"Thank you," she said simply.

"What was that about?" Annbeth asked crossly as they walked back to Jr. Girls.

"You tell me. Weren't you listening?" Ceit said with an amused smile on her lips.

Annbeth stopped walking and placed her hands on her hips. "I'm trying to take care of you. If you had any idea of what is waiting for you out there . . ."

"I'd be glad to be locked up in a home for disruptive children?" Ceit swiveled to face her. "Is that it? She told me that a missionary warned her not to take me in. Those are your people."

Annbeth shot a look up and down the hall. "Be careful with your words, child."

"Damn my words," Ceit retorted. "I didn't have to be locked up here at all. Why are you keeping me here?"

"You are a child who needs extra attention. You have anger issues and emotional disturbances. Your file is thick, and you have caused two psychologists to quit the field outright. In addition, you may have even been involved in the death of your great-grandmother and the attempted murder of your own mother. You belong here, Ceit." She spoke slowly, locking eyes with Ceit as she enunciated each syllable.

Ceit let the words absorb. It was clear that Aoife's warning was timely. She had to find a way out of MacLaren Hall before Annbeth's people did it for her.

33

SESSION NOTES: 07/26/1987

Subject: Ceit Marie Robertson (hereafter referred to as CR)

Doctor in Session: Dr. Sonia Katz (hereafter referred to as SK)

*The events precipitating this session are outlined in the minor child's case file. From this point on, the State of California will hold sole custodial guardianship of CR, as the father, Boyd Robertson, has signed away parental rights for CR. The mother, Grace Robertson, has been deemed to be in a vegetative state, thus rights were terminated on medical grounds.*

SK: Hello, Ceit. I'd like to talk about your father today.

CR: He's changing his name.

SK: Let's talk about that. Robertson was your mother's name?

CR: Yes. In the Society, where I grew up, a man took his wife's name.

SK: That's a bit unusual but not unheard of.

(inaudible noise)

CR: He's changing it back. Alan told me in a letter.

SK: Your brother Alan? Is his name being changed as well?

CR: Yes. I think they're leaving the state or at least the city. Alan didn't say. I don't think he knows.

SK: How do you feel about all this, Ceit?

CR: How long do I stay here?

SK: At MacLaren Hall? I can't say. I know that we will work to find you a foster family, maybe even a permanent adoption.

CR: No. I mean, how old do I need to be before I can be emancipated and leave this place?

SK: Eighteen. But, Ceit, we will work to find you a placement.

CR: I think we both know that will never happen. My father is changing his name and taking my brother away so I will never find them. You think a stranger will want to adopt me?

SK: Why do you think no one will want to adopt you, Ceit?

CR: I think that the minute they do, something will happen to scare them off. I think they'll be threatened by someone they don't know. They'll feel like someone is watching them, and they'll be right. I think I'll be here at MacLaren Hall until I am eighteen unless I disappear.

SK: There's a lot to discuss there, Ceit, but why do you think you'll disappear?

CR: (inaudible rustling, indiscernible language)

End of Session

34

ANNBETH SAT ACROSS THE TABLE IN THE ACTIVITY
room, glaring at Ceit. Ceit lined up her Scrabble tiles and, after
deliberation, spelled out DECAY.

*"We used to be on the same page,"* Annbeth said to Ceit using
only her mind.

It had been awhile since Ceit had opened herself up enough to
hear Annbeth's chatter, but she didn't want the other girls eavesdropping right now.

*"Were we?"* Ceit asked back, as Annbeth added OR to her D.

*"You've put yourself on the watch list, little girl."* Annbeth glared.
*"They think you're paranoid. They want to give you meds. You know
what that will do to you? You want to lay in bed high on clozapine?
You need to trust that I'll get you out when the time is right. You will
not be fostered out to just anyone."*

Ceit added EAD to Annbeth's D. *"Yes, I remember. I'll get to go
to the ones who keep using Mormons to do their dirty work."*

Annbeth sighed, staring hard at Ceit for a moment. "*It has all been in your best interest. And those of my organization who have been sending messages have many methods. That is but one. And no one was threatened. They all agreed of their own will.*"

Ceit slammed her hands down on the table, the little square letters rattling out of their boxes. "*My cousin said a missionary was planted outside her house night and day. She said she thought they would kill her. That's not a threat?*"

Annbeth cocked her head, took a deep breath, and added OWL to Ceit's Y. "*So, you want her to take you in? That wasn't always what you wanted. You used to trust me.*"

Ceit glared and added ORDS to Annbeth's W. "*I'm beginning to wonder if I trusted in the wrong things. Why do your people need to steal the bodies and minds of others to communicate? I grew up in a world not so far from what you claim you want to bring me to, and we never stooped to such low tricks.*"

Annbeth sighed and said aloud softly, "We needed your father to sign over custody to the state before we could move. Now that that's settled, your new placement will happen very quickly. You will leave this place before you know it. You will not spend another birthday here. You will be with those who love you."

"I don't trust you," Ceit replied firmly, and stood up from the table abruptly, sending the tiny letters flying. As she walked with an even pace back to Jr. Girls, she thought back on her dream of the Matrarc. She needed to wake up, but she didn't know what that meant. The thing that had spoken through her mother at the stones so long ago had said the same thing. It said they would be waiting, and when she decided to wake up they would be there. The Matrarc indicated that Ceit did not know who "they" were, but she knew the other "they" that lay behind Annbeth and the hapless missionaries who allowed themselves to be so easily overtaken were the wrong path. She stared out the window of the girl's dormitory and plotted her course. It was time to disrupt the mundanity of this system. It was time to break what was being pieced together.

## 35

BOYD HASTILY PACKED THE BOXES IN THE KITCHEN. He didn't have much, mainly a utilitarian set of pots and pans. What food was in the cupboards and fridge, he would leave.

"How's it coming in there, buddy?" he called down the hall to Alan's room.

The door swung open and his son stepped into the doorway, his face sullen. "I'm almost done."

"Good!" Boyd responded too cheerily. "We can load the car and be off first thing in the morning."

"Dad?" Alan said hesitantly. His voice held none of the adult certainty that Ceit's always had. Even from the time she had first strung words into sentences, her lineage had always defied her physical form. But Alan, he was easy. He sounded like a child, he acted like a child, and right now, he was as confused as a child should be.

"Dad?" he started again, his thin voice shaking a bit. "Why are we leaving? We're leaving Ceit behind. Why aren't we taking her?"

Boyd stopped packing and crossed the room, taking the little boy into his arms. "Look, kiddo, I know it's confusing, but Ceit can't come with us. We have to leave this place."

"Why can't we tell anyone?" Alan asked in a whine that wanted to be a cry. He held it in and waited for an answer.

"It's just better we don't for now, son. We'll get settled and start over. And besides, darlin', San Diego isn't that far away. I can keep my job, and it doesn't rain as much there." Boyd knew his promises sounded thin, and Alan's face was unconvinced. "Just go pack for me, all right? We'll order a pizza tonight, okay?"

The little boy nodded miserably and returned to his room to pack the few possessions he had. He had arrived with a duffel bag full of clothes and a backpack full of odds and ends. He had little else to add at that point.

Boyd crossed to the fridge and poured himself a tiny bit of the vodka he kept in the freezer. It steadied his nerves, but his hands were still shaking. In truth, he wanted to leave tonight—he wanted to leave this minute—but Boyd knew that for Alan's sake he needed to keep up the illusion that this was a normal move, a transfer, a fresh start.

Boyd Healy. That was what his new driver's license said. Alan's revised birth certificate with his name change had arrived last week: Alan Michael Healy, born to Grace Robertson and Boyd Healy. Boyd had tucked the documents away carefully in the leather portfolio he kept by his bed.

The Home Depot manager had been confused as to why he was changing his name, but he hadn't asked many questions. Boyd was grateful he hadn't had to get into explaining the odd practices of the Society. They needed men in the new San Diego store. It was south of the city, close to the Mexico border. The houses were cheaper the closer you got to Tijuana, and the company was willing to offer a bonus that could go toward a down payment. Boyd had a chance to get away. On the surface it all looked perfectly legit. He wasn't hidden, but the ones who followed him here might stop, might see it as a sign that he would leave Ceit be and not interfere with any of their plans.

The doorbell had rung on a Friday afternoon. Boyd was home from work early and waiting for Alan to arrive from school. The bus dropped him off only half a block away, but Boyd still worried that something would happen. He worried a damn missionary with whatever level of demon inside would approach the boy. He worried that there were people watching, memorizing their schedules. Boyd jumped at the sound of the doorbell and opened it cautiously. A woman in her midforties—thick build with a sun-worn face, coveralls, and a tool belt around her waist—stood at the entry.

"Hi there. I'm Kelly from Sears Home Repair. You called about your fridge?" Her voice was measured and polite, a perfect mimic of its owner.

"Who are you really?" Boyd asked.

The woman laughed, a deep belly sound. "Oh, Boyd, you're getting too good at this!" She looked past him and into the living room. "Let me come in and take a look at that fridge. This one is on a service call somewhere in this building, and if I stand out here too long I'll have to figure out how to repair something!"

"Or you could go the fuck away and leave me be," Boyd said coldly.

"Good lord, that language!" Not Kelly laughed again. "You surely didn't speak that way in the cul-de-sac!"

"Lots of things have changed," Boyd said. "Why are you here? I did what you asked the first time. I left my girl in that place. I haven't asked any questions. I even stopped going to see her..."

His voice broke a bit at that. The guilt he felt was a constant tide, ever present, and at the mention of what he had done, it swelled and crashed on the shore.

"Yes, you have. And now we need a bit more from you," Not Kelly said cheerily. "Know what? I'm just gonna come in. You can get me an iced tea or something." She pushed past him and stood in the living room. "Do you have iced tea? I am parched. This one works way too hard for my taste."

Boyd glared and crossed to the kitchen, where he poured a glass of water and then handed it to the woman.

"Well, this will do." She drank it all in one gulp. "I tell you, we target the clergy, missionaries, the little ladies who put those Beware of the Devil pamphlets on doorways, you know the type. Anyhow, we use them when we can because, to tell the god's honest truth—which isn't much to be trusted—they're easier. They don't work all that hard, and their minds are as open as the day is long, at least in some regards. You say demon, they say jump!" Not Kelly paused. "You know what I mean?"

"Is that what you are? A demon?" Boyd asked coldly.

Not Kelly ignored the question. "But this one, well, it was the best we could do in a pinch. She is in sad, bad shape, I tell you. She smokes, which will be the end of her. I barely got up all the stairs out there without wheezing up a lung. I think she must've eaten half the deli counter for lunch. I can just feel the weight of all that dead flesh hanging off her bones... but couldn't be helped. There were no devil-fearing little ladies around, and the Mormon Temple has stopped sending missionaries to this block. That last one—Elder Dallin, I think his name was?—well, he went and told the Temple that this block was a lost cause. We usually do a better job of cleaning them out when we leave. Our bad."

"What do you want?" Boyd said more firmly.

"I came to tell you of a slight change in circumstance." Not Kelly's tone changed, and she placed the empty water glass down on the counter. "You need to terminate your parental rights to our Ceit. We're ready to move her, and she will be adopted as soon as we can file the paperwork."

Boyd felt ice thread itself down his spine. "Terminate my rights? Wha... what does that mean?"

"It means, Boyd, that you need to quit playing. You signed over custodial guardianship, but for young Ceit to be fully adopted, she will need to be completely free from any interference on your end. We need her. She will be well taken care of and raised in a manner conducive with her potential. You need to go to the Child Protective Services office and file the paperwork immediately. There's a bit of a process, you see. You will go through all the hoops and sign all the papers and go to every legal proceeding necessary. But you will do it." Not Kelly's voice lowered to a growl, and she stared at Boyd.

"But I can't... she's my daughter. What about my wife..." Boyd sputtered, his body growing numb.

"Your wife is as good as a vegetable. She will never wake up, and you will do as you are told." Not Kelly took a step and looked out the window. "Your boy is due home any time now, right?"

Boyd nodded numbly.

"You know this one has a criminal record? Not surprising, really. She got in a bar fight years back, broke a guy's jaw slamming his head into a table. She was on parole. It's been years, but violent behavior is known to resurface. It would be a real shame if she had a relapse. Your son would find worse than a broken jaw. That would be a real shame." Not Kelly turned and grinned, showing a row of broken and stained teeth.

"I have to sign away my parental rights forever."

"That's my boy!" Not Kelly exclaimed. "You got it. We need to place our Ceit with our people, and you need a fresh start. This is a lousy neighborhood for a little boy. The damn Mormons won't even come to this block!" She laughed at her own joke. "Maybe it's time for a change of scenery. Think about it."

With that, the woman in the coveralls had left the apartment. Boyd saw her later, as Alan was coming up the stairs to the apartment. She was leaning on her truck, smoking a cigarette, her face wrenched in confusion. Boyd knew she remembered nothing. The ones who followed him made sure of that. When Alan entered the room, Boyd wrapped him in a hug. The little boy was confused by the outpouring of emotion, but the child had grown used to the regularity of his father's tears. And later Alan had listened quietly when Boyd told him he thought it might be nice if they got out of the city. And maybe a new name so no one would ever ask him about all that business with his great-grandmother ever again.

Boyd poured himself another swallow of vodka and then put the bottle away. That had been weeks ago, and he had done as the creature had asked. Even still, he looked outside the kitchen window to see a primly dressed little lady standing in the middle of the parking lot. A bag full of pamphlets hung on her shoulder. Her dark eyes were locked on Boyd's window. She waved cheerily as she saw the curtains move. Boyd knew she would stand there all night and into the morning until they left. They were being watched, and the only chance he had of giving Alan a normal life was to leave this place and his girl behind.

*36*

CEIT SAT ON A HARD BENCH OUTSIDE THE COURTROOM. The Child Protective Services attorney had requested that she attend the last hearing before her father's parental rights were officially severed and she became a ward of the state. Termination was deeply frowned upon, and Ceit knew that the lawyer hoped that seeing her face would turn her father's mind. She also knew it would do no good. The hearings had been going on all summer, and now school was due to begin again. She had been left out of the actual proceedings so far, only told and counseled on what was happening. Her father had been driving up from San Diego to finish the process. Boyd Healy—as he was known now—had filed a statement that his daughter required intensive psychiatric care, citing the incident with the glass and Melanie's lost eye and her counseling sessions wherein she indicated she felt she was being followed.

When Ceit had been told, she grew so angry that a full coffee-pot brewing in the corner of the room had imploded as though crushed by a large and strong hand. The lawyer and her case-worker, a middle-aged lump of a man named Frank, had jumped to their feet. But obviously it wasn't Ceit's fault. She was just a little girl sitting on the opposite side of the room. She couldn't have had anything to do with that. Regardless, they refused to meet her eyes ever again.

The Matrarc had come to her in another dream. This time Mór Ainsley was walking down a city sidewalk, dressed in a fashionable suit and heels. She was younger, and her hair was cut in a short, boyish cut. The gray was gone and replaced with platinum blonde and silver. Only her pale eyes were the same, but Ceit knew her instantly. In the dream, Ceit stood planted on the sidewalk as people streamed around her, taking no notice. She felt a fool in her sneakers and cutoff shorts. The Matrarc stalked down the sidewalk toward her, sleet-gray office towers on either side, the sky a steel-cut slab. A blur of cars and taxis rushed by on the street. The sound was muted but present. The air smelled of rust and dead things.

In the dream, Mór Ainsley had stopped directly in front of Ceit and stared.

"You're running out of time," she said. "If you let those fun house magicians take you away, you'll never return. They will drain you. They will turn you into a punch line. I'm sending someone for you. You will know when he is near. You cannot trust anyone but me, not even yourself right now. You need to demand to see your mother. Just once is enough." She then flipped her jacket over her shoulder and stalked around Ceit's frozen form, continuing down the sidewalk. At that, Ceit had woken. That had been two nights ago, on the full moon. Ceit had been shaken and then reassured.

Ceit had a plan for this last hearing. She knew the Matrarc was right; once custody was officially severed, it would be just a matter of time before Annbeth's people came for her. They would look like a nice couple who wanted to give this poor girl a second chance. She could see them in her mind's eye already. Not too conservative, not too hippy, they would be the right mixture of confident and open. They would convince all the oblivious masses that surrounded her that they were perfect. And Mór Ainsley spoke the truth when she said that if Ceit went with them, she would never escape.

"Ceit?" The lawyer poked her head out the door. "You can come in now. You ready to do this?"

Ceit nodded and stood. Her father looked thinner than he had when she'd seen him last. His last visit had been before Christmas, and now here he was, so many months later. He shrank back slightly as she entered the room. Ceit sat at the long table next to Frank the caseworker and the lawyer. The judge was dressed in a nicely tailored business suit, her graying hair pulled back neatly. She nodded and smiled at Ceit as she sat.

"Hello, Ceit. I'm Judge Conners. This is rather informal, so no need for all the pomp and circumstance. We just wanted a chance to make sure that this was the best choice for everyone before any final decisions. Do you understand what is going on here today?"

Ceit nodded. "My father is signing me off to the state. He doesn't want me anymore." She pinched the inside of her arm hard enough to cause tears to well in her eyes. Under the table, she wrenched the bit of skin around so that she gasped with the pain, which was taken as a stifled sob by the adults in the room.

Her father, the newly named Boyd Healy, broke down. "Oh, Ceit, no, that's not it at all..."

The stiffly suited man next to him put a hand on his shoulder, indicating to him to stop talking. The judge looked from one side of the table to the other.

"I think I might speak with Ceit alone for a minute," she said quietly and firmly.

Without question, the adults all stood and exited out the door to the hall, her father shuffling his feet, his face wan. When they had gone, the judge stood and moved to the chair next to Ceit.

"Hello, Ceit," she said simply.

Ceit's stomach dropped. This was no ordinary judge. Now she understood why the proceedings from her father's request had happened so fast. Some of the other girls at Mac had been in court for years, and Ceit's case had taken a matter of months. It all made sense now.

"I know you came here with a plan," she said with a frown. "There's no need to hurt yourself." She reached over and took Ceit's arm. An angry welt was already forming from the pinch she had given herself. Ceit felt all hope quickly dissipate.

"You're everywhere, aren't you?" she said with a smirk, the tears gone.

"Not everywhere, but many, many places," Judge Conners said.

"Are you really who you say you are, or will poor Judge Conners wake up on the sidewalk later not knowing her own name?" Ceit asked dryly.

"Oh no, I'm really Judge Conners, just as your Annbeth is really Annbeth. Some of us are really who we are. Others come and go as needed." Judge Conners paused. "We're working hard to bring you home, Ceit. I'm going to need your cooperation in that. You get your father all worked up, and he won't sign the last papers. He doesn't sign the last papers, and the easiest way to bring you home is as an orphan. Do you understand?"

"Yes," Ceit said. "So Frank and my feckless lawyer from CPS, are they yours too?"

Judge Conners smiled gently. "No, they're not. They petitioned to bring you in today, and it would have been very suspicious for me to disallow it, so I acquiesced. But I do need you to play along. You need to be stoic and understanding. You need to let your father feel good about signing the papers. And then we can worry about the business of the rest of your life."

"I have a demand," Ceit said firmly.

Judge Conners blinked in surprise. "What would that be?"

"I want to see my mother in the care center. I haven't seen her since she was in the hospital. I want to see her one last time before whatever happens happens." Ceit looked into the woman's eyes, dark with a lightness in the shadows.

"Very well," Judge Conners said, a bit confused. "I can't see how it would hurt. But I need your word that you'll let us get through this today with as little drama as possible."

Ceit nodded. It wasn't the plan she arrived with, but it would do.

Judge Conners stood and went back to her seat at the head of the table.

"One thing..." Ceit said suddenly as the judge went to press a button that would let the others know to reenter. "These sessions are always recorded. How will you explain this conversation?"

Judge Conners laughed. "It never happened, Ceit." She pointed to the security camera in the corner and the audio recorder on the table. "This equipment is old, some of it from the seventies. A few minutes of garbled audio, and all the camera shows is me comforting you. No one cares much." With that she pressed the buzzer, and the rest of the party entered.

For the next thirty minutes, Ceit answered every question stoically. She told her father it was for the best she stay at MacLaren Hall. She thanked Frank the caseworker and her lawyer. She shook Judge Conners's hand. She gave her father a stiff and stilted hug.

He seemed as one whose life had been drained from his veins. His pale face was nearly translucent, his eyes dead. Ceit knew that whatever torments she had been subject to, he had endured worse. With no malice in her heart, she said goodbye to Boyd Healy.

## 37

THE INGLEWOOD CENTER LONG-TERM CARE FACILITY
was a long, squat building flanked on one side by a decaying
doughnut shop and the other by a recycling plant. As Ceit got out
of the MacLaren Hall van, Frank the caseworker following her, the
roar of a compressor filled her ears. Frank cast her a sympathetic
look and surveyed the scene.

"I take it you've never been here before?" he said quietly.

Ceit shook her head. The last time she had seen her mother was
in Cedars-Sinai Hospital right after the incident. Her mother had
been in intensive care then, and Ceit had had to look through the
glass at her. Grace Robertson had lain in the bed attached to all
manner of tubes and wires. After a time, a nurse had led Ceit into
the room and let her hold her mother's hand. That had been nearly
two years ago, and Ceit remembered being confused as to what
exactly lay in the hospital bed. Was it the creature that manifested
itself at the stones? Was it her mother? Her body now void of the
Sluagh and Rabharta? How much did she remember?

Two years ago, her mother's eyes had shot open, and the nurse had jumped back, obviously surprised. She had immediately pressed a call button on the side of the bed to request more personnel.

"I'm sorry, honey, I'll have to ask you to step out. This is the first time your mother has regained consciousness, and we need to check her out." The nurse started to lead Ceit away, but her mother's hand clamped down on Ceit's to a painful degree. Her pale eyes, a mirror of her daughters, locked on Ceit, and her mouth started moving—silent words, but Ceit had known what she was saying.

"Múscail, inión."

It was then that Ceit had known her mother was long gone. In her place, a shell with a lingering memory of horror remained. The Sluagh had dug their claws in deep and were licking the bones of their conquest as they bided their time. They would leave Grace Robertson eventually, but not until she was entirely sapped and ruined. The nurse had pulled Ceit out of the room as a fleet of doctors took her place.

After that, Ceit had declined to see her mother. The various psychiatrists had been concerned but had not pushed the issue. Her father—back in the days when they had visits—had told her once, rather hesitantly, that her mother grew upset at the mention of Ceit's name. Ceit did not doubt the truth of what he was saying, but the intent of her mother's emotion was entirely different from what her father thought it to be. The Sluagh were still trying to call to Ceit. While they waited, they would hunt the weak and tired souls of the living. In her mother's place, a black hole had opened up. As long as the doctors kept her heart beating and her blood flowing, the spirits of the restless dead would circle around her in an invisible storm.

Frank laid a meaty hand on her shoulder and led her to the door. Annbeth had been incensed that she was not allowed to go on this visit. It was a relief that it was entirely out of Ceit's hands. Even if she had requested and pleaded for Annbeth to accompany her, the request would have been denied. The MacLaren Hall staff was too swamped with new arrivals and the encroaching start of the school year to go on field trips; that was what the social workers were for. Ceit had heard Annbeth arguing about it in the front office and had smiled to herself. She wouldn't be able to assign fault to Ceit if she tried. Annbeth did not even know where they had gone, which relieved Ceit's nerves even more. They had been en route when the driver had received word that Grace Robertson had been moved the week prior to the Inglewood Center. If Annbeth did try to send a naïve missionary, or anyone else for that matter, they would find themselves at the wrong location.

The air smelled of antiseptic and urine, and one of the overhead lights was flickering. A gaunt nurse sat at a chipped counter at the front entrance.

"You here from MacLaren Hall?" she asked, glancing behind them to the van.

Frank nodded. "Ceit Robertson here to see her mother, Grace Robertson."

The nurse nodded and disappeared around a corner. She was replaced with another woman with short, rough hair and dark skin who wore a name tag that read "Mariane."

"Hello, Ceit," she said kindly. "I'll take you back." She looked up at Frank. "You can wait here or come with—"

"I'll wait," Frank said abruptly, and sat down in a plastic chair.

Ceit followed Mariane down the hall.

"Your mother just joined us, so we haven't gotten to know her very well yet." Mariane cast a sympathetic look over her shoulder to Ceit. "Maybe you can help us, tell us what she likes, her favorite foods…"

"I wouldn't know," Ceit said. "I haven't seen her in nearly two years. If you read the case file, you'll find out."

Mariane nodded, obviously perplexed by the oddness of Ceit's response. She paused before an open door that revealed a figure on a bed beyond.

"Here we are. I should warn you, she hasn't spoken to us, not yet. She can eat and drink, so if she wants water or anything, you can ask us to get it. It would be nice, actually. So far she hasn't had much of a response to anything." Mariane paused. "I just want you to be prepared, young lady. Your mother is likely not as you remember her. Would you like me to stay close while you visit?"

Ceit shook her head. She had known what it was she was visiting, and while Mariane's honesty was refreshing, it was unnecessary.

The woman on the bed had greasy long hair pulled away from her face. Her expression was void of emotion, and her eyes stared out the window. Her frame was bone against skin, cheeks sunken, her collarbone sticking out beneath the faded gray T-shirt she wore. A sour smell emanated from her skin. Ceit knew she would not live long in this state. Ceit could see the memory of her mother in this creature, and the resemblance made her swallow back the emotion that welled to the surface. On Sinder Avenue, in the cul-de-sac, Ceit had never seen the end of the world. She had thought she would grow to become the next Matrarc and lead the old ones the way her great-grandmother had. In her child's mind, she had seen her mother by her side. She had never accounted for the calamity that had sent the sky crashing to the ground.

As she stared at her mother's unresponsive form, she knew the old ones had been right to call her precocious, pompous. She knew Mór Ainsley was right to scorn her confidence and dismissal of the traditions she'd hoped to uphold. Perhaps it was for the best she had been locked in a prison of sorts for the last two years; it had given her a perspective on all she had lost. Ceit reached out and took her mother's hand, even though she knew the spirit of Grace Robertson was long gone. It had flown that night at the stones. This was a shell, a holding place for the darkness that had consumed her.

The figure on the bed slowly turned her head to look at Ceit. A slow, deliberate smile spread across her lips.

"Hello, daughter." The voice was raspy and dry from disuse.

"Why was I told to come see you?" Ceit asked, trying to stop her hands from shaking.

"Good to know you still listen to your dreams," the creature on the bed whispered, showing her yellowed and rotting teeth. Ceit cringed. Her mother had always been meticulous about her appearance. This was a particular indignity that would sadden her mother's spirit, wherever it was.

"The Matrarc said to come, so I am here. What do you have to tell me?" Ceit swallowed the heaving tide of emotion that threatened to break her in half.

"You are so much more than the Matrarc now, daughter, so much more." The figure in the bed motioned with her head. "Come closer, daughter. I cannot move this shell any more. You need to come closer."

Ceit took a step in and leaned as close as she dared. The bitter stench of rot and unwashed skin overwhelmed her. She felt her bile rise, and with a hard gulp that left her throat raw and aching, she swallowed her disgust and turned her ear to the creature's mouth.

"A man is coming for you. He will have dreams of you. You need to find the Ch'įįdii."

Ceit shook her head, confused. "I don't know what that is."

The creature on the bed croaked a laugh. "It is the dreaming dead of a people who still believe in magic. They will come to you in your sleep if you allow them in. We need to hide you in a place where the ones who seek to bind you will never look. We need you to reclaim your throne, my daughter. And when you are ready, you will rise from your hiding place and soar to the sky. You are more than just our Matrarc—you are the Bandia Marbh, the goddess of the dead. You bring a new age, a new rule, and those who seek to control you have no idea of your power."

Ceit reeled back and stared at the figure in the bed, so thin the skin sagged on the bone, her eyes dead and already glazed.

"How?" she stuttered.

"You will know when the one we will send is near. Until then, seek the Ch'įįdii. Call to them in your dreams, and they will lead you. Only then, when you are of mind to take what is yours, will the spirits of the anamacha caillte rise. Go now, daughter, and do not trust those who claim to help you while they lock you in a cage. Go. Now." The creature on the bed collapsed back, the air rushing from her body.

Ceit stumbled back toward the door, Mariane appearing and catching her just in time before she fell to the floor.

"Ceit? What happened?" she asked urgently as white-jacketed doctors and nurses ran past her into the room. Ceit heard the chatter of the staff. The monitors had sent off an alarm. They were pumping at her mother's chest. Mariane led Ceit quickly from the room.

An hour or so later, Mariane came to where Ceit and Frank sat in the dingy lounge.

"I'm so sorry, Ceit. Her heart just gave out. We tried everything to help her, but there was nothing we could do." Mariane waited for a response. "I can't say how sorry I am that this happened today."

Ceit nodded. Frank put a hand on her shoulder.

"This was a long time coming, Ceit," he said softly. "Your mother has been sick for a very long time."

"It's important you know you did nothing wrong, Ceit." Mariane took her hands. "I rather believe that maybe she was waiting to say goodbye to you before she left."

Ceit nodded. Her chest felt raw. The words of the creature that had once been her mother were ringing in her ears.

"My brother, Alan...he didn't get to say goodbye," Ceit said softly.

Mariane looked to Frank, her face conflicted. "I'm sorry, honey. They were here yesterday. I think he understood how sick she was. I hope you can—"

Frank cut her off with a motion of her hand. "There's no contact with them right now. We'll help Ceit."

Mariane shut up immediately, her face a bit horrified. Ceit knew she felt she had blurted the wrong thing.

Impulsively, Ceit reached out and touched Mariane's elbow, causing her to jump. "It's okay. Really. I'm glad he was here. I hope he will be all right."

With that, Frank led Ceit back to the waiting van, and then they rode silently back to MacLaren Hall. Even Annbeth stayed away and let Ceit curl up in bed. She felt a great emptiness, void of grief and void of emotion. It was numb, static. Her mother had died that night at the stones; Ceit had always believed that. Still, she had held on to hope that a bit of her soul stayed on, and maybe the grip of the Sluagh could be relieved enough to let it rise back up. But now she knew she had always been wrong. Her mother was dead, and the Sluagh had taken her dying breath. Her soul had joined the ranks of the restless dead. It had been this way for two years now, since that night at the stones.

Ceit stared out the window at the waking chaos that accompanied the Santa Ana winds. A storm was rising. As the trees outside the glass pane bent to the point of breaking, Ceit summoned the strange spirits that the creature had told her to call. "Ch'įįdii, hear me," she whispered.

*38*

SESSION NOTES: 09/17/1987

Subject: Ceit Marie Robertson (hereafter referred to as CR)

Doctor in Session: Dr. Sonia Katz (hereafter referred to as SK)

*Please see file #587 (attached) for details concerning the passing of the minor child CR's mother, Grace Robertson.*

SK: Ceit, I'd like to talk about your mother's memorial service. Are you up for that talk?

CR: Does it matter?

SK: Well, yes, it does. We don't have to talk about that today, but I will want to someday soon. However, it is up to you if you're ready to speak about it.

CR: It's fine.

SK: Okay. I understand you were with your mother when she passed.

CR: She died two years ago. The thing that was left in that bed wasn't her, not anymore.

SK: I think that is a very natural reaction, Ceit. Your mother had never been the same since her injury two years ago.

CR: Do you think I'm responsible?

SK: For her passing? Of course not. No one thinks that. She had been very ill an—

CR: Not that. The injury, the incident, the accident—whatever you want to call it. Do you think I'm responsible for that?

SK: No, I do not think you were responsible then either. Do you feel like people blame you?

CR: They do blame me. Go ahead, ask me what you want to ask. Ask about the funeral.

SK: Okay, why don't you tell me about it in your own words, Ceit.

CR: You have my story in the file in front of you. Why don't you ask me about the bits you are confused on? It will save us all time. (inaudible rustling)

SK: Okay, Ceit, we can do it that way. (inaudible rustling) I am curious about the ceremony that your grandmother and the other women from your old neighborhood performed. Can you tell me what it meant?

CR: I'll tell you what it is supposed to be, and you can see in your file how it worked out. It's called Caoine. Traditionally the body of the dead has to be washed in seawater and wrapped in an eslene, a sort of shroud. What's supposed to happen is the body sits in its home for seven nights until Caoine starts. That marks all sorts of ungodly moaning and wailing for three damn days and nights. Three, can you believe it? And then—as if that's not enough—they have a feckin' meal, a feast that's supposed to be right there in the room with the body. That's not what happened with my mother.

SK: Have you seen this done in the way it's supposed to happen?

CR: (inaudible rustling) Yes, twice. The first time I was very little and didn't have to stay for all of it. The second time wasn't too long before everything happened. Máthair Lisel died. She was old, really old. I had to stay the whole time. She died in June. The house was hot, and the smell... They kept her body in the living room. Not our house—Máthair Lisel's house. The neighbor on the other side of the cul-de-sac called the police over the smell after a week. The women raised hell, but thank god the coroner took her away.

SK: I'm sorry you had to see that, Ceit. That's a very upsetting thing for a child to see.

CR: Is it? The old ones didn't think so.

SK: What happened in your mother's service that was different?

CR: You have it in your notes. (inaudible rustling) Okay, they didn't get to wash the body with saltwater because my father had my mother cremated before the old bats could get to her. It's the first brave thing he's ever done.

SK: You think he was brave?

CR: I do. They hadn't been to see her or cared at all for her since that night, and then here they all came with their buckets of ocean water, all ready to start wailing and moaning.

SK: Was that what caused the argument at the service?

CR: That and other things. The argument started because I was there.

SK: In the file, it says it became physical and several of the older women at the service caused a disruption, throwing things and attacking your father.

CR: He is angry, my father. And he blames me, as maybe he should. The old ones pulled him back from attacking me. They were trying to protect me in their way. The things they were throwing were supposed to be offerings to my mother. (inaudible noises) They know I'm bound here, and they have no wish to make an enemy of me.

SK: What do you mean? Bound?

CR: Trapped. They still fear me and know I will leave this place one day.

SK: Ceit, I'd like to ask about what you said at the service.

CR: I'm done talking about this. You have your notes. You know what I said. (inaudible rustling)

End of Session

*39*

BOYD SAT AT THE KITCHEN TABLE AND LOOKED OUT at Alan rolling a truck back and forth on the concrete patio. Their home in San Diego was near the desert. It was hot all year, and he missed the ocean breeze. An empty bottle of vodka sat in front of him. He knew that if he stood, he would go into the garage and take another from the box behind the folding chairs and camping gear he had bought when they first moved here but had never used. He knew that if he stood, the world might swirl in front of him, but he would still feel the stabbing ache in his gut that never seemed to entirely go away. Alan looked up and met his father's eyes briefly and then went back to pushing his truck. He wasn't exactly playing; he was pretending, so that everything would look okay. They were all pretending now.

The funeral had been two days ago. Alan hadn't slept, and he'd hardly eaten. Boyd knew that Alan's circumstances were getting dire, but he couldn't bear to leave the house. A good father would take his boy to see someone—a counselor, a doctor, someone. But

Boyd was in no shape to leave the house right now. The Protective Services office had called to check in with him an hour ago. There were still mandated appointments and sessions. Up to this point, Boyd had been meticulous in keeping every one, filling every obligation. But now he'd missed an appointment and a session with their joint therapist. He knew his boy needed help as much as he did, maybe more, and all Boyd could do was stare at the empty bottle in front of him.

When he'd arrived at the morgue, her body had looked as though it had been deflated. The skin had lost all color, and he could see the outline of every bone in her body through the translucent wrapping. She had spoken, the nurse had told him. She had spoken to the little girl. They talked for several minutes, and then Grace had what they thought to be a massive stroke. She'd talked. That was what Boyd was stuck on. Grace hadn't had a cohesive conversation since that last night at the house. Even when he had visited her early on, her talk had been in rhymes and nonsensical, disconnected words. Then she stopped talking altogether. But not to Ceit—she talked to Ceit, and the damnable little witch killed her.

Boyd clenched his fists and then released. That wasn't fair. Ceit hadn't done a thing, had she? The nurse had been there, close enough anyway. And who blames a soon-to-be twelve-year-old for causing a heart attack in a terminally ill patient? It was ridiculous... and yet, it was what it was.

The funeral had been a circus, as he'd known it would be. He'd been privy to the Caoine from his own childhood. Boyd knew what the old women would do if they could. He knew that even though they hadn't been to see Grace in two years, since the accident, they would show up in droves now that she was finally dead.

He had her cremated as an impulse, but also because the idea of

Alan seeing his mother's body like that again was unbearable. They had been to see her the day before she passed, before Ceit. Alan had held his mother's hand and told her all about San Diego and the house and his new friends. He had chattered on in a hopelessly optimistic voice and then cried for the three hours it took to drive home. He didn't understand why she was sick, he didn't understand why Ceit was gone, he wanted to go home, he wanted to see his grandmother, he wanted, he wanted, he wanted.

Boyd drank. He had never drunk alcohol when he lived on the cul-de-sac in Venice. The Society didn't disallow it, but they certainly didn't encourage it either. Boyd's first taste had been with the men at the Home Depot warehouse in Torrance. After that, he had taken to keeping a bottle in the fridge, just a little treat. Now he bought it by the case and hid it from his son, although he knew he failed at that endeavor.

All he could see was Grace's golden-red hair, the way she looked on their wedding day, her smiling up at him when she first held newborn Ceit. He remembered their arguments, how her eyes would flash with anger. Her voice would drop to a deep tone instead of a yell, which was by far more frightening. Boyd always found himself backing down from whatever he had proposed to be right. He remembered the feel of her body and the smell of apples in spring that lived on the soft spot behind her ear. He saw her decayed and destroyed body lying on the metal table. He saw the gray urn of ashes she was reduced to. He picked up the empty vodka bottle and slammed it back down again.

The old women. They had clustered together in their huddle at the cemetery. Ceit and a woman with dark hair and eyes that sent shivers up his spine stood opposite them. Boyd and Alan stood alone. No one else came. No one else was left. Ceit had approached Alan before the service started. He had run to her, sobbing. Boyd had ripped him away, and his daughter's pale, incriminating eyes had locked on his, judging him, condemning him. She had whispered to Alan that it was okay and then something else that Boyd could not make out, and then she had gone back to her caretaker while the little boy had sobbed on Boyd's leg. His whole body heaving, he alternately cried for his mother and for Ceit. Máthair Shona broke from the pack and held Alan's hand, glaring at Boyd. She wiped the little boy's tears away while the preacher spoke.

Boyd had no idea who he was. The care center said he was their pastor and had spent time with Grace. That was fine. The old women let him speak of God and everlasting light for a full five minutes before they started their infernal chanting. They threw bits of cloth and bread into the hole where the ashes would go. They threw handfuls of salt and coins. The pastor stopped, confused, and Boyd had stuttered an apology. From across the fray, Ceit locked her eyes on his and raised one eyebrow, daring him to stop it. The wailing of the Caoine grew to a fevered pitch, and Boyd lost control. He shoved Alan into his grandmother's arms and rushed at the women. He screamed at them to stop, told them to fuck off, told them he wished every single one of them were in the ground instead of his Grace. He had felt himself outside his body. He had no control as the old women pushed him back. Then he turned to his only daughter, her pale eyes so much like her mother's and her grandmother's and on and on and on. He called her a murderer. He told her she was evil.

He woke up on Máthair Shona's sofa. He had no idea how he'd gotten there. He still didn't. Alan was sobbing in the next room. Máthair Shona was sitting across from Boyd, watching him with her own set of pale eyes.

"I've my own sins to repay for Grace's death. I've only just returned to this world entirely, you know. It was hard for me to understand everything that happened. I was culpable in every way for what they said I did. I should have stopped it." She had narrowed her gaze and then continued. "The girl is not one you want to make an enemy of. She is above the things of this world, and you have always known it. Take your boy home. Make a life for him."

So here Boyd sat, his son a pale imitation of the child he was two years ago. God only knew the damage that had been done. Boyd knew with certainty that hell was real, and there was no greater sin than destroying your children.

40

ANNBETH PLACED A PIECE OF DRY SHEET CAKE IN FRONT of Ceit.

"Happy birthday," she said flatly. The other Jr. Girls were milling around the cafeteria, eating the October birthday party cake, casting sideways glances at Ceit. One sad balloon hung from the back of a folding chair.

Ceit laughed, a dark, scoffing sound. "Thanks." She said and pushed the cake away. Another birthday at MacLaren Hall. She had started the sixth grade at Madrid Junior High. School was the same nonsense as it had always been. She liked the idea of walking from class to class better though. People looked at her less, and teachers took less notice. She blended in with the sea of people. No one asked her how she was feeling. No one called her freak.

Ceit stared out the grimy windows and unconsciously rubbed her arm. She had five stitches right above her wrist. It had happened last week. Ceit hadn't been able to sleep. She had walked from the Jr. Girls' hall to the communal bathroom, where she stood in the fluorescent light and stared at her reflection. She was trying to figure out what she was feeling. It wasn't grief exactly. She had known for years that her mother would never recover. It wasn't guilt either. Wheels had been set in place in the Society long before she was born that brought the Sluagh to their door. She might be a beacon for the dark energy, but she hadn't invited it in. No, that had been done without Ceit's help.

She had wandered back down the hall barefoot, taking her time going back to her cot. The windows were high up on the slab of a wall and covered in wire mesh, so the moonlight looked as though it were divided into one thousand separate bits. She had been staring at the prism of refracted light when she had felt herself reeling forward. The shock of the movement numbed her, and she nearly didn't react in time to stop the fall with her arms. When she turned, she saw one of the orderlies who worked the Sr. Boys' hall. He was a slight, wiry man, with a face pinched like a weasel. His eyes were a muddy gray and his skin pockmarked with acne scars. The other girls made fun of him constantly. He was the butt of their jokes. They giggled that he was their boyfriend and then squealed in disgust. Ceit knew he heard this. She had never participated in any of the giggles and cruelty, but she doubted that mattered now.

"Not supposed to be out of bed, little girl," he hissed. "Come with me. We'll take you to see the dean. He'll love to straighten you out." With that, he grabbed her by the arm, hard enough to cause what would turn into a purple-black bruise by the next morning. Ceit felt herself pulled to her feet and then dragged along, and she stumbled to keep up with the pace. For a small man, he was surprisingly strong. He stunk of tobacco and stale sweat.

"I'd let go, if I were you," she managed to say with a semblance of calm in her voice.

"My job is to monitor the halls. You were out of your dorm, so

I'm taking care of it." He turned his head and grinned. "You think I don't hear how you and your friends talk? You think you are so funny, eh?"

"They're not my friends, if it matters," Ceit said firmly while trying to wrench her arm away from his grip.

"It doesn't," he replied coldly.

Ceit knew they weren't headed to the front office. She gathered her waning strength for what she might have to do. The man stopped in front of the Time Away room, a cramped and windowless cell that locked from the outside. The man flung open the door and gestured for Ceit to enter.

"No," Ceit said simply.

The weasel-faced man laughed. "No? I'm in charge, little girl. You don't have a choice."

His hand still gripped around her arm, he shoved her forward, but Ceit caught the motion and swung away from the door. As she collided with the concrete wall adjacent to the opening, she reached back to where she had seen the man's keys hanging from a ring on his belt. The feel of the metal secure in her hand, she pivoted back, breaking his grip on her arm.

"Little bitch!" the man swore, and grabbed at her again.

With one solid movement, Ceit raked the keys down his face. He squealed in pain, an ugly, frightened sound. Ceit stepped back and muttered the words that had lain dormant for nearly two years.

"Ceanglaím tú dorcha."

She felt the floor begin to tremble, and the little man began to cry. Ceit felt a wave of anger rise up in her—anger at this wretched little creature in front of her who sought to harm her; anger at her father and his empty, cruel words; anger at Annbeth and whatever force had kept her in this place for far too long; anger at the moon and the sky and the night. She seethed with it. Her entire body shook, quaking with the fire she felt building from her core. It wasn't enough to bind this little man, to stop him from doing harm. He needed to pay, and he needed to be sorry for what he had planned to do to her, for what he had done to others. Never breaking her eyes from his, Ceit stabbed a key into her forearm and dragged it across. A stream of dark blood welled to the surface and dripped to the floor. She knelt, never breaking her gaze from the frightened and cowering creature before her. With one hand she traced the image of the serpent in the blood that was now gushing from her open wound. The serpent was the harbinger of war. It cast fear into the heart of the enemy. Its poison, once ingested, never left your flesh. You died from the bite of the nathair for all your days, your life-force slowly draining, the pain you inflicted on others coming back tenfold, its vengeance lodged in the very marrow of your bones. As she outlined the shape, she muttered a curse.

"Ag fulaingt go léir do laethanta."

Ceit could hear voices in the hall and knew others had heard the man's shrieking. They would be upon them any moment. She smiled at little man, whose acne scars would now be punctuated with jagged lines that ran from his forehead to his chin, mercifully missing his eyes. She hoped he would suffer all his days.

The hall was soon filled with people, from the night staff who had been dozing in the front office to curious faces from the adjoining dormitories. They saw what they wanted to see: a little girl, bleeding from a wound obviously inflicted by the hysterical orderly on the ground. No one paid any attention to the strange symbol smeared in blood on the linoleum floor—no one except Annbeth, who had run from the front and had known immediately what had happened when she saw Ceit's face. Annbeth had offered her a shocked nod of approval and then jumped back to clearing

the hallway of curious onlookers. Ceit was taken to the community hospital and stitched up. The orderly was taken to the psych
ward after he wouldn't stop shrieking.

In the days to come, several girls would quietly come forward
and tell horrible stories about things he had done. The front office
administration would listen and then quietly cover up every
instance of misconduct. But justice for the girls wouldn't be lost,
not entirely. The wiry little man with the leering eyes and the
pinched face would never leave the psychiatric hospital. He would
never stop screaming. Even after his vocal cords burst from the
strain and no sound could be uttered, he would continue to sound-
lessly choke out a strangled shriek. One day he would hang himself
with a bedsheet, and no one would miss him. Ceit knew all this as
they closed the gash on her arm with five neat stitches. It was fair
and right.

That had been two weeks ago, and the stitches would come out
soon. Ceit had turned twelve two nights after the incident, and
Annbeth had left a note on her pillow.

"It's almost time."

Ceit had been forced into an uneasy truce with Annbeth.
Begrudgingly, Ceit had admitted to herself that after the shitshow
that was her mother's funeral and in the cleanup from the incident
in the hallway, Annbeth had been her only ally. She knew it was a
form of Stockholm syndrome—the one who was responsible for
her confinement was also her only friend—but it was all she had.
Still, she remembered the words that had come from her mother's
lips and the dream warnings from the Matrarc, and she kept her
eyes open to the signs that this would end.

41

THE CURSE THAT CEIT HAD CAST ON THE ORDERLY
was like nothing Annbeth had ever seen. She recognized the image
of the serpent from the drawings in the holy book they kept at
the altar of the temple back in Salt Lake. The Codex Gigas was a
mystery to her, as it was to most of the congregation. But the Maga
read from it in the ancient Latin, and Annbeth had seen the image
of the serpent coiled around the elaborately illustrated pages. The
massive leather-bound text was sacred to the temple. The Maga
had found it in the very back of a used book shop in Providence.
The owner hadn't wanted to part with it, but she had convinced
him that it was going to a grand home. The old man had warned
her that the magic the book contained wasn't meant to be practiced by just anyone, but ultimately, he collected a sizable payment
and parted with the text.

He needn't have worried; the magic in the book was out of the
reach of even the Maga herself. She had taught herself to read the
Latin, and the senior members of the temple pored over the images

and tried to pull meaning from the language, but it was far beyond them. Annbeth didn't need to be told that the curse that Ceit had managed to cast on the scumbag in the hallway was part of a tradition of magic that the Maga would never obtain. She had nodded at Ceit when she walked onto the scene, but inside she had been in a whirlwind. This changed everything. The temple had told her that Ceit's powers could not fully manifest until she came of age. Early adulthood was when the spirit was the strongest, they had said. She is a child, they had told Annbeth, and she is just beginning to see what she is capable of.

This made Annbeth question everything they had ever told her. This "child" had summoned a curse from the ancient magic—and done it with seemingly no struggle or strain. The temple thought they would take her to their enclave and Ceit would complacently lead them, teach them, protect them. The Maga thought she could control Ceit. Annbeth leaned against the doorway of the darkened dormitory, watching Ceit's sleeping form on the far side of the room. They were wrong. This girl was not to be ruled over.

42

THE PERFECT COUPLE WAS EXACTLY WHAT CEIT HAD
expected. The man was in his midthirties. He wore a suit jacket
over his striped T-shirt. His jeans were stone-washed and his
sneakers clean. His wife was in a long, hippie wrap skirt that wove
every color together in a shimmering rainbow. Her skin was the
lightest shade of cocoa, and her long black hair was pulled back
in a million tiny braids in a wrap that defied gravity on the back of
her head. They said all the right things: they wanted to give Ceit
a chance to have her childhood back, they had a little ranch up
in Oxnard, they had fostered kids before, they knew she needed
her space as much as she needed their support. They smiled and
nodded at the right times. The wife, with her perfect yoga-toned
arms, reached out and took Ceit's hands in hers while they talked.
They were the perfect combination of conservative stability and
edgy compassion.

   Ceit knew that if she left with them, she would spend just
enough time at the little ranch in Oxnard to fool the Child

Protective Services office into thinking she was in her forever home. They would do their perfunctory checks, and then as soon as they moved on to more urgent affairs in their already over-burdened office, Ceit would be moved to wherever the center of Annbeth's people were. She knew the seemingly perfect couple in front of her in the dayroom knew she knew this. Annbeth knew this as well. They were all supposed to be on the same side. Ceit was growing doubtful of the promises made to her at her mother's bedside and in the dreams of the Matrarc. She wondered if anyone was coming to get her.

She had tried to escape from the junior high last week and failed miserably. Ceit wondered if that was the reason the perfect couple had shown up now. Annbeth was afraid she was going to bolt, and she was not wrong. Ceit had lingered after class, pretending to do homework. She knew the van was outside waiting for her and the other girls from Mac. She also knew that one girl wouldn't be able to open her locker and would be late, thanks to the penny Ceit had crammed in the hinge during passing period. She would be the distraction, and Ceit would slide out the side gate and run to the nearest city bus stop.

The escape plan had fallen apart almost immediately. She had made it out the gate, but the assistant principal had seen her exit. He called out to her and followed. She was caught. He mercifully didn't tell the van driver, just placed a hand on her shoulder as they walked to the front, where she was supposed to be exiting. He had muttered some sort of encouragement, and Ceit had ignored him. The girl's locker she'd sabotaged turned out to be a much bigger deal. For her trouble, Ceit ended up sitting in the hot van for an hour while the janitor pried the door open. Annbeth knew there had been a delay at the school and suspected Ceit was responsible, but as far as Ceit knew, she wasn't aware of the escape attempt.

But Ceit had also begun to wonder how many people at the school were a part of Annbeth's world.

So here she sat, the perfect couple chattering across the table, Frank the caseworker nodding happily. Ceit knew that Frank was ready to be rid of her. After the fiasco that was her mother's funeral, he had stopped hiding the dread on his face when they had their weekly meetings. Frank was supposed to have been the one to accompany her to the service. Ceit had known all along that Annbeth would never let that happen. Ceit wasn't sure what trouble Annbeth had caused to make it happen, but when the time came to leave, it was Annbeth, not Frank, who led her to the car. It had landed on Frank, however, to clean up the mess that was left behind. He had had to sort out the details and collect statements from her father, the old women, and the poor, traumatized pastor. He had had to transcribe the notes and ask Ceit to spell out what that old women reported she said: "Ar ais go dorchadas anois."

It wasn't a curse or a blessing. It was a way of settling down the restless spirits that, if left unattended, joined the ranks of the Sluagh. Back to darkness, back to your fate, back away from the living world. That was what Ceit had uttered as chaos reigned while the gray urn that held her mother's ashes sat forgotten in the center of the fray. As her father screamed curses at her, as the old ones threw their trinkets, and as Alan sobbed quietly in Máthair Shona's arms, she had raised her arms and called out the command. It had silenced the mayhem immediately. The old women understood, but no one else—not even her father. Though he had grown up in the Society, he had never understood the ancient ways, not the language and not the balance that needed to be maintained between life and death.

Frank had been tasked with the paperwork, cleanup, and filing of that day. Ceit did not blame him for wanting to ship her off to the first foster family to apply. In truth, Ceit knew that according to all the official rules, she should have been at Mac no longer than thirty days. She was going on two full years. The sooner she left, the sooner the front office could make that oversight disappear. Not like she was the only one. There were girls and boys who had spent far longer than Ceit at Mac and had no chance of release; they were in prison until they left at eighteen.

"So let's get this ball rolling!" the man in the striped shirt and tailored jacked said sunnily, smiling at Ceit.

"Yes, let's," his wife agreed, giving Ceit's hand a little squeeze. Her flesh was cold and slick, like the serpent that Ceit had drawn in her own blood on the hallway floor.

"Ceit?" Frank asked, his face hesitantly optimistic.

Ceit shrugged and got up from the table, walking away from the artificial conversation to look out the window. Where was her sign? Where were the Ch'įįdii that her mother had promised? She would have no choice in leaving with these people if it came down to it. They would sign all the papers, and she would be taken from here. She closed her eyes and sent a silent signal out into the world. *"Hurry,"* she said. *"It's time."*

43

Subject: Ceit Marie Robertson (hereafter referred to as CR)
Doctor in Session: Dr. Sonia Katz (hereafter referred to as SK)
*This session marks the final counseling session at MacLaren Hall. The minor child, CR, will be placed with a foster family, effective on 11/1/1987. Therapy will be transferred to the Oxnard Psychiatric Center, close to CR's placement home.*

SK: Ceit, this is the last time we will be meeting.
CR: Are you sad?
SK: Are you? Are you nervous about your foster home?
CR: A bit, but not for the reasons you think. Are you relieved?
SK: I am relieved you will be with a family. I think that will be a good experience for you. And the (inaudible rustlings) Pierces are a lovely family. They've fostered many teenagers and older kids before. They will take very good care of you. They have a swimming pool, and there are animals on their ranch. Do you like animals?
CR: More than people, if you want to know. What if I told you that

the Pierces are part of a cult that has the power to control people's minds? What if I told you that the Pierces are only holding me until the rest of the cult can get to me? What if I told you that this same cult had intimidated my father and cousin and who knows who else into not taking me in? What if I told you that they can take over people's bodies? Not just anyone, but the more susceptible, superstitious among you—missionaries and the like. What if I told you all that? Would you still ask me if I like animals?

SK: I would say that you have a very good imagination. Ceit, I know you are worried, but we really do check out our foster families very carefully. We wouldn't let you go with someone who would cause you harm. All this sounds like you have some anxieties. Would you like to talk about them?

CR: If I leave with the Pierces, I will stay at that ranch in Oxnard just long enough for all of you here to forget about me. That won't be long—a matter of weeks. After that, I will disappear, and no one will ever look for me. You should ask Annbeth about that.

SK: (inaudible rustling) Do you intend to try to run away from your foster family, Ceit?

CR: I don't think I could if I tried. I would expect they will have rather tight security up there at their ranch with all their animals. No, my best bet is to break out of here.

SK: Ceit, I understand that you are feeling overwhelmed. I can only tell you that Eric and Kara Pierce have worked with Child Protective Services before, they have fostered kids your age and older, and they really want to make a difference. They aren't part of a cult. Eric Pierce is a financial analyst who works from home. Kara runs a yoga studio near the house. Both of them will have lots of time for you. It will be a good change. I feel like they are very different, perhaps, from the people you grew up with.

CR: You have no idea how similar they are.

SK: I'm sorry you feel this way. I hope they can change your mind.
CR: I'd like to tell my brother where I'm going.
SK: I hate to have to tell you this, Ceit, but your father has requested no contact. However, if you write a letter, I can see what I can do.
CR: When do I leave?
SK: On November 1. I really want you to try to stay positive about this, Ceit. Try not to find reasons not to like them. Tonight, I'd like you to list all the positive things about going to a foster home. Don't let your imagination make you unhappy.
CR: It doesn't need to.

End of Session

## 44

BOYD STARTLED AWAKE AT THE POUNDING ON THE front door. His head throbbed, and for a minute his vision blurred.

"Mr. Healy? Are you home?" a man's voice called at the door.

Boyd tensed immediately. It was another damn repairman or missionary or some spy sent from god knows where. It wasn't enough that he'd signed away his daughter, denounced her, and was living in an entirely separate city. They still wanted more. He looked to digital clock on the nightstand—10:03 a.m. *Goddamn.* Boyd cringed at the movement it took to swing his legs out of bed. Alan would be gone. He had taken to getting himself off to school without waking his father. If Boyd let the guilt of that in, he would never leave the bed again, so instead he pushed it back down along with the sea of regrets that lived at the bottom of his being.

"Mr. Healy?" The voice called again "We really need to talk, Mr. Healy. My name is Brad Carpenter. I'm with Child Protective Services. Can I come in?"

Boyd groaned and pulled on a pair of stained sweatpants that lay on the floor near the bed. His T-shirt smelled of booze and grease. He knew what he looked like, his beard shaggy and unkempt, hollows under his eyes. It was clever, them sending an actual CPS agent, not the typical little lady with Jesus pamphlets or the damn Mormons. He knew he didn't have a choice; he could hide in his filthy bedroom all day, but Brad Carpenter or whoever the hell he really was would knock all day.

Boyd shuffled to the door and looked through the peephole. Very clever indeed. This one was wearing a button-up and suit jacket—very professional. Boyd chuckled darkly as he opened the door and stared Brad Carpenter in the face.

"Just drop the act. What do you want?" Boyd said coldly.

"Mr. Healy, I'm not sure what you mean. My name is Brad Carpenter. You can call me Brad. I'm from Child Protective Services. You've missed several check-ins, and we've received a report from your son's school. Can I come in?" The man looked over Boyd's shoulder at the living room. There were dirty plates on the side table and laundry strewn over the sofa. An empty bottle of vodka had rolled onto the floor. The wood floor was filthy, covered in mud prints and remnants of the trash that Boyd had knocked over last night. Boyd realized that Alan must have tried to sweep up at some point, and he felt a pinprick of shame in his chest.

"What message do you need to tell me? Just out with it. I'm fucking sick of your games. I did everything you asked. Why are you still following me?" His words caught in his throat and he coughed. He could feel bile rise and fall in his esophagus, and he gagged.

"Mr. Healy, I have no idea what you are talking about. Here is my identification. I'm here from CPS, and this is rather serious. Can I come in so we can talk?" Brad's voice was firmer, and he narrowed his eyes a bit.

*Clever*, Boyd thought. *He's sticking to the role.*

"Is it Ceit?" Boyd asked. "She's all yours. Isn't that what you wanted? I told them no contact, I signed all the damn papers— what else could you possibly want from me?" Boyd's voice raised and cracked. The creature in front of him furrowed his brow and squared his posture.

"Mr. Healy...Boyd. I don't know what you are talking about. You are on the edge of losing custody of your son, again. And this time it could be permanent. You had very specific obligations you needed to fulfill. You have missed appointments. Your son's school filed a report stating that he appears unwashed, his clothes aren't laundered, and he frequently does not have either a packed lunch or money for school food. According to the report, they have tried contacting you and have received no response. We are aware that your wife passed recently, and we are very sorry for your loss. However, it is a very real concern that you may no longer be capable of caring for your son. We understand that you are no longer employed? Is this true?" Brad locked his gaze on Boyd. "I am sorry to be speaking of these things here, outside. I would prefer for your sake to have a private conversation."

Boyd took a deep breath and considered the man's words. They were trying to drive him mad, that was it. The damn demons or monsters or whatever the hell they were had taken to driving him until he broke completely.

"Get the fuck off my steps," Boyd growled. "Go back to whatever hell you came from. Let this poor sap go. Leave him on the sidewalk, wipe his memory, do whatever you do, but leave me the fuck alone." With that, he slammed the door.

He heard a halfhearted "Mr. Healy...please," before the creature shuffled away and Boyd was left alone. All his courage dissipated immediately, and Boyd collapsed onto the filthy floor. His hands were shaking, and his head was spinning. What more did they want from him? He had done everything. Was it the old ones on Sinder Avenue that kept sending these monsters? Boyd had never known them to be so capable as to do such a thing, but who else?

It was all because of the damn girl. She had killed her mother. She had ruined everything. If it weren't for the little witch, he would be living with his golden-haired wife in their little house. Maybe they would've left. The two of them and Alan would be in some sweet little suburb by now. He'd be an electrician or a carpenter or something, and she'd stay home and care for the garden and the house. They'd have a dog and a car with four doors. But none of that could happen now with that little bitch of a girl fucking everything up.

Boyd lurched to his feet. He had a plan. It was a three-hour drive to LA. He left a note on the table for Alan saying he was sorry, and he left a stack of crumpled one-dollar bills so the boy could order a pizza. It was the last cash they had. The creature at the door had been right; he had lost his job. But that wouldn't matter soon. It would end tonight, one way or the other. His boy wouldn't grow up alone on account of that little demon sitting in her palace in Los Angeles, fucking up their lives with the nod of her head.

45

ANNBETH STEADIED HERSELF AGAINST THE DESK IN THE
front office. The desk manager, a squattish woman named Deirdre,
matched Annbeth's furrowed grimace.

"I can alert the gate security to be extra cautious, but it would
help if you would tell me how you got this information," Deirdre
said with worry in her voice.

"I can't exactly. I have some contacts in San Diego who saw
Boyd Robertson—or Healy or whatever he calls himself now—
they saw him acting erratically, and they told me he was headed to
Los Angeles. That's all I know. But I'm worried for Ceit." Annbeth
had told some of the truth. The fact that her contacts had followed
him up the I-5 until he lost them by weaving through traffic had
been an unnecessary detail. Deirdre also didn't need to know that
her initial contact was a gardener whose mind had been overtaken
by the high priestesses of the temple. It would be very hard to
explain that the team who had followed Boyd up the freeway in
a mad chase was really just a car full of teenagers high on pot and

cheap beer. Deirdre likely wouldn't understand that the real drivers of the car were hundreds of miles away in a meditation circle in an underground worship hall in Salt Lake.

"It's very hard to explain, but you have to trust me. Can we call in more security for the entrances and exits?" Annbeth asked, lowering her eyes a bit, trying not to look as frightened as she felt.

"There really isn't much we can do now, with the holiday and all. But I'll let the gate know. I'll radio the security officers and tell them to keep an eye out." Deirdre reached out and took Annbeth's hand, making her jump. "I know you worry about that one. I think we all do, especially after that terrible incident…poor little thing. I could just shoot that man myself. But from what I heard, he's in pretty bad shape. Complete nervous breakdown, they said."

Annbeth just nodded. It was so much more than that. She squeezed Deirdre's hand and then paced back down the hallway to warn Ceit.

46

CEIT HATED HALLOWEEN. SHE HAD HATED IT AS A CHILD in the cul-de-sac, and she hated it even more here in Mac. The rest of the residents from Jr. Girls had dressed up in devil horns, angel wings, zombie makeup, and vampire teeth. The counselors had made a middling effort at entertainment by setting up candy stations at various points in the building. *One could trick or treat, if your idea of fun was running around a prison and collecting stale candy,* Ceit thought darkly. For her part, Ceit lay on her bed, staring out the window at the night sky.

They never celebrated Halloween on the cul-de-sac. Samhain was the same night, and the elders made a big show of chanting and offering gifts of salt and bread to the moon. It was the night that the elders believed the veil between the worlds was thinnest—the night when the dead could be contacted and communicated with. The Matrarc would lead two or three of the most respected elders to the stones, where they would ask for guidance for the year to come. Ceit had never attended these Samhain ceremonies, and it had always irked her, even as a very little girl. She suspected that if the world hadn't fallen apart, then she would be of an age where she would follow the Matrarc to the beach where the veil would be lifted and they would have entered the layer of reality that lay just below the surface.

But the world had fallen apart, and Ceit was here, listening to the girls giggle and carry on from the hallway. The counselors had tried to banish the devil costumes, but that had made them only more popular. They had tried to banish all sorts of things they suspected to be evil, including Madonna, a variety of heavy metal bands that Ceit could care less about, and the *Smurfs* cartoon on Saturday mornings that really only showed in the Pixie ward, where the babies and toddlers were kept. None of it had stuck. Ceit had laughed at their attempts. She knew for a fact that there was a group of Sr. Boys who played Dungeons and Dragons in the boiler room after lights-out. She had seen them sneaking down the hallway when she was on one of her roaming night walks. They had their books and little bags of dice. Ceit wondered if the counselors knew how appealing they made devil craft sound by the very nature of banning such things.

The Pierce family would be at Mac tomorrow morning to take Ceit to their ranch in Oxnard. She had packed her few belongings and listened to the entirety of Annbeth's rant following her last counseling session.

"Do you want to stay at Mac forever?" Annbeth had asked. She had been approached, she told Ceit, because her name had been mentioned in the session. "What did you say?"

Ceit had shrugged. She knew the good Dr. Katz couldn't share the transcripts of the session without her consent, and she knew no one believed anything she said. She also knew that Annbeth had seen the notes that her paranoia was increasing, her inability to connect with or trust the staff was inflated, and the CPS psychologist had serious concerns about the placement that had been arranged.

Annbeth had raged at Ceit for nearly an hour. "We're helping you," she had whispered in a steely tone. "We're getting you out of here, out of this system for good, don't you see?"

Ceit had refused to respond, instead meeting her eyes and offering as little reaction as possible. It didn't matter. Ceit couldn't see how this would possibly end in any other manner than her leaving with Kara and Eric Pierce tomorrow morning. Even the psychologist's concerns weren't enough to delay this.

Girls dressed in bedsheets rushed into the dormitory and then, in a flurry of chaos, crashed into each other and ran back out. Melanie had left Mac finally, a placement in a foster home somewhere in East LA. The girls were starting to forget the incident with Melanie's eye and starting to not be openly frightened of Ceit, but they still were unnerved. She had become a curious oddity, a harmless sort of freak, someone to giggle at, the butt of dares. Ceit sighed. If she were to be here for any longer, she would need to address such things, but it was hardly worth it now.

Just as she closed her eyes, trying to block out the noise and light, she heard Annbeth's steps approaching the bed. Annbeth's energy was a blackish swirling cloud, like soot. Ceit didn't need to open her eyes to know that she was silently staring at her.

"We have a problem," Annbeth said. Her voice didn't sound angry any longer; rather, it sounded borderline panicked.

Ceit opened her eyes and propped herself up on her elbows. "Oh?"

"Yeah... my people in San Diego, they've been keeping an eye on your father. They say he took off a while ago. They tried to follow him, but he lost them in traffic." She sounded the words out slowly as though trying to figure out what they meant.

"What would this possibly have to do with me?" Ceit asked, but her interest was piqued.

"He was headed north, probably to LA. There's not much he'd come back here for. They called me because they're concerned he's coming here." Annbeth sat on the edge of the cot.

"Your contact, did he talk to my father directly?" Ceit asked.

"No, they've been keeping their distance. But they overheard him bawling out a CPS agent. Guess your father's fallen apart a bit. Lost his job, looks like he's been drinking," Annbeth answered nervously.

"What about my brother?" Ceit asked sharply. "Who's taking care of him? He's only eight."

"I don't know," Annbeth said. "I suspect that very soon CPS in San Diego will be looking after him. Sounds like your father's missed appointments, and there have been complaints."

"Why do you think he's coming here?" Ceit asked, narrowing her gaze. "You know more than you're telling me."

Annbeth paused. "He's been in a bad state for a while now. I guess his last interaction with the child protection office concerning you was rather angry. He had to file a no contact order. I'm sorry it had to be this way, kid."

"Save it," Ceit said coldly. "I don't want your apology. Far too late for any of that. When did this happen?"

"Around ten or eleven this morning." Annbeth looked nervously out the window. It was just about five thirty. The light was quickly dimming outside, and the bell signaling dinner would ring soon. "He'd be here by now. I'm keeping an eye out, and I told the office. The security guards at the gate are on alert."

"That doesn't actually make me feel better," Ceit responded curtly.

Ceit tried to carry on with her day as normally as possible, but

Annbeth's news clawed at the edge of her thoughts. She pushed food around her plate as the ghouls and angels around her giggled and unwrapped their candy in place of the flavorless meatloaf and reconstituted potatoes on the cafeteria tray. The boiled carrots were sour, and Ceit suspected they were the same batch they'd been eating since last week.

Ceit was on kitchen duty that night. Annbeth stood in the doorway of the washroom while Ceit, donning long plastic kitchen gloves and an apron, scraped food into the trash. She stacked the plates in the industrial dish rack and then passed it down to the next girl to spray down. Annbeth paced nervously. The clock over the entry read 6:40 p.m. If Ceit's father had come to LA, he would most certainly be here. But getting into Mac would take some work. He had cut himself off the guest list, so getting past the locked gate, at night and unannounced, would be a feat.

By the time Ceit was spraying down the cafeteria tables with vinegar and wiping the surface clean, Annbeth was looking notably more relaxed. Ceit could hear her thoughts pinging off the walls: *He'd be here by now. He probably turned around and went home. Probably never even left San Diego. He'd never get through the gate anyway. He'd never know where to find her. She's safe here...*

Ceit hung up the apron on the hook on the kitchen door and walked down the hall to the dorm. Around her the others still shrieked and ran up and down the hall dressed in their homemade costumes. The counselors ignored the chaos. Order would resume tomorrow, but tonight they had given up. She curled up on her bed and opened her new book, which had earned the same distinction as heavy metal and Madonna. It was strictly forbidden by some of the counselors and tolerated by others. Ceit didn't like it quite as much as *Heaven*, but *Cabal* by Clive Barker was gruesome and made her feel more adult than usual. She longed to find Midian, the town that lay beneath the cemetery. Boone only wants to escape, but Ceit suspected that she was more Night Breed than human anyhow. She put a pillow over her ears to drown out the giggles and squeals that came and went from the dorm. She had just let herself fully dissolve into Boone's flight from Midian when she heard the screams in the hall.

Ceit sat up. It had to be the girls in their costumes, scaring each other. The next scream confirmed that she was wrong. Annbeth rounded the corner into the dormitory.

"Come on, fast!" Annbeth motioned and kept glancing at the door. "Now!" Ceit jumped off the bed. She was barefoot, and the cold concrete floor was jarring. She ran toward Annbeth. She didn't need to be told what had happened. Her father was here, and something was very, very wrong. In the hall, girls in halos and fairy wings ran past, their faces frozen in fear. From the end of the hall, Ceit heard a shriek and loud male voices. Annbeth pulled on her arm.

"C'mon, now!" She was pulling her in the direction the others were running, but Ceit stood her ground. She needed to see him. Was it actually her father, or was it the Sluagh wearing his skin as these girls were wearing their devil horns and bedsheets? She had never been able to hear her father's thoughts, and try as she did, she could not hear them now. The screaming terror of the girls in the hall filled her head, ringing in her ears. She did not feel the presence of the Sluagh or the Rabharta near, but that did not mean they had not taken hold of her weak-hearted father. Her little brother sat alone in a house far from here. He had been neglected, left behind. Ceit seethed with anger, and it rooted her in place even as Annbeth pulled on her arm.

"No," Ceit said firmly, and looked Annbeth in the eyes. "No. I need to see him. I can stop this."

"Ceit, come with me now!" Annbeth shouted, and pulled at her arm as more girls screamed their way past. On the far end of the hall, by the front office, Ceit could see the space clearing. Those who could run had, and anyone left was not there by choice. Ceit walked toward the office, Annbeth screaming behind her to listen, to run, to turn around and follow her. Ceit ignored her.

She felt her heart racing and her anger rising. A single bloody handprint adorned the wall as she neared the front doors. Ceit paused and considered. She hadn't heard a gunshot, so it must be some other manner of weapon. A knife perhaps. He had come to kill her, she knew that with certainty. She wondered how he'd gotten past the front gate. A chain-link fence ran the length of the property. A locked gate let authorized personnel, vans full of kids, and registered visitors in and out.

"Hello, my girl." A quiet voice drifted from outside the door. Ceit took a deep breath and stepped through the threshold. Boyd Healy sat in a cheap office chair at the front desk. Red-black blood smeared the counter, and Ceit saw the edge of a foot sticking out from the corner. She heard a raspy wheezing coming from the form, and Boyd turned his gaze to the figure. "I'm sorry. Really, I am. I didn't come here to hurt you." He looked up at Ceit. "More blood on your hands."

Ceit narrowed her focus. "How many people have you hurt to get here?"

Boyd stood. His face was skeletal, the skin hanging off the bone. Dark circles lined his eyes, and his greasy, matted hair stuck to his head in clumps. She could smell him from the doorway, unwashed skin and the stench of vomit and sweat. This was not the Rabharta; it was a much crueler form of madness. No, the Rabharta had no interest in one so far gone. He would provide no nourishment at all in this state. Even the demons of the old world had forsaken him.

"A few." Boyd held up a long knife, stained red. "I'll never be free of you. Alan will never be free of you. I'm sorry, my girl, really I am. They won't let me go. They keep watching and whispering and waiting, waiting, waiting." He stopped and spun around, the knife flailing. Ceit took a step back and waited for what he would do. "You know what your mother said to me when you were born?" He whispered, his voice barely audible. "She said she wished you'd been born a boy, that she wished all our children to be boys so the madness of your damnable Society would end." Then Boyd locked his eyes on Ceit, and in a mad scream unleashed, "But it did matter, you little bitch, it mattered! You ruined all of it. Your killed her—you killed them all!"

Ceit felt her anger boil to the top of her being. "Enough." Outside the doors, she could hear sirens approaching rapidly, and she knew the authorities would be inside in moments. "I can't decide if your punishment should be a locked cage, just like the one you left me in, for the rest of your days... or perhaps something from home. I could send you to the place where the Sluagh would pick at your bones for eternity. What would you like, Dad?"

Boyd started chuckling. It turned into a mad sound that filled the room. Without warning, he slid over the desk and rushed across the room. Ceit was startled at his speed. He looked as though he could barely stand, but he flung himself across the space. She heard the commotion of the officers entering the front doors. In the microsecond before Boyd closed the space between them, she whispered the words.

"Ceanglaím tú dorcha."

She was a fraction of a second too late and felt the knife pierce the flesh of her shoulder—not deep, he lacked the strength for it—but it was all she needed. As he reeled back, in the blood that sprang from the gash and fell to the concrete floor, she outlined the image of the crescent moon with the winding lines of the binding symbol cutting it in half. Urgently, Ceit whispered the words a second time.

"Ceanglaím tú dorcha."

Boyd Healy stopped deadly still, teetering before collapsing completely. It all happened in a matter of seconds. As Boyd's head hit the concrete, Ceit leaned in and whispered in his ear, "I cannot save you from your madness, but I can stop you from doing more harm."

Behind her, Ceit could hear the footsteps and the orders of the officers for Boyd to stand down, to put his hands up, to drop the weapon. With that, she fell back, shrieking in pain and begging for help she didn't need. The officers saw exactly what they wanted to see: a little girl, attacked and bleeding, and a madman with a knife. As the weapon fell from Boyd's hand and spun out of reach, they rushed in, pulling Ceit away as she whimpered and cried. She forced the tears out of her eyes, and the panic-stricken young police officer looked as though he would cry himself. She saw Boyd being pulled away, his voice already raw from screaming. But unlike the orderly, his senseless shrieking would stop before his throat was shredded and his mind folded in on itself. Ceit had bound his mind. Before he reached the ambulance, he would drop into a deep and dark sleep, never to fully awaken. Ceit let a memory flash before her eyes—"my girl" he had always called her in his soft voice. Whatever had driven him here had killed the man she had known. She closed her eyes and let the darkness overtake her.

When she awoke it was in a clean white hospital room. Her shoulder was bandaged, and she wore a blue gown that tied at the back of her neck. Annbeth sat by her bedside, dozing. Ceit regarded her for a moment before waking her. She felt thirsty but overall fine. Her father was gone; she didn't need anyone to tell her that.

He was trapped in a never-ending nightmare. Never again would he be free from the screams of the restless dead. Ceit's binding would provide him with sleep, but she could not offer him peace. It was beyond her sight to heal what had already been broken. She also knew that she wouldn't be leaving with the Pierces today. Boyd's breakdown had bought her time. She closed her eyes and waited for the sign that was promised. She would leave this place. The Ch'įįdii would come for her.

47

ANNBETH HAD SEEN BOYD HEALY'S FACE AS THE
ambulance carried him away, his arms cuffed to the gurney even
though it was clear to everyone that he was beyond harming
anyone but himself. Deirdre was rushed out in the same ambulance
as Ceit, her face smeared with blood and her lips moving silently,
sending up little crimson bubbles that popped in the October air.

The image of a crescent moon with swirling lines crossing it
was scrawled in blood on the office linoleum floor. Annbeth didn't
need to be told what had happened. When she had reported the
incident with the orderly to the temple, they had brushed her off.
It's not possible, they had said. The girl isn't powerful enough to
access the old magic. The man was obviously deranged to begin
with. They had told her to stick to the plan. The foster family was
arriving on Monday. They would take her to Oxnard, and then
Ceit could be transferred to her proper home in Salt Lake soon.

Annbeth knew they were mistaken. This little girl could not
be contained. The Pierces would be found dead on their ranch in

Oxnard. The girl would break free from all the attempts the temple made to restrain her. Annbeth could see clearly now. Ceit did not need what they were trying to force her into. She would burn down the temple and destroy the enclave of little houses with little more than the force of her will. The Maga was mistaken. Ceit was far beyond them; she had always been.

Annbeth needed to realign her loyalties. She longed for the comfort of her home, but she knew that if she helped bring Ceit there, it would never be a comfort again. Ceit was a caged tiger who was just beginning to understand that her captors were powerless against her. Once she fully awakened, Annbeth knew that the little girl would destroy them all.

She could already feel the girl creeping into her head. Last night she had dreamed of the serpent. It had slithered toward her on black marble floor. As it approached, it split into a thousand separate snakes with scales the color of night, the black marble transformed into a mass of the dark-scaled creatures. As they reached her ankles and began to climb up her bare legs, she opened her mouth in a scream she knew would never end. She had woken with the certainty that it had been no ordinary dream. Ceit was expanding her reach. Her powers were becoming more focused, and those she perceived as her enemy would feel the true power of the ancient magic the girl was just beginning to command.

48

THREE DAYS AFTER CEIT WAS SUPPOSED TO HAVE MOVED to a ranch in Oxnard with the Pierces, she lay on her cot at Mac, staring at the ceiling. She had arrived back at MacLaren Hall that morning. Her new departure date was set for Monday, which gave her a total of four days to figure out what it was she was going to do. She had spent her nights calling for the Ch'įįdii, trying to follow the advice of the creature that spoke through her mother, trying to listen to the dreams of the Matrarc, and nothing had happened. Her shoulder ached dully, and she adjusted a pillow under her head to relieve the pressure on her bandaged laceration. Between that wound and the stitches that still held her wrist together, Ceit was looking less like a little girl and more like she belonged at Mac.

Annbeth had been nervous. She didn't offer much information, but Ceit suspected the Pierces had grown hesitant. She was supposed to leave from the hospital with them, but instead Frank the caseworker had shown up in the Mac van.

"They want to make sure you're in good health," he had said

flatly. "They've delayed your pickup so you can heal without the shock of a new place."

Ceit wasn't the only one who thought that smelled of bullshit. Her former therapist, the good Dr. Sonia Katz, had scheduled another session with her even though their last meeting was supposed to be the end of their time together. Ceit suspected that Dr. Katz was prepping her for the reality that the Pierces might not show up at all.

This would have been good news, except Ceit knew perfectly well that if it wasn't the Pierces—with their quirky, edgy perfection—it would be someone else, and soon. Annbeth was itching to get her out of Mac. All their hurdles were now eliminated. There were no parents or family members to object. There was no one left to look for her when she mysteriously faded from the system. If she left with Annbeth's people, Ceit knew she would be forced onto the path the Matrarc had warned her of in her dreams. She stared out the window and muttered the name of the dreaming dead who were to show her a sign, a path out of this prison. "Ch'įįdii," Ceit mouthed the words silently, "*Ch'įįdii, we're running out of time.*"

The swirling black cloud of anxieties that preceded Annbeth made itself known at the foot of Ceit's bed. She sighed and turned her head.

"Yes?" she asked irritably.

Annbeth's face was slightly flushed, and she rolled the bit of cloth on the end of her plaid shirt back and forth in her fingers. Intrigued, Ceit sat up, wincing at the effort.

"You're nervous," she stated.

Annbeth frowned for a moment and then sat down. "We're having a program tomorrow morning. There are some people you need to meet. They're coming in to do a thing for the whole center, for all the girls, but I need you to sit down with the head of the district."

Ceit considered Annbeth's words. They often had special speakers or programs on Saturday mornings, whoever the counselors could rope in to be motivational. There was some sort of Avon or Mary Kay thing happening tomorrow. She could not have been less interested, but now she was curious despite herself.

"The makeup thing?" Ceit asked with a smirk.

Annbeth rolled the end of her shirt back and forth in her fingers, staring at the bed blankly.

"We're having some issues with your placement. Your medical issues have necessitated that you have more follow-up visits and medical clearances. It's becoming complicated..." She trailed off.

"You're nervous," Ceit repeated. "You're never nervous. You've held me here for two years—what's a few more months? Seriously, what aren't you saying?"

Annbeth looked up and met her eyes. Without using any spoken language, she thought the words into Ceit's consciousness. The thoughts were fuzzy and broken. Ceit realized that Annbeth was using every bit of her energy to transmit the message, whereas before it had seemed effortless.

"*My temple believes there are others after you. I have had dreams, and I haven't slept in days. I can't think straight. The district head wants to move you. She's afraid. She has an emergency plan to keep you safe.*"

"Safe?" Ceit scoffed out loud, making Annbeth jump.

"Ceit, I need to talk to you about the plan the temple has." Annbeth spoke in a hurried whisper, making Ceit lean in to hear the words. "They don't know you. I can't make them understand..."

Ceit bristled with frustration. "Understand what, exactly? You keep telling me this is all to keep me safe. I've ended up in the hospital twice in the past month. My own father gutted the gate security guard before stabbing the desk manager five times. Did you know she will likely lose function in her left arm? He would have killed me, and you are talking about handing me off to the Avon lady so I'll be safe. That's a good one." Ceit swung her legs off the bed and then stalked out the room. She knew Annbeth was still sitting on her bed, her mind swirling.

As she exited, she let a small smile play on her lips. Maybe the Ch'įįdii were coming for her after all. If Annbeth's people were spooked enough to resort to something as risky as this, the nightmares the dreaming dead haunted them with must be powerful. The program tomorrow was an opportunity. The girls from Jr. and Sr. halls would be in unorganized chaos. Ceit slid into the empty counselor's lounge and switched the television station to *Days of Our Lives*. Agent Brown's ring is in Carrie's purse. Roman is in love with Marlena but has to settle for Diana. Everyone lies, and everyone is duplicitous. Ceit knew that the sooner the deceit of her life here at Mac was over, the better for everyone.

49

DIRECTOR CARABUS STRAIGHTENED HER BLOUSE AND
pinned a name tag on her chest; it read "Leanne." She turned and
grinned at Annbeth.

"You like?" she asked. "I knew an Avon lady named Leanne
once. Always did like that name."

Annbeth sighed. The program was due to start any minute. The
rest of the WonderGals crew was clueless. Director Carabus, a.k.a.
Leanne, was the only member of the temple's Los Angeles team to
join them. The rest were at the gas station across the street from
Mac, waiting for the signal that would not happen until nightfall.

"This is easy. Not even you can mess this one up," Director
Carabus said with a pointed glare, which made the thick, cake-like
makeup surrounding her eyes crack. "We know what you told the
foster family. We understand you got rattled by this most recent
incident with the father, but you have to pull it together, girl. The
Maga will forgive your transgressions if you can play your part
tonight."

Annbeth sighed and watched the director as another of the WonderGals crew approached and pulled her away, showing her something to do with the makeup stations and mirrors they were using for this morning's program. Free makeovers—the common room would be in chaos. Ceit would be able to meet the director, and she would pass her the message and instructions. Annbeth's job was to make sure Ceit was ready for extraction that evening.

It was all bullshit. Annbeth felt her skin burning with the strain of the nightmares she had been suffering from. She knew the director had had them too since she had been in Los Angeles. The temple was blaming them on some outside group that was also interested in Ceit. Annbeth knew they were wrong. If they didn't come from Ceit herself, they were part of the old magic that surrounded her. Annbeth also knew she was in terrible trouble with the temple. She had called the Pierces and told them Ceit wasn't ready to leave. She had told them the girl was sick, an infection, and she needed more time. It hadn't been hard to dissuade them. Eric Pierce had mumbled in agreement and then told Annbeth about the nightmares he and his wife had been having. They both dreamed their ranch was being consumed by flames and they were chained to their bed. They dreamed of burning alive, all the way to the bone and ash. They dreamed of screaming endlessly even after they were reduced to a pile of dust and mineral.

The temple had known who was responsible when the Pierces said they needed to wait to pick up the girl, that they needed to think about it. Annbeth had been relieved until she realized the temple was just going to take Ceit anyway. They had sent Director Carabus and the rest of the LA team to extract her and take her straight to Salt Lake. They had thought of everything, they'd told her. Annbeth would be dealt with later.

*50*

"YOUNG LADY. YOU ARE GETTING AWAY WITH MURDER for how you're neglecting that skin. And those eyes—my land, those eyes. I think we'll go with a nice, natural glow with just a touch of Heavenly Shimmer on the edges to bring out those eyes."

Ceit could see the line of foundation rimming the border of the woman's face. She smelled of dryer sheets and baked goods. Her eyelids were colored with a rainbow of pink sparkles and a flaky turquoise substance that had broken into individual continents, each one threatening to come thundering down on her high-necked blouse with its magenta floral print. A cloth bow was tied around her neck.

In Ceit's book of fairy tales, there was a story of a princess who had a bow tied around her neck. She wore it all her days, until one day when it was untied, and her head fell clean off. As Leanne from WonderGals dabbed Heavenly Shimmer on the crease of Ceit's right eyelid, she wondered if the same would happen if she pulled at the magenta bow that bobbed back and forth with

Leanne's every movement. She wondered how far the head would roll before the first person screamed. She wondered if the layer of cosmetics that was slathered all over the woman's face would slow the decomposition process.

Annbeth had pulled Ceit from the Jr. Girls' dorm and into the common room promptly at ten o'clock. There was a smattering of others there already, the older girls from Sr. hall mostly. The WonderGals Makeup Crew had little stations set up at the dingy activity tables. Each girl got a makeup lesson, a mini-makeover, and a little gift bag to take with them, customized by their WonderGals representative. It was intended to be motivational. Ceit supposed it was at least a nice try. She knew, however, that her visit here had nothing to do with eye shadow. Leanne had a steely glint to her gray eyes. Under the thick layer of makeup, Ceit could see the same signs of fatigue that were showing more and more on Annbeth. Leanne wasn't sleeping. The Ch'įįdii were working their magic on them both, and she guessed on others as well.

Ceit, on the other hand, had slept well last night. The Matrarc had appeared in her dream as a child younger than Ceit. She had Ceit's pale hair and eyes, and she stood at the edge of a great canyon filled with dusty red rocks and green shrubs and trees. A hawk floated above them on the wind, his wings spread so wide he blocked the sun. The image was slightly blurry, as though Ceit were seeing it through a filter or a smudged pair of glasses. The child Matrarc hadn't spoken but pointed out across the expanse. Ceit squinted, and in the distance a ranch-style house became clear. It sat in the far corner of the great canyon, surrounded by leafy green trees. The red dirt swirled and danced in front of the structure. A woman stood on the front porch, her hands clutching the rail. Her skin was a deep copper and her eyes dark and strong as they stared out across the landscape. Her long gray hair was loose and wrapped itself around her like a night veil. The image faded out in a flash, leaving Ceit reeling. The child Matrarc then pointed the opposite direction, away from the canyon. There sat a dented pickup truck with faded reddish paint. There was no driver. Ceit strained to see any defining marks. The only thing she could make out through her altered vision was a tiny cartoon roadrunner hanging from the rearview mirror. The child Matrarc nodded at Ceit and then took a step toward the canyon edge. Ceit felt herself rush forward instinctively, but her body was slow and sluggish. The dream figure with her same pale hair and eyes stepped forward once again and disappeared off the edge, her arms and legs spread as she plummeted through the red dirt and desert wind. Ceit opened her mouth to scream, but it was a soundless, wasted motion.

Ceit had woken knowing the two images—the woman standing in front of the house and the old pickup truck—were connected, but she had no idea how. She knew with certainty, however, that she was nearing the end of her time at Mac.

As Leanne smudged her eyelids with a pinkish shimmer, Annbeth walked up and leaned over Leanne's shoulder.

"Well, this is the most girly I've ever seen you," she said flatly.

"This little girl is going to be a bona fide knockout before you know it," Leanne chirped, leaning close to Ceit. Her breath smelled of coffee and mouthwash.

Ceit stared forward. She knew there was more to this plot than a makeover and a customized gift bag. Girls were filling the common room now, half of them made up in a style that would make rodeo clowns jealous. Ceit saw the front office director standing in the doorway, looking uneasy. Security had been tight since the attack, and Ceit knew this seemingly motivational event had almost been canceled. The front office director was fidgeting. Ceit could see what she was apprehensive about: unauthorized visitors, the over-all chaos of the girls roaming around, the distracted counselors and staff. One of the caseworkers was getting her own makeover in the corner while a fascinated semicircle of girls watched and giggled. The director saw potential for trouble, as did Ceit. But she needn't have worried. Ceit knew Annbeth would never try anything as risky as moving Ceit during the day. No, whatever was coming, they would wait until night had fallen.

Leanne handed Ceit a rose-colored cloth bag with WonderGals printed on the side.

"Here you go, my dear! I have given you a trial size of the colors I used on your eyes, a foundation stick, and a few little surprises. You look beautiful...like a true queen."

She paused on the last words, and Ceit felt a shudder run up her spine. Leanne smiled broadly and patted her on the back. Annbeth motioned for Ceit to follow her, but she ignored the request. Another girl eagerly took Ceit's spot, and Leanne imme-diately started cooing over the size of her pores. Annbeth's broken, distracted thoughts tapped at Ceit's consciousness.

"*We need to talk. Meet me in the cafeteria.*"

Ceit had no intention of going to the cafeteria. She paced back to her bed, where she dropped the rose-pink bag and grabbed her toiletries. As she scrubbed the paint off her face in the bathroom, she considered her options. She needed to avoid Annbeth as much as possible; she knew that with certainty. She also needed to figure out how to keep the girls' wing of MacLaren Hall as chaotic as possible. Whatever plan Annbeth and Leanne had dreamed up would be significantly harder if security was on high alert.

She stared at her reflection in the mirror. Two years she had wasted here. She wondered how she would have spent her time if she'd known then what was to come. Ceit pressed her hands to the mirror and rested her head against the glass. Would she have cursed the lot of them, bound them against harming her? Would she have summoned the Rabharta to root out the weakest among them? Would she have pulled the Sluagh from her mother's decrepit form and cast them out into the world to destroy it from the outside in? She knew it was useless to wonder. She hadn't been powerful enough to bind another or call the nathair when she'd arrived here. She had thought she was, but these two long years had taught her that there was little she could have done to escape until now. She still doubted she could summon the Rabharta or Sluagh on her own. One day perhaps, but they came and went as they wished. To summon these ancient evils required a root level of power that Ceit had seen only in the Matrarc. The most important revelation though, the one that superseded all else, was the fact that she knew she was not the Matrarc, at least not yet. She was not yet the Bandia Marbh, as the creature who spoke through her dying mother had called her. One day perhaps. Ceit also knew with certainty that if Annbeth and her illusionists took her away to wherever it was they hid, she would become none of these things. Ceit knew that in their captivity, she would wither and die forgotten, her power wasted.

She slipped out of the washroom, watching for Annbeth. She put away her toiletry bag and then moved silently down the hall to the nurses' lounge. Annbeth never came to this place. She said the other employees were slobs, and Ceit could only agree. Half-empty coke cans littered the table, and a trail of sugar ants led a march from the cracked window to the trash can. Ceit heard a rumble of thunder in the distance. She looked out the grimy glass window, intrigued. Lightning and thunder were rare in Los Angeles. A storm was coming and would likely land by nightfall. Ceit smiled as she adjusted the bunny ears to catch SOAPnet. *Days of Our*

*Lives* was available around the clock if you knew where to look. Patch leads Kayla and Benjy to an abandoned mission. The priest lies, and Patch pulls Kayla from the doorway as an explosion levels the building. Ceit smiled to herself. Tonight she would create her own sort of explosion, just enough to distract the ones who sought to lock her in yet another cage.

## 51

ANNBETH PACED THE FLOOR OF THE CAFETERIA. SHE felt dizzy from lack of sleep and nerves. She had gotten no more than two hours of sleep in the last three nights, and those had been wracked with nightmares. She tried to transmit a thought to Ceit, but all she felt was static. Her brain was too jumbled to communicate.

The girl didn't trust her anymore, and Annbeth hardly blamed her. She should have fought harder to keep Ceit with her father years ago. She had listened to the Maga and the directors when they told her it was necessary to eliminate the girl's ties, get her officially fostered to a host family (of their choosing, of course), and then and only then move her to the temple. They had insisted it needed to be painstakingly legal up until the point when the system relaxed enough to avoid scrutiny. Annbeth had told them for two years that they were wasting time. Six months after the girl was moved to Mac they could have taken her to Salt Lake, and no one would have done more than a cursory search. The directors didn't understand the Child Protective Services system into which they had waded.

What if Ceit had been taken to the temple two years ago? Would she have learned the screaming curse? She shivered at the thought. Would she have grown complacent and cooperative? Annbeth doubted it. The temple did not know Ceit. They still saw her as a pliable ten-year-old who acted ages older than her natural age, which Annbeth recognized to be a particular sign of her lineage. No, they should have left her with her father. He would have tempered her, and Ceit would never have done anything to harm or scare her little brother. In their efforts to sever her connections to the world, the temple had created the perfect environment for Ceit to build her strength—and Annbeth knew who Ceit's target was.

One way or another, Ceit needed out of MacLaren Hall that night. Annbeth had no idea where the girl would go if she didn't leave with Director Carabus and her team. But Annbeth felt the bone-deep dread of what was to come if Ceit ended up in Salt Lake. Director Carabus had an extensively researched plan. They would be out of the state by dawn. It would cause trouble, and there would be extensive searches. Annbeth was to stay behind and play at being shocked and worried. She would find and present the note they would plant in Ceit's bed, which read that she had decided to run away to find her brother. From there, their San Diego people were working on fabricating a case that she had been taken across the border at Tijuana. The ruse was meant to keep the powers that be distracted for at least six months until they figured out it was bullshit. By then, Ceit would be safely ensconced in the Salt Lake temple, her identity effectively changed and her new life underway.

Ceit wasn't going to show for their meeting in the cafeteria.

Annbeth knew this with certainty. She was probably holed up in the counselors' lounge watching television. It would be impossible to catch her, however, as she always sensed Annbeth no matter how hard she tried to mask herself. There was no way to tell Ceit that she wasn't the enemy Ceit thought she was.

She wished she could tell Ceit how similar they really were. Annbeth had begun watching Ceit years before the incident in the cul-de-sac ever happened. The Maga had seen Ceit in a dream when the girl was just an infant. She had told the congregation that very night that their messiah had finally been born in the flesh, that this infant girl would grow to lead the world entire.

As soon as Annbeth came of age, she had been sent to Los Angeles to join the handful of temple devotees who were assigned to watch the strange cult on Sinder Avenue and keep an eye on the child who had been promised. Her first job had been in the Special Victims Unit of LAPD. With the help of a judge who worked for the temple from downtown LA, she had gained the proper credentials to work as a clerical assistant in the SVU office. It was wretched, grueling work. She transcribed recorded interviews, filed paperwork, set up meetings, and arranged countless appointments for the detective staff. It had, however, given her access to the files concerning the Society.

The cult had gained the attention of the LAPD over the years. Small stuff, really. There was the matter of homeschooling in the early years and properly filing the children with the state. There were petty concerns about the manner of plants the Society grew in their backyards. And then there was the occasional matter of their burial practices, which violated about every state law there was. None of it equaled much to investigate, but the SVU unit had an open file and added information as needed.

By the time Ceit and her brother had started in the local public school, much of the scrutiny had fallen off. The cul-de-sac residents were seen as eccentric but harmless. It was a cult, but not one that was likely to mix up a batch of Kool-Aid anytime soon.

Annbeth had moved to Social Services as a file clerk. The reports were still available to her, courtesy of the same family court judge who filed a few papers on her behalf, and the work was far more interesting. Her real job, however, had been to watch Ceit Robertson. Annbeth had watched Ceit grow up. She had seen her playing with her brother in the cul-de-sac, walking to and from school. She knew the marks she received from her elementary teachers. She had been watching Ceit for over ten years now.

By the time she met Ceit at MacLaren Hall, Annbeth felt like she was meeting a long-lost family member. She wanted nothing more than to tell her how the enclave of houses in Bountiful, just outside Salt Lake proper, was so very similar to the cul-de-sac where Ceit had grown up. She wanted to take Ceit's hands and tell her she understood the oppression from the elders in her Society. She knew the danger of the old magic that followed Ceit, as she understood the terror of the ancient rituals performed in the underground worship hall in Salt Lake. She understood the expectations, the impossible nature of the life she was expected to lead, the weight of the oddness that never left her consciousness. Annbeth wanted to protect her, and all she had done was convince the girl that she was an enemy.

Annbeth sat down and buried her head in her hands. She felt dizzy with lack of sleep and tension. In the nightmares, ravens clawed at her eyes and snakes wound their way around her ankles, knees, and then chest until they forced open her mouth and burrowed deep inside her stomach. Thousands of scarab beetles surrounded her immobilized form, eating the flesh from her bones as she silently screamed. Annbeth shuddered at the remembered images. This was old magic, far beyond what the Maga was capable of.

Annbeth had chanted the banishing and cast the pentagram in hopes it would alleviate the nightmares, if only for a few hours. They were only escalating. Even now, wide awake, she could feel the sensation of the dream snakes winding their way up her legs. Her muscles tensed with the phantom pain of the scarab bites. Only Ceit held the sort of power that could end this, and Annbeth knew that the torment would only increase if she were taken to Salt Lake. In order to save herself and the temple, she needed to stop this.

The conflict tore at her. They were the only family she knew. Her birth parents had given her up at birth, and her adoptive parents had had her baptized in blood in the worship hall. The temple had been her entire life. It had been years since Annbeth had been back to the temple, and she might never have a chance to return unless she was taken there for the final judgment of the Maga. But that was unlikely. It would be easier to dump her body off the San Pedro pier and let it wash up in the tide after the seawater bloat had destroyed the manner of her death.

The worship hall was beautiful, and Annbeth felt a raw ache in her core at the realization that she might never see it again. It was carved from the volcanic rock exposed when an underground tunnel collapsed in an earthquake in the 1930s. The tunnel itself was long abandoned. The temple members entered from a grate near the edge of town leading out to the Wasatch Mountains. Annbeth missed the cold, crisp air of the tunnel. She remembered the excitement she felt as she would walk down the concrete steps and follow the dimly lit path, illuminated by battery-powered torches, until the worship hall revealed itself. The stone floor was lined with carpets and pillows, all facing the great pulpit where the

Maga took her honored place. It was large enough to fit nearly fifty people, more if you crammed into the nooks and crannies along the sides. That was Annbeth's favorite part; she and her friends would tuck away into the breaks in the irregular surface and giggle silently as the services proceeded.

The tunnels ran for miles, but the children were not allowed to explore—too dangerous, the adults always said. But Annbeth had often snuck down into the worship hall when no one was looking. She and the other children would climb over the makeshift barrier put in place to keep anyone from wandering. They brought flashlights and giggled madly as they crept down the pitch-black space. No one ever had the nerve to go very far. It had been a good childhood, and for that she was grateful.

She would never be able to explain to the Maga that what she had to do tonight was to save the temple, save the Maga herself. Annbeth would be reviled—cast out at best, disposed of at worst. She would be a cautionary tale to all the children about traitors. They would never know how very much she loved them all and how close they had come to their own destruction.

It would all be over soon. Annbeth knew it was time to lift the bars of the cage and free the very thing she had been trying to contain. With a sigh, she paced down the hallway, waiting for the sun to drop and night to begin.

# 52

NOT SURPRISINGLY, THERE WAS A NOTE IN THE WonderGals goody bag. It was rolled tight and taped to the underside of a Shimmer Joy eye shadow container. Ceit closed her eyes to see if she could sense if Annbeth or anyone else was near; the air felt empty. She sat on the edge of her cot and unrolled the tiny note. The script was printed in immaculate block letters.

It is time to come home, dear girl. Meet at the locker room
at the far end of the gymnasium after dinner. Annbeth will
guide you. We welcome you, my child.

Ceit rolled her eyes and crumbled the note into a ball. She could run to the main office and show them, ask for help, but she knew exactly what the reaction would be. They would tell her it was one of the other girls playing a prank. They would ask Annbeth, who would nod sympathetically and tell them she was just looking for attention, feeling a little insecure. There was no help here.

No matter; Ceit had other plans. She removed all the books from her backpack and shoved them under her bed. She hadn't attended school regularly in a month. Between the stitches in her arm and then her father's attack, it hadn't been a priority. Quickly and quietly, she took a change of clothes and rolled it tight, placing it into the bag. The fairy tale book was too big and heavy to carry, so with a sigh, she placed it aside along with the rag doll. She added her mother's jewelry, her father's watch, a bottle of water, and a lunch bag full of odds and ends she had lifted from the kitchen—a couple of apples, a hunk of stale bread, a small bag of beef jerky. She had been collecting it over the last few days. She had no idea where she would be going or what the conditions would be like. On second thought, she added two more pairs of socks.

Ceit spent the next several hours lying on her bed rereading *Heaven*. It had marked her imprisonment, and now it would see her escape. Heaven was a fool to ever go back to Winnerow. If Ceit ever made it out of this pit, she would never return to Los Angeles. Cal is disgusting, but he isn't her father. But, then again, neither is Luke Casteel. Everyone lies, and no one is what they say they are. Ceit closed her eyes and waited for nightfall.

## 53

CEIT WAS PUSHING THE SHAPELESS LUMP OF TUNA casserole around her plate. Annbeth watched her from the entryway, where she was supposed to be supervising the dinner hour. In truth, she was fidgeting with the cuff of her shirt and hoping Ceit would eat even slower than she already was. Director Carabus had officially left with the rest of the WonderGals after the program but was unofficially waiting in the girl's locker room by the gymnasium. A van was parked at the entrance to the gym. Inside were two more members of her team. The rest were across the street at the gas station with walkie-talkies, ready to create the distraction that would cause the entrance gate to be unlocked. The whole thing hinged on Ceit leaving willingly, and Annbeth suspected the girl had no intention of doing so.

Finally, Ceit shuffled off to the kitchen to drop off her plate for the kids on cleaning duty. Annbeth watched carefully. She was under orders to herd Ceit to the gymnasium, where the director would then escort her into the van. Instead she followed her, keeping her distance even though she was sure Ceit could hear her heart pounding. *Where is the girl going*? She passed Jr. Girls and headed to the Pixie ward. Intrigued, Annbeth stepped up her pace to see what Ceit was up to.

She rounded the corner to find Ceit in the nursery. There was one infant right now—a stringy, sickly little boy who had just been detoxed from the meth addiction he'd been born with. His mother had been found dead next to him, and the father was unknown. So here was baby boy Hector, named after the nursery counselor's grandfather.

"Hector was a hero in Greek mythology," Annbeth had told Ceit a week or so ago, when the little boy arrived.

"Hector's body was dragged behind a chariot by the heels around the city of Troy as an example to his father," Ceit had replied. She wasn't wrong.

Ceit was sitting in the aged rocking chair, holding tiny Hector while the nursery counselor sat at the desk and watched with a contented smile on her face. Annbeth realized that the girl must come here quite often if the nurse was that comfortable with her. It was a side of the child that Annbeth hadn't paid attention to.

Ceit was an enigma. She could destroy them all with a few words, but she chose to spend her time with this sickly little infant. Annbeth took a deep breath and entered the nursery. She had to talk to the girl. The director would be waiting, and soon she would grow impatient. The nursery counselor looked up and smiled.

"Well, we have lots of company tonight, don't we, Hector?" she said softly.

Annbeth nodded back. "Think I could have a word with Ceit?"

The nurse gave her a curious look. "I suppose. I need to go get a load of towels from the dryer anyhow. Just please don't leave her alone. Ceit and I know how to take care of this one, but with everything that's gone on recently, the office would have my head."

Ceit offered her a small smile, and the nurse left.

"Are you here to escort me to the locker room?" Ceit asked directly.

Annbeth sat down opposite her in a matching worn rocking chair.

"No," she said firmly.

Ceit looked surprised. "I found the note," she said softly, in the tone of a lullaby, as she stroked Hector's puckered little face. He stirred in his sleep and contentedly reached up to clasp Ceit's thumb. The image made tears spring to Annbeth's eyes. Ceit should have been home taking care of her own brother. It had been Annbeth's work that had severed that tie, and it could never be repaired.

"We need to get you out, but not with them. I have no plan. I just know that it is a mistake for you to leave with them…" Annbeth realized how alone she really was. She didn't know anyone in LA that wasn't connected to the temple. She had no allies in this, no safe place she could take Ceit, no way to get her out. All she could do was buy more time.

"How are your nightmares?" Ceit asked abruptly, looking up from Hector.

Annbeth swallowed the emotion in her throat. "Who is sending them?"

Ceit smiled. "The Matrarc—the true Matrarc. I am not that, at least not yet. Nor am I the Bandia Marbh, not yet. But your temple is not the cocoon in which I wish to make my transformation."

"I don't know what to do," Annbeth said in a small voice, their roles reversed. She was the child here, and the girl who sat opposite her was all-knowing.

Before Ceit could answer, the nurse came running back in.

"I'm afraid I'll have to ask you to go back to your dorm, Ceit.

There's something going on outside, and they're asking us to go on lockdown." Her voice was a model of controlled panic. "I'm sure it's nothing, but with everything that's been going on, I think they're being extra cautious."

Ceit nodded and then kissed little Hector on the head. Annbeth could see her whisper something in his ear, but the words were inaudible. She stood carefully and handed the infant to the nurse. Hector squawked his complaint and then fell back asleep.

Annbeth nodded at the nurse as Ceit left the room.

"I'll make sure she gets back," Annbeth said. "Did they say what's going on?"

The nurse looked up from laying Hector back into his crib. "Some commotion across the street, but I guess the police were called. It's the front office being paranoid—not that I can blame them. I went to see Deirdre yesterday. She's going in for another operation on that arm. It's not good."

Annbeth nodded, a migraine creeping behind her eyes. "Send her my best," she said, and left to follow Ceit.

The girl was, predictably, gone from the hallway when she emerged. *What the hell happened*, Annbeth wondered. The dinner hour wasn't even quite up, the director would not be missing Ceit yet, and the nonsense they were planning at the gas station wasn't supposed to happen until they were given a cue from the director. And it was supposed to lead to the gate being left open, not the facility being put on lockdown. Something had gone wrong.

Annbeth broke into a jog as she reached the Jr. Girls' dorm. Ceit was not there, but neither was the backpack that normally hung at the end of the bed. With a migraine spreading out to her temples, Annbeth ran to the cafeteria, where the last stragglers were taking their plates to the washroom.

"Ceit? Are you in here?" she called out desperately.

No one had time to answer. Annbeth was thrown to the floor by the force of the plate glass windows on the far end of the cafeteria imploding. The sound was a mad cacophony of splintering glass and screams from the remaining residents. Annbeth lay face down, her entire body covered in razor-sharp beads of glass. A girl wailed at the far end of the room, and the sound of adults shouting filled the air. But there was another sound aside from the chaos; it was the roar of wind, as though the sky itself were being ripped from its holdings. It was intermixed with lost screams and siren wails and was overwhelming. Annbeth bolted to her feet, her hands dripping blood from a thousand cuts. Outside the shattered window, the sky held a greenish tint. The long, thin funnel cloud whipped upward to reveal a spreading blackness. The base widened, and the battered metal picnic tables on the quad were ripped from their casings and pulled into the sky. Annbeth screamed Ceit's name, knowing the girl was long gone. She felt hands on her shoulders, dragging her out of the room and into the hall. As quickly as the tornado touched the ground it was gone, replaced with a torrential wind that whipped through the ruined cafeteria, sending spirals of glass shards flying into the air.

Annbeth could hear the other adults yelling at the rest of the kids to get to the hallway, to put their heads between their knees, standard disaster protocol. But this was far from standard. Annbeth knew this was Ceit. The temple had no control over nature like this. This had been Ceit's plan all along. She did it here on the farthest end of the complex from the nursery, when most of the kids would be out of cafeteria. She did it to cause chaos, not harm. She did it to escape. Annbeth didn't know whether to cheer or scream.

She felt a strong pair of hands on her arm and was pulled down the hall away from the growing chaos. Director Carabus and a man in a black hoodie looked at her desperately.

"Where is the girl?" the director snapped.

"I have no idea." Annbeth pressed her bleeding palms to her shirt, trying to stop the flow of the blood, instead discovering there were still shards of glass within.

"They radioed from the gas station that the van caught on fire. The owner called 911, so our guys had to run. Someone knows we're here," the director said hurriedly.

"You underestimate her," Annbeth said, feeling the weight of the tension she had been carrying for so long begin to lift. "You have no idea what she is capable of."

"She is a child. And your job was to contain her and help her come home to us," the director hissed.

"I cannot contain what does not wish to be caught," Annbeth said as the hallway filled with Mac residents. Another counselor ran past, pausing to cast a confused look at the director and the man in the hoodie.

"Annbeth, come with me. You're bleeding," the counselor said.

"These two are unauthorized to be on the grounds. They broke in. I need security! Security!" Annbeth raised her voice and screamed the words as the director stumbled backward. A security officer in a black uniform came running from the end of the hallway. Annbeth pointed at the director; her companion had already run and was likely out the door by now. As the officer led Director Carabus away, Annbeth wrapped her hand in her sleeve and headed to the infirmary. She didn't know what had become of Ceit, but she knew her role in her captivity was finally ending.

## 54

THE PICKUP HIT ANOTHER BUMP, AND CEIT CLUNG TO the side to keep her balance. Her shoulder ached and made her grimace. The bed cover gave her just enough height to sit with her head touching the top, and the boxes on either side kept her from rocking back and forth too terribly much. The metal underneath her felt like ice. She suspected it went to the other extreme when the sun rose and hoped she would not have to stay hidden that long. Ceit had no way of knowing where she was headed, except she was certain that it was far away from MacLaren Hall and Annbeth's temple. There was no hope of sleep, and Ceit would have been too afraid to even try. She adjusted her backpack against the small of her back and leaned back as best she could. Through a small plastic window in the bed cover, she could see the sky. She slid the window open just a hair, enough to let in a hint of the rushing air. She didn't mind the darkness; she'd never minded it really. The things that made other children afraid held no terror for her. She knew there were far worse monsters in the night than those that lived in fairy stories.

They had likely not noticed she was missing yet. That would happen later as bed checks were conducted and after the grounds were thoroughly searched. No, she probably had until daybreak before anyone became alarmed. Even then, the police would waste time by conducting another search of the facility and the surrounding grounds. They would figure Ceit had been spooked by the storm and freak tornado and had hidden somewhere. By the time they clued into the fact that she was truly missing, she would be long gone. No one would be looking for her in the back of a rusted pickup truck on I-40 headed east. The interstate name and direction didn't matter to Ceit; it was all about the truck. It was the one the Matrarc had showed her in the dream. The Matrarc had whispered in her ear where she would find it and how to call the winds that would conjure the tornado. The power to do so was on the edges of Ceit's burgeoning ability; the control necessary to keep the winds from destroying the whole of Mac and killing everyone inside threatened to slip from her grasp. She still felt the ache in her muscles and a slight ringing in her ears. She had finally grown to be powerful enough to let the Matrarc's power help her leave this place, powerful enough to reach the Ch'įįdii—not quite grown but close enough to feel the simmering potential of what she was truly capable of.

As the cafeteria was reduced to a pile of twisted metal and concrete, Ceit had made her exit out the small window in the back of the dry food supply closet. She had had to throw her back-pack out first and then wiggle one shoulder and then the other to fit through, but she did it. She had always been small. It was exactly what had always led others to discount her that allowed her to escape. Once out, she had run through the wind and the torrential roar of the destruction to the tall security gate, which had been ripped to pieces by the storm. She'd barely felt the wind on her. It wasn't there to hurt her; it was protecting her, guiding her. It was the force of the fallen Matrarc, making sure her great-granddaughter was led to safety.

The truck had been parked at the gas station, and Ceit had known immediately it was there for her. The driver—a man with sad, dark eyes and rivers of age through his copper skin—hadn't asked many questions. Ceit had seen a glow surrounding his form, a sort of aura, but not the kind the older girls at Mac claimed to see. They would sit in circles in the common room or outside by the worn play field, holding hands and claiming to be calling the spirits. One had a tarot deck, cards filled with fanciful pictures and meaningless symbols. Ceit shifted in the truck bed, her legs long since numb. She knew it was unfair to say they were meaningless. In the right hands, the cards spoke the truth—not just of the future but of the soul. In the hands of the silly teenage girls at Mac, however, they were no different than playing cards.

No, this man had a moon-silver shimmer that traced the outline of his body. He had been standing next to his weather-beaten pickup truck at the gas station, watching the funnel cloud tear into MacLaren Hall when Ceit had run up, carrying nothing but her backpack.

"I need to leave this place. Can you help?" She had rushed the words and knew they sounded mad. She also knew she did not have much time. The storage shed outside the gas station had caught fire, and though it had been extinguished, two police cruisers were still parked on either side. Ceit knew the fire was also the work of the Matrarc, a stray bolt of lightning cast down to strike this small target. The fire was connected to Annbeth's temple in some way. And everyone but this man was hiding inside the gas station. They were watching the first tornado in their memory to touch down in El Monte. The man had turned and regarded her for a full minute before speaking.

"I know you," he had said. "Saw you in a dream."

Ceit had nodded.

"You were among the Ch'įįdii but not one of them. I recognize your eyes." His voice was calm and not fearful. Ceit had felt her trembling body grow still, her heart slow to a steady beat.

"I need you to take me from this place. Will you help?" she had asked in a voice much smaller than she was accustomed to. There was no need to unnerve this man. He knew her for what she was and, unlike Annbeth and the others, did not respond based on what she might do for him.

He had pointed to the bed of the truck. She knew without asking that it would be too risky to ride up front. They needed to get past the crouched figures in the gas station. Once she was reported missing, the truck would be a target if she were seen. So the old man had moved several heavy bags of dry concrete to the side and laid down a blanket, and she had situated herself in the bed of the pickup.

"When it's safe, I'll stop and you can ride up front. Until then, no one will look for you here," he had said as he helped her climb aboard.

Now, hours later, Ceit found herself wondering if the man was going to keep his word or if she was to remain wedged between the bags of concrete powder and utility buckets. She finally felt the truck slow and rumble to a halt. The back shook and then opened. The man stood staring at her with the same impassive expression.

"Come up front, little one. No one will watch for you now."

He helped her down. She limped to the passenger's side door, her legs numb and cramped from her uncomfortable quarters. The interior of the truck smelled of mildew and long-ago smoked cigarettes. The man climbed in beside her, and the engine growled to life.

As they pulled onto the road, Ceit cleared her throat. "Thank you," she said softly.

The man nodded.

"Where are we going?" she asked.

"I'm taking you to my home. Get you rested. From there, we'll help you to a safe place," he said with quiet authority.

"Why did you help me?" Ceit could not help but ask. Everyone else, even those who knew her for who she was, was hesitant to offer blind help. Most kept their distance. The ones like Annbeth sought not to help, but to contain, to control. She shivered, and it turned into a full body shake.

"I was told to. I had a vision—a dream, you would call it. But this was a dream that passed into the spirit world. You were among the Ch'įįdii. You told me that a day would come that you would appear and I would recognize you even though your human form was not the same as your spirit self. You said you would need help, and I was to offer it freely." He stared straight ahead as he spoke.

"What would've happened if you'd refused?" Ceit asked, genuinely curious.

"Guess I'd be up shit creek," he said flatly, and Ceit snorted a laugh. He looked at her sideways, a slight grin on his creased face. "Course, I might be there already. Can't imagine someone's not looking for you by now."

Ceit sat back and sighed. They ones who should be looking for her, the officials from Mac, likely had no idea she was gone. It was the others that worried her far more.

Ceit cursed her bad judgment. When she'd first arrived at MacLaren Hall, she had taken Annbeth as an ally. But now she saw through the veneer. Annbeth was the same as the others. She had enough of the sight to see Ceit for who she was but not the wisdom to be of use. Her temple sought to use Ceit, to bring her to some underground vault in Salt Lake, to put her on display, and to lock her in a cage surrounded by the black candles and burning sulfur in salt piles that they believed were demanded by the dark one. They knew nothing of how the world worked. Their faith came from terrible books written by paranoid old men. It came from wretched movies wherein the dark one ran rampant with smoke pouring from his nostrils and a pitchfork in one hand. Everything they knew was wrong.

Ceit had lain dormant all this time, and now it was time to wake up. She had left the nursery, the smell of baby Hector's skin still in her head. He had the same silver-moon glow around him that this man had. She did not understand what it was, but Hector was so much more than what the world would perceive him as.

Ceit had gone to her dorm and grabbed the packed backpack from the bedpost, Annbeth's words sitting uncomfortably in her mind. She had worked for two long years to keep her in Mac, and only now she was questioning her temple? Only now did she see them for what they were? Ceit had shaken off the nursery conversation. She needed to focus. The Matrarc had been whispering in her head all afternoon, repeating the incantation that Ceit must chant, repeating the order in which things were to happen.

So just as the harvest moon glowed from amidst the first evening stars, Ceit had stood in the cafeteria and lifted her arms to the sky, commanding her fingertips to catch the wind. It had been difficult to feel the vibrations through the concrete and plaster of the ceiling. If she had been outside, the stars themselves would have burst from the effort she put forth. Ceit had pushed the annoyance aside and concentrated her thoughts. She needed the storm, she needed the noise, and she needed to terrify everyone in Mac. She needed their fear to distract Annbeth and these people from Salt Lake who waited for her. From outside she had heard the first patters of rain and the low growl of thunder. It had comforted her, and the calm it brought made the pale-orange flames that had emanated from her fingertips glow brighter. Her flesh had burned, and Ceit had felt her spirit disconnect from her body. It had hovered right outside her flesh, commanding the bolts of energy that flew through the ceiling of the cafeteria and into the sky. The rain fell harder and turned to sleet. Lightning flashed in quick succession. The last straggling children in the cafeteria had seen Ceit standing near the windows, reaching to the sky. They'd considered the oddity of the weather and her actions and quickly dismissed her. They saw exactly what they wished to see.

She had heard the roar of the approaching storm as the wind whipped through the courtyard on the other side of the plate glass windows. Across the facility, errant tree branches had shattered windows, and the violent thunder and the bright flashes of lightning chased everyone from their beds to the hallway, as was the protocol. With a methodical wave of her fingers, Ceit had stirred the sky above her, the fire and energy of the atmosphere building to an intolerable intensity. With a swoop of her hands, a thousand hairline cracks had appeared in the plate glass. Ceit had then turned and walked with fast and deliberate steps to the dry storage room, where she knew the window was unlocked and no one was looking. She'd caught the eye of the last stragglers awed by the weather and standing dumbstruck in the cafeteria.

"Get out of here," she'd said quietly. They had nodded numbly and walked slowly toward the washroom, which would be safe from what was to come. Ceit was half out the window when she'd heard Annbeth scream her name, followed by the dissonant roar of the tornado. By the time she had extracted herself from the tiny opening and landed on the sodden grass below, the funnel cloud was ripping the metal picnic tables from their posts and sending them crashing into the remains of what had been the cafeteria. The gas station had been barely visible through the swirling dirt and debris, but she had run straight into the wind, feeling it wrap around her body and propel her forward through the mangled security fence and toward a vision she had, as yet, only seen in a dream. By the time she had reached the truck, breathless and legs trembling, the funnel cloud had started to wind its way back into the sky.

Ceit shivered in her seat, leaning against the worn door of the pickup truck. She wondered how much of a head start she had really given herself and how trustworthy this man really was.

"Take this." The man handed Ceit a glass soda bottle. She accepted it eagerly and guzzled the cola, a burp emitting from her throat against her will. He chuckled.

"Where is your home?" she asked.

"Canyon de Chelly, yisdá, little one," he said softly.

"How do you know the ones who are looking for me won't find me there?" Ceit asked in a quiet voice.

"Everyone has forgotten us, álchíní. Why should the ones who seek you be any different?"

## 55

THEY DROVE ALL DAY, THE MAN STOPPING ONCE FOR gas and to bring Ceit a tuna sandwich wrapped in aluminum foil from the gas station cooler. Ceit crouched on the floor of the truck, out of sight, until they were back on the road, although the ancient man sitting on the front steps of the two-pump gas station in a sagging lawn chair looked as though he was well accustomed to not paying attention. Scrubby desert greenery flashed by inter-mixed with blank space from which heat rolled upward in waves, even in the November sun. Finally, as night fell again, Ceit relaxed and closed her eyes. She had been asleep for several hours when the man gently shook her shoulder.

"Wake up, little one. We're nearly there. I'll take you to the ranch in the morning. Not safe to take the horses at night unless you're used to the ride, and I assume you've never ridden before."

Ceit shook her head. It was dark outside still. She wondered what time it was and why she needed a horse to get to their destination.

"I live here with my sister and her children, áłchíní. You can get some sleep, no worries here. She will take care of you tonight, and I will be back in the morning to take you to the ranch," he said softly. He climbed from his side of the truck and circled around to Ceit's door. Opening it for her, the man gave her an expectant look.

Before her, in the darkness, sat a little house—quite small, put together in a ramshackle sort of way, with no one style favored over another. It had a small front porch of the sort you might find in Venice Beach and the rounded logs used in mountain cabins. The roof caught the moonlight, and Ceit saw it was made of slabs of overlapping metal, seemingly held together by gravity.

"This is okay with her? Your sister?" Ceit asked hesitantly. She was unaccustomed to feeling unsure. Even with all the upheaval of the past two years, she had always felt she had the upper hand. Now, for the first time, she felt like a child, and utterly at the mercy of this man and whatever sort of person he turned out to be.

"My sister will see what is in your eyes same as I did, áłchíní. She will take care of you. You are safe here," the man said while glancing over his shoulder at Ceit as he fit a key into the lock of the front door. Ceit noted that the door looked to be another mismatched part; it was more like the door of an office than a front door. It held a single key lock, none of the security bolts and reinforcements that Ceit was accustomed to. She nodded and followed him inside. Once there, she saw it was not so different from her home back on Sinder Avenue. A thin rug covered a chipped linoleum tiled floor, and the furniture was threadbare and saggy with the weight of its age. There was a faint scent of dog in the air. Ceit breathed a sigh of relief. It felt familiar and could have been her own living room from so long ago, before the Sluagh, before the Rabharta and the message from the stones that ended the comfort of her life.

A woman shuffled down the hall wearing a pale-pink bathrobe.

Her long black hair was piled on top of her head, and she swallowed a yawn as she saw Ceit standing by the door. She looked questioningly to her brother, and he motioned to Ceit to wait. He led the woman around the corner. Ceit could hear muffled voices but could not discern the words. When they returned, the woman was holding a thick blanket with a Teenage Mutant Ninja Turtle print on it and a thin pillow.

"Hello, young lady," the woman said in a gentle voice that matched her brother's. "My brother says you need a bed for the night. I'll set you up here. In the morning, you can help me make breakfast. Sound okay?"

Ceit nodded as the woman spread the blanket over the worn sofa and fruitlessly fluffed the pillow before setting it at the armrest.

"There's a bathroom in the hall. I think I even have an extra toothbrush in the cabinet," she said softly.

Ceit nodded. "Thank you." Her voice was barely audible. She didn't recognize herself. She had never been this unsure of her surroundings or her fate. The feeling was overwhelming, and she was hit with a wave of regret for her decision to run from Mac.

"You're welcome, kiddo." She gave her brother a pointed look. "I need to speak with you privately." He nodded, following her back to where Ceit assumed the kitchen must be.

Instead of going down the hall to the bathroom, she crept closer to the corner of kitchen, straining to hear their voices.

"Are you crazy?" the woman whispered, her voice a combination of anger and frustration. "You can't just bring a runaway here! The kid has a family somewhere. She probably got in a fight with her mom, and you basically kidnapped her!"

"You don't understand, adheezhí. This is no child, at least no ordinary one. Look into her eyes. I have seen her before. So have you. I saw her with the Ch'įįdii, but she is not one of them—separate somehow, more powerful than them," the man said with a soft intensity.

"In the morning, I'm calling the reservation office. I'm telling them she hitched a ride on a truck, ended up here, and you found her on the side of the road. That is our story. I will give her a bed for the night, feed her in the morning, and then turn her back over to where she belongs. You are talking crazy. The Ch'įįdii are a child's story, an old man's superstition. Next you'll be crying Yeibichai and scaring the kids half to death," she said low and soft, her voice measured. Ceit felt her body tense and her mouth go dry. If this woman turned her back over to the police, she would end up back at Mac...or worse.

"Sit with her, adheezhí. Look her in the eyes, and tell me you don't recognize her. If you truly do not, then call the office tomorrow and we will send her home. But I am telling you, I've seen her before—not in this form, not as a child, but as what she is to become, what she has always been. I was told to help her." His voice was intense and level, a cadence driving the beats like a chant.

"You'd best be right. Wrong and you will set the łigai to fits, and then we have trouble. We have not had trouble in so long. She is dangerous, no matter how right you might be. Someone is looking for that child." Her words rose slightly, tension breaking her calm exterior.

"I don't know. As I drove onto the land, I felt the áhí behind us. I think it follows her, or maybe she can call it like the elders can. But I do not believe they will ever seek her here."

Ceit heard the shuffle of movement, and she slipped away from the wall and into the small bathroom. Her face was pale, with smudges of dirt from the bed of the truck on her temple and cheek and in her hair, which was matted to her head. She sighed and picked it clear with her fingers. The woman had been right; there was an extra toothbrush in the cabinet, still in its plastic wrapper from Smile Dental. It was child sized and had grinning alligators lining the neon-green handle. It made her think of Alan. She wondered if she would see him again. Alan would never grow up to know how the world he had been born into really worked. She wondered if her grandmother would take him in or if he'd be cast into the foster care system like she had been. If he did end up back on Sinder Avenue, the elders would scare him with stories and their useless, wasted magic. Their energy had been made impotent when they betrayed Ceit. She was their true Matrarc, and one day she would be ready to lead them. Without her, they were withered old women, trapped by their ridiculous superstitions and stories.

When Ceit emerged from the cramped bathroom with its narrow shower stall and cracked pedestal sink, the man and his sister were standing in the living room. The man's face was tense, his sister's a mask of controlled concern.

"Come here for a minute, child," the woman said softly. "Sit with me." She indicated the sofa. "I'm not trying to scare you—no harm will come to you here—but I would like to look into your eyes. My brother says he has seen something in you that, to our people, means you are someone very important."

Ceit nodded. The woman was talking to her like she was any other child. It was refreshing, and Ceit knew she would miss it when the woman truly looked at her. Ceit sat down next to the woman on the Ninja Turtle–covered couch and looked up at her. The woman closed her eyes a moment, mouthing a chant or maybe a prayer. When she opened her dark eyes, the intensity that flowed from her made Ceit waver. She was accustomed to being around powerful women, but this was a sort of energy she had not yet encountered—older and more primal, more powerful than anything that lived on Sinder Avenue. The woman stared at her without blinking, her eyes narrowing and digging still deeper. Finally, she sat back and regarded Ceit for a long moment.

"It appears my brother is sometimes right," she said softly. "Pardon me, child. I did not see before. You have a powerful hwó surrounding you."

Ceit nodded. "I am running from those who claim to worship me. They think I am something I am not."

The woman listened, a line of concentration furrowing her forehead. "I imagine there are lots who would claim you are theirs. You are in such a fragile body. I wonder the logic of the gods sometimes. You are too vulnerable."

Ceit smiled. "I won't be for long. And I am less fragile than I look."

The woman returned her smile. "I am sure you are. You should rest now. You are safe here. It turns out my brother—who I think has a bit too much of the yá—is also right about where you must go. The best place for you now is at the ranch. It's down in the canyon. Best way there is by horse. Our aunt lives there. She's good people. She raises horses and goats and has a grove of peach trees. It's a quiet place. You can stay there as long as you like. No one will find you in the canyon. We are far from the White House Ruin, where the tourists hike."

"Thank you," Ceit said quietly. "I don't know your name, or your brother's."

The woman smiled. "Nor us yours—the name you go by, that is. We all know the name of what you are. I am Yanaha. You can call me Yani. My brother is Yiska. People around here call him Benny."

Ceit gave him a curious look.

"It's a long story, for another time perhaps," Benny said with a soft smile.

"I'm Ceit."

"It's nice to meet you," Yani said. "Now get some rest." She settled the blanket around Ceit's shoulders as she lay back on the pillow. Her body trembled with the memory of her mother, before the trouble, before any of the trouble. Her mother who used to tuck her in and sing soft songs. Her mother whose auburn hair smelled like licorice.

"You're safe here, child," Yani whispered. "Now get some sleep."

*56*

CEIT WOKE TO A GOLDEN-SKINNED CHILD OF ABOUT
five staring her directly in the face. She started a bit as she opened
her eyes and met the large brown pair fixed upon hers.

"Hello," Ceit said simply.

"She's alive," the child confirmed, her breath smelling of Cheerios.

"Were we in doubt?" Yani's voice rang from the kitchen. Ceit
was hit with a wave of smells—bacon and something else, a bread
smell that made her stomach contort with hunger.

"I was," the child answered.

"I'm very alive. No need to worry," Ceit said quietly, sitting
up and regarding the child, who wore Ninja Turtle pajamas and
whose long, shiny black hair was in a knot at her neck.

"I wasn't worried. But if you had died, then my blanket would
have dead person on it," the child responded, making Ceit stifle a
laugh.

"Mosi!" Yani yelled from the other room. She poked her head
around the corner. "Never mind Mosi. She has her priorities out
of order."

"It's all right," Ceit said with an amused smile on her face. She pulled the blanket off her and folded it neatly before handing it to Mosi. "Here, all yours. Thank you for letting me use it."

The child nodded solemnly, took the blanket, and disappeared down the hall.

"You hungry?" Yani asked. "There's breakfast on the table."

The last meal Ceit had eaten was yesterday's gas station tuna sandwich. She had been far too concerned with other matters to notice, but her stomach was complaining of the neglect loudly, and her hands were shaking. She walked on unsteady feet to the small kitchen and found the pressed wood table was filled with food. A plate of bacon, another of a flattish sort of bread, and a bowl of what looked like beans with onions and chilis. Another black-haired child, a bit older than Mosi, sat at the table. He was happily munching on a strip of bacon and regarding Ceit with curiosity.

"This is Niyol, my son. You met Mosi. Sit, eat," Yani commanded.

Ceit did as she was told. The first bite awakened still more hunger that she had been denying.

"Wow," Niyol remarked as Ceit reached for a third piece of the flatbread.

"Stop that," Yani scolded. "Never mind him, Ceit. Eat up. My brother will be here soon, and you have a bit of a trek ahead of you." Yani sat down and took a bit of the flatbread.

Ceit pointed to the bread. "What is that? It's delicious."

"Fry bread?" Niyol answered, his voice incredulous. "Haven't you had it before?"

Ceit shook her head.

"Jesus, you'd think my kids were raised in the woods with the mą'iitsoh." Yani gave a pointed look to Niyol, who grinned and swiped another piece of bacon before he scuttled from the table.

"Am I welcome on your aunt's ranch?" Ceit asked quietly, aware that the children were listening from the hallway.

"Yes," Yani said. "You'll meet a couple of others she has collected in the past few years, not like you—there's no one like you—but who were also in need of a place. My aunt is an ataa' in the tribe, an elder. She has the sight. Many seek her out for help. She will know exactly why you are there."

"If people seek her out, won't I be seen?" Ceit asked.

"Those who go to an adiłgąshii do not speak of it. You will be safe there, and she can help you. You are young yet. While I see what you will become, you are not that yet. She will guide you to where you need to be. My brother is right—there is a strong hwó surrounding you, but that will wear thin as time passes. I have a sense of who is looking for you, and you do not want to sit in plain sight much longer." Yani popped another bit of fry bread into her mouth as Ceit considered her words.

"No, I suppose I don't," Ceit said softly. "What language are you speaking? I have never heard it, but it reminds me a bit of Gaelic."

Yani looked surprised. "It's Navajo. You're on reservation land, child."

"Does everyone speak Navajo here?" Ceit asked, intrigued.

Yani laughed. "No. In fact, I think Benny and I speak more than most. I'm a teacher at the reservation school here. I teach a course in Navajo, among others. But the young people here, they don't much care. I use it as much as I can, hoping the kids pick it up a bit. My aunt will speak it a bit. You'll catch on. They say Navajo is a dying language. It would be nice if someone picked it up." She sighed and leaned back in her chair.

"How does a language die?" Ceit asked, her head buzzing with a vague sense of déjà vu, an odd feeling that she had had this exact conversation before in this place.

"Like anything else, I suppose," Yani said. "Something new takes over and makes it obsolete. This place is dying. I often wonder if my children will raise their families here or go to the city like all the others."

The buzz turned into a hum, growing in intensity. It followed the beating of Ceit's heart and the throb of the blood in her veins. She could see below the surface of Yani's skin. It appeared as translucent as glass, the blue and red blood flowing from one place to another. The pulse of the hum turned into a driving beat, and when she looked around the room, the walls seemed no more consistent than a dream.

"Yani," Ceit said in a metered tone. "You need to get the kids and run. Now."

Yani looked up, alarmed.

"No time." Ceit closed her eyes, the certainty of her words throbbing in her ears. "Get the kids. Go out the back door. Someone is here. Go. Now."

"But…" Yani stuttered.

"Go," Ceit whispered, the energy behind the front door palpable. "I will be fine. You will not. Go."

Without further hesitation, Yani shot to her feet. The kids, who had been eavesdropping, popped out from around the corner. Yani grabbed both their hands and pulled them toward the battered door leading from the kitchen to the outside. With a glance behind her at Ceit, she slammed the door behind her. Ceit heard the roar of a truck as they pulled away. From the small kitchen window, she saw the dust fly into the morning sun, and she breathed a sigh of relief.

*57*

ANNBETH STARED OUT THE FILTHY WINDOW OF THE
Days End hotel room where she had spent the last two nights. The
walls and comforter reeked of ancient cigarette smoke, and a faint
odor of gas hung in the air. Under normal circumstances it would
be cause for concern, but potentially being killed by a gas leak was
the least of her problems. She hadn't waited to see what would
happen to the director, nor where the other members of the LA
team had hidden themselves. They would be looking for her, and
she knew they would not stop until she was found.

As she watched the sun climb into the sky, peeking over
a decrepit swimming pool filled with leaves and mildew, she
wondered if Ceit had gotten away. She wondered if Ceit was
hidden well enough to escape the temple. They had people all
over, it seemed. They were invested in raising ambassadors, as
they called them, to work in every major city. They had judges,
police officers, teachers, lawyers, and people like Annbeth, who
were juggled into whatever position they needed. They would all
be on full alert. And while the search for Ceit was, of course, the

priority, Annbeth was now a traitor, and her actions would have consequences. She had needed to get out of town.

On the night of the tornado, she had bandaged her hands and then slipped outside. The van the director had left by the gym was still there, dented and a window broken by the storm, but relatively untouched. The temple members were long gone, lost in the chaos that still reigned. Annbeth had jumped inside, found the key in the ignition, and taken off out the twisted front gate. The guards were huddling in the storm shelter, so no one took any notice. She had made it to Barstow before the gas light came on. She was able to limp the van to this wretched motel. The Days End was appropriate. If they found her here, that was exactly what would happen. Taking the van was a terrible risk, but in the panic of the moment Annbeth hadn't been thinking clearly. A Mac van would have been even more obvious. At least the temple favored neutral black, which was intended to be unnoticeable.

She hadn't had enough for the room, just a crumpled pile of dollars in her pocket. But the desk clerk, who looked to be no older than sixteen, had taken the bills and given her a key. "I'll give you three nights. We're empty as fuck right now. Don't drink the tap water," the kid had muttered. Annbeth had nodded a thank you and then locked herself in her room.

So far, the meager continental breakfast had provided all her food. She had taken the entire tray of stale croissants when the teenager at the desk (a new one for the morning) had stepped into the back room. The edict not to drink the tap water hadn't stuck, as she had no alternative. It was a temporary solution that would end when the sun rose tomorrow. She had no idea where she would go next. Annbeth watched water bugs scoot across the filmy surface of the pool and hoped Ceit was waking to a kinder dawn.

*58*

THE RAPPING ON THE FRONT DOOR WAS CORDIAL AND polite. Three raps, a pause followed by three more, another pause, and then a single, inquisitive knock. Ceit sat up, staring at the door from her seat at the kitchen table. She knew it didn't matter whether she opened the door or not; they were coming in whether or not she gave her blessing. She wasn't sure quite what they were. The energy rolling off the entities on the other side of the battered door, with its chipped paint and simple knob lock, was unlike anything she had ever felt before. She knew there were multiple people there—if, indeed, they were actually people.

Another single knock, quiet, as though they were trying not to wake the inhabitants. There was no urgency. They knew Ceit was there, and they knew she was alone. Ceit could feel the blood in her neck begin a rhythmic pulsing. She looked down at her arms and saw the blue and red veins and arteries throbbing, pulsing. Her mind felt disconnected from the rest of her body, and her limbs took on a heavy, almost numb feel. She sat straighter in her chair and then, with great effort, stood. Ceit walked to the door and stood staring at a spot of scratched paint for a moment before she reached for the doorknob. The door swung open to reveal a man with deathly pale skin, wearing a striped fedora and a Hard Rock Cafe Miami T-shirt with a matching striped suit vest over it. His jeans were artfully ripped at the knee and his feet ensconced in white Converse sneakers.

Ceit narrowed her eyes. She had distinctly felt the presence of multiple beings here, but the man with the unnaturally pale eyes of no particular color stood there alone. He smiled, revealing a mouth full of too-perfect teeth.

"Miss Ceit, I presume?" he said in a voice that Ceit suspected could sound like a great many things but in this moment sounded like the slow flow of syrup.

Ceit nodded. "What are you? How did you find this place?" she asked, keeping her hand on the doorknob even though she knew she lacked the ability to keep him from entering this space.

The man smiled, his pale lips disappearing into his gum line. "It's true what they said. You do have a strong—what do they call it here?—hwó. But that doesn't cover up your stench, not entirely. One might say I simply followed my nose. Don't take it personally. I rather like it. But it is, as they say, an acquired taste." He smiled and looked around at the room behind her. "All alone? That's good. You were the one I was coming to see anyhow, and I'd rather not have to take care of any prying eyes or ears."

With that, he slipped past Ceit into the living room. She felt no more than a breeze as the creature moved past her, his presence insubstantial as air.

He stood in the center of the room, surveying the worn furniture and cheap, fake wood paneling on the walls. "Shame what's become of these people, isn't it?" He glanced back at Ceit, who felt the door close of its own accord, neatly clicking shut. "Real shame. I'd be surprised, quite frankly, if Chinle had another fifty years left in it. Whose fault is it? Whose fault indeed. Do you know?" He swiveled and turned to Ceit, his pale eyes narrowing.

Ceit stared at him impassively. She could feel what was at the core of his being—a storm of various influences, but no particular beginning or end. This creature was the culmination of many things, but no one thing in essence. She could not figure out how it had found her. In the cul-de-sac as a child, she had felt things similar to this on occasion. The Matrarc had called them the Spiorad Aisling, a sort of creature spun from bits of dreams and fears. She had pulled the veil down around them when they approached. "Not gone, but hidden," she had said. Ceit had not felt their presence since then, and she was unsure of how to block its presence now. Her abilities felt impotent and weak. Her hands shook for fear, and her throat was dry. With a start she knew this was the same Ch'įįdii, nightmare spirits, demons that walked the periphery of the waking world.

"Little one, I'm the least of your problems. Do you have any concept of the humans who are chasing you? They will find you eventually, stupid as they are. It will take time, but a little blonde girl hidden in a place where little blonde girls are rare will not stay hidden long. Here, sit. Would you like to hear a story?" He tipped his hat and nodded to the worn sofa.

Ceit's feet moved of their own accord, and she sat on the edge of the cushion. Her skin had started to pulse with the rhythm of the man's words. He sat down opposite her in the tattered armchair.

"Not too far from here is a set of great caves that stretch far into the earth. Today, tourists follow a staircase down into the bottom where they've hung lights. You can even buy a cup of coffee at the center of the earth. Imagine? But before they were turned into a commodity, before the soul of the caverns was sold to the highest bidder and chiseled out to make room for a safety rail and gift shop to sell T-shirts and commemorative shot glasses, the caves sat empty of human life. Bats flew in and out. You get the idea. Deep at the center, where you can now buy a stale turkey sandwich, sat an ancient creature. The people here call it the Yee Naaldlooshii, a skin-walker, but it's older than all that. It could turn to a bat, or a puma, or a coyote, or whatever it pleased.

"One night when the moon was new and so slight it didn't show even a sliver of light in the night sky, the Yee Naaldlooshii flew from the caves, through that endless darkness, all the way to the desert. It was hungry, but the desert creatures it normally fed on had become tiresome. It needed more than the blood and flesh of animals. It flew until it found the first people. Primitive as they were, all they saw was a monster. As one of their own was plucked off and pulled into the night sky, they began to create the myth of what they had seen. They drew pictures and told stories. They created elaborate rituals and danced the Yeibichai in circles on the nights when the moon was so slight it did not show in the sky.

"It didn't matter. The Yee Naaldlooshii came and went as it pleased, picking off children who had wandered too far from the tribe, men who dared to hunt alone, women who sat outside under the stars at night. It didn't care who. It was hungry. It was no more monster than the coyote or hawk. Is the snake a demon for swallowing the mouse? The mouse would certainly say so, but without it, the snake would perish. Are you following?" The man leaned in, propping his thin elbows on his knees. Ceit nodded, her head numb. The walls of the small house seemed to be permeable. She could almost see through the plaster to the sun outside.

"Good," the man said with an edge to his voice. "My point is, dear Ceit, that all the superstition in the world couldn't save the people from the Yee Naaldlooshii. You have nothing to fear from me. I am here to remind you of what you are, little one. You are the Bandia Marbh, and the people of this place are a superstitious lot. I know where they want to hide you, and I can only tell you to follow at your own risk. You could start to believe your own hype. The Yee Naaldlooshii is a force of nature, as are you. You have existed in this world as long as there has been a world to exist in. You are the dark to the light, the reason that an honest man can't buy a drink on a Sunday. But I think you know all that, am I right?" He smiled his lipless grin.

"I will be the Matrarc of my people," Ceit said softly, her voice unsure.

"My dear," the man said, his face quizzical, "you are so much more than that. That is like saying the DeLorean was just a car. Your people, that dying cult stuck in a cul-de-sac, could never contain you. Why do you think they cast you out? Why do you think the Sluagh found your mother? They underestimated you, Ceit. The ones who called the ancient evil to your door did not see you for what you truly are. It wasn't her they were after, my dear. But you are far too powerful for them, so they picked off the weakest near you, like a hawk with a rat."

"What do you mean?" Ceit asked, leaning forward. "Who summoned the Sluagh? Who allowed the Rabharta to rise?"

The man laughed, a shrill, dissonant chime that filled the room. "Not for me to say."

"Why isn't it?" Ceit demanded. "Someone called the darkness that killed my mother. Who was it?"

"Not. For. Me. To. Say," the man hissed, his tone a warning.

"Should I have stayed with Annbeth and gone to Salt Lake?" Ceit asked, feeling a chill seep into her skin with each elongated word the man spoke.

"Good lord no, child," the man said with disgust in his voice. "You might be ignorant, but your instincts are intact. Those dungeon masters with their pentagrams and goat heads are as far from what you are as your beloved Matrarc. They want to fit you into their mythos, plant some horns on your head and cloven feet on the soles of your sneakers. They want some role-play fantasy creature, a cartoon, a mockery. They are dangerous in their surety of who they think you are. You are more than all that."

"What are you?" Ceit asked suddenly, her heart beginning to slow, her back becoming straighter.

He laughed, a thin, sporadic sound. "Your Matrarc wasn't wrong. I am the Spiorad Aisling, at least to your people. I am called many things. Here they call me Ch'įįdii. In other places I am something else. I am your servant, your valet, your personal assistant. I am at your service. My job is to make sure you reach your potential and don't get caught up in the hilarities of superstition that exist in waves around you. You are young yet, and up until this point have had only a hint of knowledge as to what you really are. But as they say, the more you know…"

"What do I call you?" Ceit asked, feeling for the first time like her heart and head were connected. Her very bones felt stronger. She sat tall, her spine made of iron.

"Amon is my preferred moniker," the man said. "I've been called a great many things, but I am the Scotty to your Captain Kirk, your own personal Bo Brady, ready to do your bidding."

Ceit smiled slightly. "Bo Brady isn't terribly good at his job. If he worked anywhere other than the Salem Police Department, I'm not sure he'd make it."

"Touché," Amon said, matching her smile.

"I need you to not harm Yani and her family," Ceit said firmly.

Amon nodded. "As you wish. If you are planning on following

them down into the canyon, I will stand back and be quite invisible. But practice caution. They are better than the lot back in Los Angeles, yes, but in their own way just as dangerous. I know you were sent here by your fallen Matrarc, but superstition is a powerful thing, and there is prodigious danger in becoming an imitation of yourself."

"How do I call you when I need you?" Ceit asked.

"Catch the reflection of the sun or moon in this." Amon handed her a bronze cast locket on a chain. On the surface was carved a curious symbol of a double circle and A M O N, each lettered in the place of the four directions. In the inner circle, there was an ornate design—a rectangle with three curved edges and the letter I in the center, a line with swirls at each end through the center. Ceit opened the locket to find a tiny silver mirror. She looked up at Amon and nodded.

"Until then, I will be watching. On your word I will not harm the people you have chosen, but I cannot speak for anyone else. My job is to protect you. Now that you have seen your true self, I will not hesitate to make sure you live to a ripe old age in this ridiculous form you have chosen for yourself. There are plenty who would like to see you destroyed." At this, Amon tipped his fedora and crossed to the door, turned the handle, and then disappeared in a gust of wind.

59

BENNY'S TRUCK PULLED INTO THE DRIVEWAY IN A STORM of dust.

"Yani called me from the gas station, said to get here immediately." He stood in the door, breathing heavy, his face flushed. His eyes grew confused as he looked around the empty room. "You're alone." It was as much a question as a statement.

Ceit nodded. "I had a visitor. He is gone now, and he has promised not to harm you and your family."

Benny nodded slowly. "I suppose that makes as much sense as anything has in the last couple of days." He looked back at the truck. "We should get going. Get your things."

As Ceit brushed her teeth with the alligator toothbrush, she regarded herself in the mirror. She wondered if Amon was to be trusted and what he meant by "this ridiculous form you have chosen for yourself." It had never occurred to her that she had a choice. Until the creature who had overtaken her mother had spoken to her in the neglected care center, she had never considered the possibility that she was anything but the leader of the Society. She had never seen herself anywhere else but in her home, leading the generations of women who had lived there since long before her time. She had heard of the Bandia Marbh only in the oldest of the stories the elders told. The deity was both a blight and a savior; she could destroy as well as she could heal. She was to be deeply revered. The Bandia Marbh purged the dark souls from the world of man and controlled the night sky, sending her minions out to pick the weakest of the lot from the face of the earth. Ceit understood why Amon had told her the story of the Yee Naaldlooshii. She also knew that she was the only one among the Society who would, one day, be able to raise the veil and reach the other world. There was a certain satisfaction in knowing that it would be closed to them forever now, that her banishment had relegated them to the bowels of the news, a forgotten sidenote. As she placed the toothbrush in her backpack, Benny knocked softly on the door.

"We need to go, little one," he said quietly.

Ceit opened the door. "I would like to thank Yani. Is she back?"

Benny shook his head. "No. The children were scared. I will tell her. She will understand."

The truck rumbled out of the driveway and down a dust-filled road. Bright tourist signs pointed in the direction of hiking trails and pull-off spots for Canyon de Chelly. Benny passed them all and kept driving.

"We're going to a place the tourists can't get to. On the north end, near Massacre Cave. Tourists have overlooks, but only the locals can get into the canyon from there. Our aunt isn't far once we get down the canyon," Benny explained as he veered to avoid something covered in gray fur that darted across the road.

Ceit caught her breath as the truck tires found solid road again. "Why is it called Massacre Cave?"

Benny looked at her sideways. "Spanish murdered our people there back in 1805. Women and children, old men. They stood on the far end of the canyon and fired on them while the men were out hunting. Killed them all before they had a chance to run. Our people had never seen guns that could kill from so far away. The cave had protected us from the Ute and the Apache in years past, and they thought they were safe."

"It's a tourist spot?" Ceit asked softly.

Benny nodded. "The bilagáana take family photos and throw rocks to see if they can reach the other side."

Ceit looked out the window. "Do you think it offends the dead ones that they do this?"

Benny was quiet for a minute, and Ceit turned her head to watch his profile.

"No," he said finally. "But it makes me wonder how long it will be before a massacre happens again. Not in the same way—our people know better than to hide in caves—but we've stopped counting how many ways there are to kill. It reminds me of the sandstorms out in the desert. Have you ever seen one?"

Ceit shook her head. Benny gave her a small glance and then nodded back at the road, slowing before he turned left onto an indistinguishable dirt path barely wide enough to accommodate the truck.

"The wind catches the sand and lifts it into a funnel cloud. Dust devils are what shimá called them. They dance across the desert. When they collide, they either fall to the ground destroyed or they combine and grow even taller. They're beautiful in a way." Benny slowed the truck and pulled off to an area filled with rough grass. He looked at Ceit, his bright brown eyes intense. "The power to destroy is a strange thing. One can combine forces with it or be destroyed in the process. I suppose the bilagáana and their cameras have made their decision. They chose to not care that blood was spilled in that place. I have chosen to remember. We are all dancing across the sand, and one day we will collide. I do not know who will be left."

Benny opened the truck door and climbed out, motioning for her to follow. "From here we ride."

Ceit walked through the bramble and rough field grass, following Benny. As she came out of a thicket, her breath disappeared. Spread out in front of her was a vast canyon. Shades of green, blue, gold, and bronze washed the canyon walls in waves.

"Where are we?" Ceit asked.

"This is local land, Canyon del Muerto—the very north point. Massacre Cave is a bit that way. You can't see it from here," Benny said. "You can ride with me—if that's okay, that is. I'll teach you to ride on your own, but your first time out shouldn't be today," he said cautiously, a wrinkle forming between his eyes.

"It's fine," Ceit said, silently relieved. She had never sat on a horse, much less ridden one. "Do I want to know why it's called Canyon del Muerto?"

"Nope," Benny replied. "C'mon. Paddock is this way."

A tawny mare with a black mane and black hooves was munching on a bit of hay in a tiny fenced square. Next to her, a chocolate-brown creature with giant eyes watched Ceit and Benny approach through the undergrowth. Saddles hung on the fence.

"We'll take Maggie. She's always up for a little intrigue and adventure." He winked at her and set to saddling the chocolate-brown mare. Maggie regarded Ceit impassively, her eyes engulfing her in their perfect darkness. Ceit reached up and stroked her nose.

Once the saddle was adjusted, Benny lifted Ceit up and swung himself up behind her.

"You don't need to do anything. I'll drive, and she knows the way. Just hold on." Ceit nodded. As the horse started down a narrow path, Ceit leaned back into the swaying motion and rested the back of her head against Benny's chest. One hand gripped the saddle, the other stroked the black-brown mane. She felt as far from the world as she could be.

60

ANNBETH WAITED NERVOUSLY AT THE COUNTER AT Black Bear Diner on Lenwood Avenue. She was early. Karen McAlister—current CPS agent, ex-SVU detective—wouldn't be here for at least another half hour. She had listened to Annbeth silently and then asked where she was. "I'm leaving in fifteen," was all she had said, but the drive to Barstow was close to two hours. Annbeth didn't have any money left, so she sat with her glass of ice water and tried to avoid the glare of the waitress. The food smells were driving her mad. The teenage clerk had grown wise to her continental breakfast theft and chased her out of the office on the second morning. Now her time was up there. The charity of the Days End was over, the van was empty and useless, and she was penniless. She had called Karen McAlister out of desperation. It was a dangerous move. She could easily be sending a squad car to arrest Annbeth, or she could be connected to the temple herself. Annbeth had no idea how many contacts the temple really had as part of their Los Angeles security network. Some had grown up in

Salt Lake like Annbeth, but others had joined the order remotely and formed their own chapters. There was no way for Annbeth to know if Karen was connected. They were instructed to never talk about it unless specific orders came from the Maga herself.

Annbeth was about to break the rule that would land her in even more trouble than she had been in for interfering with Ceit Robertson's extraction. But she hadn't known where else to turn. Karen McAlister had been the lead SVU agent on the Society investigation when Annbeth had clerked there. She had found out later that the detective had had some sort of breakdown and left the department altogether. Karen had eventually shown up at CPS as one of the head child protection agents. Annbeth suspected she had made that particular shift so that she might still watch the activity on Sinder Avenue, which could indicate that she was also working for the Maga and the Salt Lake temple. But it could also indicate that Annbeth had an ally and protection from what the temple would do when they found her.

The waitress refilled Annbeth's water and gave her a long stare. "I can give you another thirty minutes, but then you are either going to order something or go. My manager's a real asshole."

Annbeth nodded, hoping Karen showed up and felt generous enough to buy her a cup of coffee.

Right as Annbeth was about to give up hope, the door swung open and Karen McAlister stepped inside. She was beautiful; Annbeth had forgotten that. She felt the wave of attraction she'd had to stifle when they'd worked together rise back up. It made her a bit dizzy. Long chestnut hair and skin with a forever glow of the sun, she was wearing clothes far too warm for the desert but perfect for a Los Angeles fall—boots that rose to her knees over tight black pants, a man's button-up with the sleeves rolled to the elbow. She looked flushed and uncertain.

"Karen!" Annbeth called, and the woman crossed to her and sat on the stool next to her.

"Okay, so that happened," she said with a sardonic smile. "I drove to Barstow in rush hour LA traffic. This better be good. How the hell are you, anyway? No one heard from you at all after you left SVU."

Annbeth returned the smile, relief flooding from her. Already she felt ages lighter. "I'll tell you all about it. But we should maybe move to a place that's a bit more private. There's a booth in that corner over there. I hate to ask it, but I haven't really eaten, and I don't have any—"

Karen waved away the rest of the sentence. "Jesus, I'll buy you breakfast if you can help me find Ceit Robertson. Hell, I'll buy you lunch, too, for that one."

Thirty minutes later, after Karen and Annbeth had been tucked into the corner booth and Annbeth had inhaled a stack of pancakes, Karen straightened her back and shifted to agent mode.

"Okay, you no longer look like you're about to pass out, so talk. You call me out of the blue and say you know where Ceit Robertson is. Talk."

Annbeth shifted uncomfortably. "I lied a bit there. I don't know." Karen glared and then started to rise from the table. "But wait! I have more important information, and I know how to find her."

Karen stopped. "Okay. I'm listening."

Annbeth unloaded the entire story of the temple, the Maga, Director Carabus, and the Society. Karen listened and nodded. Annbeth knew it all sounded insane. She told Karen of the night the orderly attacked Ceit, of the night when her father broke into Mac. She told her about what the temple had done to Boyd Robertson-turned-Healy. She told her everything, hoping that

Karen McAlister wasn't another of the temple's pawns. By the time she finished, breakfast service was over and lunch had begun. The waitress glared at them both before giving them one final coffee refill.

Karen sat silent for a long time. "How safe do you think you are here?" she asked finally.

Annbeth shook her head. She felt tears in her eyes, and her voice cracked as she said, "Not very. They'll find me. I've seen what they do to traitors. They have people all over LA. They might be here too. I don't really know. Their focus is finding Ceit, but they'll eventually find me and take me back to Salt Lake. They'll never believe I don't know where she is."

Karen considered this. "I don't know if you're full of shit or not, quite frankly. I know the office has been going nuts since the missing person's report was filed. None of us who have followed this case believe she just ran away. How sure are you that your temple doesn't have her?"

"Positive," Annbeth responded. "Ceit got herself out, but she had a plan. She had people helping her. I guess I don't know if they were people... It was beyond anything I've ever seen..." The nightmares had stopped the night Ceit disappeared. To Annbeth, that proved that someone was trying to distract anyone who might stop Ceit, and now that energy was being put into keeping her hidden.

"You realize there's no way to explain this to anyone." Karen sighed. "Satanic Panic—that's the term for it. Your story goes right up there with kids drawing pentagrams in cow's blood and dungeon masters in black trench coats. We get this bullshit all the time. Your story will be filed right next to the reports about playing Ozzy Osbourne records backward and secret messages on Pepsi cans."

"But you believe me," Annbeth said softly.

Karen considered her for a minute. "You know why I left SVU? The breakdown everyone whispered about?"

Annbeth shook her head.

"Ever hear of the Seventh Nighters, out of Torrance?"

"I remember their early files," Annbeth said. "Doomsdayers, right?"

Karen nodded. "They thought the end was coming on June 9, 1985. Turns out they were wrong." Karen paused. "You were gone by the time the crew raided a basement on a tip from an under-cover agent. They found a little girl, although we didn't know what she was when we found her. Her hair was matted, and... they had carved up her face and hands and arms, everything. Kid hadn't seen the sun maybe ever. She screamed when the EMTs rolled her out to the ambulance. At the hospital they said her eyes couldn't adjust to the light, so they had to keep the room dim. She never spoke, didn't seem to understand any written language, couldn't communicate at all. She was starving to death. The cult had run from the location and left her there. No one knew how long she'd been chained to that fucking water pipe, left to die. She lasted eight days. Eight. The official word was she died of complications from chronic malnutrition and shock."

"Jesus," Annbeth whispered.

"Jesus had nothing to do with it. Neither did the devil. People did this. Grown men and women who murdered a child over the course of years. Who knows how many others." Karen paused and cocked her head at Annbeth. "That's why I'm trusting you. I don't believe in magic, but I believe in evil. And I believe that Ceit Robertson is in real danger, as are you."

*61*

WHEN THE SUN ROSE, CEIT'S JOB WAS TO BRING water to the horses and fill the bins with hay. The doe-eyed animals regarded her passively, except for Buttercup. Buttercup always whinnied and nudged her hand. It was for that reason that Ceit made a point to snag a carrot or apple before she left the ranch-style house that sat tucked under a crop of red rock. Taking food without permission was, strictly speaking, against the house rules. She suspected that Noni knew about it, but it had gone unmentioned.

There wasn't much that Noni did not know about, especially in regard to what went on in her house. On one of Ceit's first nights—as she lay in the twin-size bed crammed against the far wall listening to the sound of her roommate, Chooli, snoring from her own twin bed on the other end of the room—she had gotten up and wandered into the great room. She'd silently stared at the moon through the big bay window. She knew how to be silent, but still she had jumped to find Noni standing at her shoulder.

"Little girls need to be in bed," the old woman had said.

"I'm not so little," Ceit had replied, not unkindly. Her twelve-year-old body was beginning to betray its previous simplicity. Ceit had been lying in bed feeling the rolling wave of cramps across her stomach.

"I'll make you a tea," the old woman had replied, and crossed to the kitchen. "*Cordylanthus ramosus*," she'd said with authority, pulling a jar that contained what looked like dried leaves off the top shelf. "It will help with your moon cycle. The elders used to believe that it created a pathway to the goddess of the hunt, and she would, in turn, ask the moon to send healing to those who called. I think we're past that sort of superstition now. Bushy bird's beak is another name for it. Grows like weeds here in the canyon."

"How did you know?" Ceit had asked quietly. Her cycle hadn't yet started, and she'd been too embarrassed to ask for pads. She had been planning on asking Chooli the next morning, just in case she needed them, figuring the older girl surely must have some sort of supplies.

"I bet you're missing your mother about now," Noni had said, turning from the gas burner where the kettle sat, the water inside rising to a boil. "My mother wasn't around when my first cycle came either. I had to ask my sister—that'd be Benny and Yani's shimá—and she told me that I was dying, that I had the rot and I was dying."

"You didn't believe her," Ceit had said quietly. It was more a statement than a question.

"No, I didn't. But I also had no idea what was happening. When you grow up on the rez—and this was oh, what, 1947 or '48?—there wasn't exactly much talk of it. So, no, I suspected I wasn't dying, but she still wasn't much help. I ended up stuffing a sock with shavings from the woodpile and using that." She'd smiled at the shocked look on Ceit's face. "Don't worry. We have more sophisticated sorts of things now for young ladies."

Ceit had smiled back, hesitant, while the old woman poured the hot water through a strainer that contained the crushed leaves from the jar and handed the mug to her.

"Here. It tastes something terrible, but it will help." She'd sat opposite Ceit at the wooden table and stared at her. Ceit took in her long gray hair, pulled back in a single braid that fell to her waist. Noni was little, not even five feet tall, but built in a powerful manner that made you forget her height. Her golden-brown skin was lined with a life lived in the canyon's sun and wind. Her night-black eyes were watchful and took in Ceit's small form. Ceit sipped from the mug and grimaced at the muddy taste.

"Told you. Nothing for taste, but trust me, atsi'," Noni had said quietly.

"I do miss my mother," Ceit had admitted, the cramps in her belly already starting to subside. "She wasn't strong, and she could never stand up to the rest of them, but she had a beauty about her they never could pattern."

"I'll bet. You take after her, yes?" Noni had asked.

"Some. I look more like my great-grandmother. When she was young, my age, you wouldn't have been able to tell us apart. The photographs are a bit eerie." Ceit took another sip. She never spoke of her family. There was something about the old woman that made her tongue loose and her limbs relax.

Noni had nodded. "Benny was right to bring you here, Ceit. I had a vision of your arrival before he ever brought you to my door. You came to me in a dream. You know you have a shadow?"

"Yes. He showed himself before I came here. I fear he's more harm than I can control."

Noni considered this, and then she'd replied, "You are still unsure of what you are. When you embrace that, you will be less fearful. In this place there is a story of Sa, a Haashch'ééh, goddess of age. She is with you now as you turn from child to woman, and she will be with you as you ready to have children, and then as you turn gray. She watches over us all but maybe gives a special sort of attention to us women. The story goes that the war god, Nayanazgeni, tried to steal a lock of Sa's hair. It was said that all of time existed in its strands, which were blacker than the night itself. Nayanazgeni is a coward by nature, so he sent Coyote to trick her into bending down, and then Coyote was to catch Sa's hair in his teeth and run back to his master. Sa knew, of course, why Coyote was at her door. When he whined at an imagined pain in his paw and begged her to bend down to look, she stood tall and called to the sky. The clouds filled with rain, and it began beating down as Coyote had never seen. An even bigger coward than Nayanazgeni, Coyote ran all the way back across the desert." Noni had paused, considering Ceit's rapt face.

"What happened next?" Ceit had whispered, her hands wrapped around the clay mug.

Noni had smiled. "Sa looked to the sky and cried out Nayanazgeni's name, calling him out for his plot. In disgrace, the war god appeared. The rain suddenly stopped, soaking back into the earth. 'Why do you wish to steal my hair, Nayanazgeni?' she demanded. The war god puffed his chest and told her he wished to stop time to aid his warriors in battle. He wished to steal moons and suns from the Apache and Zuni, and our people would be atop them before they ever knew our breath was near. Sa listened to this with a patient heart and gently shook her head. 'You will succeed, Nayanazgeni.' She told him, 'If you steal my hair or my flesh, or any part of me, then you will stop time.' At this, Nayanazgeni's eyes grew big, and he imagined the victories he would have. With a strand of Sa's night-black hair, he would be victorious against all who came against him. His people would never want again. He would reign supreme among all the gods, for all the people would see the riches he had brought them.

"Sa shook her head and explained in a voice that held more patience than frustration, more wisdom than questions, 'You will stop time, Nayanazgeni. But if you harm me in any way—a pluck of a single hair from my head, a single action taken against my will—then time will stop for all eternity. Your warriors will turn to stone in place, their arrows pointed forever at their enemy. Children will forever lie in their shimá's arms, their lips to the breast. The antelope will pause eternally, their watchful eyes and far-reaching ears always and forever waiting for their foe. Time will stop and never again resume. Coyote, the strands of my hair still entwined in his teeth, will forever freeze in flight from my door. You, Nayanazgeni, will stare at the night sky until the end of the moons, waiting for your victory. Harm me, war god, and you stop time for all beings that live under our moon.' At that, Nayanazgeni, shaken to his core, turned and followed Coyote across the desert, leaving Sa to her peace."

"What does it mean?" Ceit had asked, her body vibrating in the same way she imagined the stars hummed in rhythm with the night.

"It means, atsi', that your shadow knows better than to pluck a strand of hair on your head."

It had been months since that early night at the ranch house on the far edge of Canyon de Chelly. As Ceit fed Buttercup a somewhat flaccid carrot, she inhaled the now-familiar scent of the barn. Outside in the paddock, the goats were restless. Chooli would be out soon to take them to pasture. The dogs were already bouncing at the barn door, ready to work. Ceit liked it here. She worked various jobs throughout the day. Her muscles ached when she lay down to sleep, and she felt more connected to her heart than she had ever before. She felt her eyes opening. Ceit rubbed the pendant that Amon had given her in his ethereal visit so many months ago. She did not need him, not yet. She needed to spend more time here and learn the truth of what and who she was.

Chooli had theories. Chooli was turning seventeen next month. Her long black hair framed her round face, accented by her black-painted fingernails and pitch-dark eyeliner. Chooli listened to Siouxsie and the Banshees and the Cure on her headphones and drew ink line tattoos on her wrist. She was planning on going to Flagstaff on her eighteenth birthday to get a real tattoo. Noni rolled her eyes and refused to comment on the plan. Ceit had liked Chooli from the start. She had been living on the ranch and tending the goats, among other duties, for two years now. Chooli's thoughts were dark to Ceit, her secrets well guarded, as, she had discovered, were all she had met in this place. Her ability to hear the goings-on in the heads of others only worked when the subjects were oblivious and open. Here, though, the canyon and the desert surrounding it seemed to keep its inhabitants on guard, their minds cloaked. Ceit welcomed the silence. Ceit hadn't asked Chooli why she was here, and no one had offered to share. No one had asked Ceit this question when she arrived either. The shared understanding that some things were beyond explaining was a comfort.

In addition to Chooli, there was a boy named Laurie at the ranch. He was in his twenties and had lived there most of his life. It went without saying that neither Chooli nor Laurie were any more Noni's blood than Ceit was. Laurie was mixed. His father was Navajo, Ceit knew that much, but his mother was something very different. Laurie had the black silk hair and golden skin, but his eyes were a tawny shade of yellow-brown. Chooli had been in love with him for years now. Ceit suspected Laurie knew and just ignored her prolonged stares. Laurie was in charge of supply runs, riding to the top of the canyon and back down with bags of rice and beans, spices, and fresh vegetables they couldn't grow in the garden. He also made sure the well pump was operational, shoed the horses, and did a mess of other jobs that kept the small ranch running.

For her part, Ceit spent her days tending the horses and working the small grove of peach trees. Noni had told her she was set to learn to preserve the fruit when harvest came.

"A good skill to have no matter where you end up," Noni had said, her sharp eyes regarding Ceit without judgment.

Ceit saw Benny every so often. He rode his chocolate-brown mare down the canyon to stop by once a month, usually bearing gifts—a bag of chocolates or saltwater taffy. He always sat down with Ceit for a talk, although mostly he listened to her stories of the horses and the birds that lived among the peach trees. For the first time in her twelve years, Ceit felt at home. The Rabharta seemed a fairy story, and the stories of Sa and the war god became more real than the cul-de-sac. She was happy.

There is a certain danger in happiness. As Ceit lay in bed at night, in darkness as pitch-black as Sa's hair, she let her awareness of the outside world become alive. She was a fugitive here. People out there in the world that ran on asphalt and gasoline were looking for her. The Sluagh and the ancient spirits that haunted the weak ones would find her eventually. She had left her pack and was in hiding. She knew that one day she would need to stop pretending she was Coyote, who could do as he pleased. One day she would have to resurface in the world again. She felt a great stirring inside her. She had some time left here. The moon had yet to see her realize the core of herself. She ran her finger over the pendant that Amon had given her. She had many enemies over the edge of the canyon in which she hid, and she would need to rise against them like Nayanazgeni—no tricks and no sorcery, just her.

*62*

THE STUDIO APARTMENT WAS CRAMPED AND DINGY.
It stank of mildew, and the tile in the microscopic bathroom had
black mold around the edges. But Annbeth had grown accustomed
to it over time. Situated in one of the crumbling mansions off
Normandie and Western, it was officially rented to one Caroline
Orellana. Annbeth had an ID courtesy of the LAPD with the same
name. Karen had used her influence to get the SVU department
to declare her a witness and offer her temporary protection, but
Annbeth knew this wouldn't last forever. The information she
had provided had proved to be useless in locating Ceit. The Los
Angeles temple ambassadors had been smart enough to never
reveal themselves, so Annbeth had been equally useless in outing
them. All she had actually done was offer up her home in Salt Lake
to observation and scrutiny. The enclave was now being photo-
graphed and surveilled as much as Sinder Avenue had been. So far
the authorities hadn't really been able to confirm that the community was any threat whatsoever. The temple members didn't dress

in the old-fashioned garb that the Society had, they sent their children to school, they held regular jobs. Annbeth knew that unless her information proved useful soon, Caroline Orellana would disappear, and Annbeth would need to fend for herself again.

She liked her new, short blondish hair. Changing her appearance hadn't been required, but Annbeth had been far too worried about being recognized on the streets of LA not to. After that day in Barstow, Karen had driven her back to Los Angeles and let Annbeth stay on her sofa bed until the police department moved her to the studio apartment with a hot plate and chain bolt on the door. They had used this apartment to house witnesses before, and Annbeth wondered how many of them had been found here. She held her breath anytime she saw missionaries walking in pairs down the street. She had nearly called 911 when an old lady with Jesus pamphlets had knocked on her door one afternoon. But the temple didn't know where she was—at least not yet.

63

ON A NIGHT IN OCTOBER, ONE CEIT HAD ALMOST forgotten to celebrate, Noni baked her a small round cake sweet with cornmeal and topped with whipped cream cheese frosting. Chooli and Laurie laughed at her surprised face as the three of them carried the little cake to the table, candles lit. She was thirteen. That night the four of them ate cake and laughed and sat on the porch to look at the stars.

"Tomorrow will be up to you, Ceit," Noni told her. "No work. Take a day off and do what you'd like."

Ceit already knew she would saddle Buttercup and ride as far into the canyon as was safe. Even under layers of clothes and a hat, she still could not let herself be seen. She would pack a small lunch and eat with Buttercup by the little creek that ran through the canyon floor.

That night she dreamed of the Matrarc for the first time since she'd come to this place. The woman appeared as she was toward the end of her life. She was an old woman, and she was sitting in

Noni's seat at the wooden kitchen table. Ceit approached her, not sure if it was a dream or reality. The old woman regarded her coldly for a moment.

"You've rested long enough, daughter. You are meant to be gathering strength. Instead you are withering."

Ceit tried to object, but her voice was mute.

"You are coming of age and must step into your role. Noni can teach you, but you have to ask. Otherwise you will pick peaches and hide from the world for the rest of your days."

At that, Ceit woke, covered in sweat and shaking. She considered the options. She could stay here for the rest of her life picking peaches. At some point, she wouldn't have to hide. Even as she allowed the thought to enter her head, she knew it was false. Though the official offices would eventually stop their search, the temple and those like them would never stop. This dream would be one of many that would plague her. She was not meant for a normal life. She was the Bandia Marbh, and she needed to learn the meaning of her power.

So on the day that was supposed to be her day off, when Buttercup looked at her from the paddock expectantly, she instead sought out Noni. She was an adiłgąshii, and the ones who sought her out did so in secrecy. Ceit always knew when she was with a visitor because the wind whipped through the canyon and the stars shone as though they would burst from the sky. There was a reason Ceit had been sent here, a reason the Matrarc had sent her the visions of this woman and this place so long ago. Ceit knew it was time to learn her purpose and take the ancient seat that had been awaiting her since birth.

Noni had known she was coming and led her deep into the peach orchard, where the trees formed a sort of a hollow. Ceit liked to come here and lay on the scrubby grass, surrounded by the heat of the sun and the desert birds that screamed overhead. But that day, the two women sat in the wooded circle facing each other while Noni taught Ceit how to breathe and control her mind.

Noni would take Ceit there every day from that point on and tell her stories of the Navajo, stories of the dead ones who walk in the night and the Yeibichai who would suck the blood from your skin, leaving it patchy and pale. She taught Ceit the art of stillness, how to listen to her innermost thoughts, how to trust her instincts.

Noni taught her that the moments of power she had experienced before—the man in the hallway at Mac, her father and the attack, the tornado that allowed her to escape—had come from rage. She explained that things that come from anger are never sustainable. Noni taught her to seek her power in stillness, in quietude, and in peace. She taught her to see.

When the winter rains and snow fell, they met in Noni's greenhouse, surrounded by the beginnings of bean sprouts and freshly spawned peach tree shoots. "It is a place where things begin," Noni told her.

By the time spring arrived, Ceit felt herself changed. She knew, with distinguishable sadness, that her time here would end. The reprieve she had been given from the chaos of her existence would come to a close—maybe not soon, but eventually. She would need to reenter the world and take her seat at the head of the table that had been set for her.

*64*

"THE DINÉ LIVE IN THE GLITTERING WORLD. THE FIRST world was black. Although it was filled with land, water, air, and language, the first spirit beings lived in darkness and longed to see the beauty of the creation the gods had made for them. The second world brought animals and the big blue water, and the first people were given souls. The physical bodies of man and animal caught and held the tenuous creation, which seemed no more substantial than the clouds. In the third world, the spider woman wove an intricate web across the sky, leaving little points of light to illuminate the darkness. The glittering world holds all these things and is constantly being created with the knowledge that the spider woman taught the first people."

Noni paused and looked to Ceit, her eyes still. "Do you understand?"

Ceit shook her head.

"You are not of the glittering world, nor were you created in the darkness of the first. Your soul was not caught by a physical form in the early days of the world. You stand outside this and yet chose to be reborn into this existence. Why do you think that is?" Noni waited for an answer.

"I do not know. I spent my childhood thinking I was the next Matrarc of my people. I know that was wrong," Ceit answered.

"It's not your fault," Noni responded. "You chose to be born to those people because it was the only place where your power would even be vaguely understood. Your people came from Ireland. The old ways are remembered there the same way they are in this place. Others too, but your Matrarc was wise to send you here. You live in this plane of existence, but you are above and within and all around. You are as much the force that moves the leaves on the tree as you are the tree itself."

"The old women feared me, as did others," Ceit said softly.

"As well they should. Death is at the core of living. All we do is designed to stave off death. And you are the Bandia Marbh—you rule over the dead and oversee their role in the glittering world. They do well to fear you, as should I, but I forgot to fear such things long ago." Noni smiled.

"I would never harm you or your family," Ceit said, but the statement was more of a question than an absolute truth.

"You will do as you must when you must," Noni said. "I will not be angry. Your mother is not angry. You did not call the Sluagh or invite the Rabharta. You had no power to truly stop them. Your magic was young then. While you did your best, you could not have saved her. Not even the ones who called the Sluagh could have controlled them once they entered this world."

"Who called them?" Ceit asked softly. It was a question she asked herself nearly every night.

"I do not know, child," Noni answered. "Someone who greatly misunderstood the nature of your abilities."

Ceit nodded. "How long am I to stay here?"

Noni considered this. "As long as you need. In the eyes of the world, you are still a child, or a young woman at least. You would be taken and put back in the same system you ran from. The ones who pursued you before would find you again, and the whole cycle would start over. Although you are more powerful now, you would still be at the mercy of others. I suspect you are here until you can be your own person." Noni smiled crookedly. "I rather like having you around, so no need to rush off."

"What if I bring harm to this place—like with my mother?" Ceit asked.

To Ceit's surprise, Noni laughed, a deep, rough rumble of a sound. "Trouble has always found its way here. Don't flatter yourself that you are the only one who could bring trouble our way. You live here on the canyon floor. Up above, our schools are crumbling, our people are leaving in droves. I cannot blame them. They live in poverty. They have to drive a hundred miles to see a proper doctor, and yet the outside world comes here to gawk. They buy keychains and take photos with us as though we are part of the scenery. My sister's grandson, Niyol—you met him once, yes?"

Ceit nodded, suddenly concerned. She remembered him clearly.

"He got jumped by a couple of bilagáana who had come here to hike the canyon. They saw him walking through town and set on him, no reason for it. Broke his front tooth, and Yani doesn't have the money to get it fixed." Noni paused. "I sent her some things to sell—some jewelry she might fetch some money for, things like that—but it's not going to be enough."

Ceit pulled at the scrubby grass of the clearing. It was their first day back in the peach grove since the winter, and the weather was mild and warm. "I don't understand," she muttered.

"It's not for understanding," Noni said firmly. "The evil of this world lives in man. It does not reside in the dead. You are no more a threat to us than a pair of drunken bilagáana."

65

KAREN'S CALL WAS SHORT AND CURT.

"Get over here now. Alan Robertson has gone missing."

Annbeth had immediately jumped into the faded yellow Honda she had bought for $300 from the corner lot. It had a bungee cord keeping the trunk in place and was missing the front passenger seat entirely; still though, it was better than relying on the bus. This was her last month as Caroline Orellana, and she had been planning her next move. The Honda would get her out of Los Angeles.

She was certain the temple would still jump at the chance to bring her back to Salt Lake, but so far she had escaped discovery. She worked for cash in the kitchen at the burger place on the corner. Most everyone worked for cash there, and the owner never even asked to check her ID. All in all, she had saved a little money. Even minus the cost of the Honda, she could get to Pismo or even farther north and try to find someone else willing to not care where she came from.

According to Karen, Alan had been in a foster home in Griffith

Park. Karen had told her the grandmother was close to agreeing to take him in, and they were trying to hurry the paperwork up and move the boy out of the system. Chances were the boy had just run off, probably looking for his sister. But Annbeth felt a dread in her stomach that told her it wasn't that simple.

By the time she reached the Child Protective Services office, her heart was pounding. Karen motioned to Annbeth from the glass-walled conference room. The long table was lined with files that she was examining as she paced back and forth. Annbeth knew this was the SVU detective at work, not the CPS agent, but old habits were hard to kill.

"His foster mom said he never came home from school. He was supposed to catch the school bus and then walk a half block to their door. He never showed. The school said they saw him talking to a guy who looked like he worked for the Department of Water and Power." Karen paused, her brow furrowed and her cheeks flushed. "I guess they were having something repaired, and the truck had been there all week. But the idiots at the school didn't think it at all weird that a grown man was chatting up a nine-year-old, so they didn't do a damn thing. He hasn't been seen since."

Annbeth felt as though she had swallowed lead. "Any other reports?"

"Foster parents say one of those Mormon missionaries tried to break into his house last week. Weird shit. Foster dad said he found the guy climbing in through a window, Bible in hand, backpack, the whole nine yards. They called the cops, but by the time someone arrived the missionary was on the sidewalk, totally zonked out. Didn't seem to remember where he was."

Annbeth sucked in her breath. Her blood had frozen in place. She never suspected the temple would go after the little boy. They must be desperate if they would stoop to such a level.

"There's more," Karen said. "The boy told his counselor that he thought people were watching him. He told her that his teacher is new this year, that she watches him all the time, that she tried to lock him in the classroom one afternoon. The school denied everything. They said he's 'imaginative.' They blame it on trauma." Karen sat down and buried her head in her hands. After a moment she looked up at Annbeth and said, "You think this is all connected."

"They're everywhere," Annbeth whispered softly. She cleared her throat and met Karen's gaze. "I know you don't believe in magic, but you told me once you believe in evil. This is what it looks like. The temple must see this as a way to root out Ceit. They must be desperate. If they can't find her, she must be well hidden. But her brother... they got to him. Everything being what it is, this will be very public. Wherever Ceit is, it will get back to her, and then she might resurface."

"The police already have surveillance of this group. If Alan Robertson appears anywhere near the vicinity, every fed on the planet will be breaking down their door," Karen said, but her conviction wavered.

"You'll never see him," Annbeth said firmly. "You're surveilling the surface, but the tunnels stretch underneath the city in all directions. The temple has used them for generations. The worship hall is underground. They can move him across the entirety of Salt Lake, and you'd never be the wiser. He's likely there already. When did you say he was last seen?"

"Yesterday at three o'clock," Karen said. "Our office wasn't informed until this morning."

"He's already there," Annbeth said.

"So what am I supposed to do?" Karen asked, swiping her hands across the files, sending papers flying into the stale air. "Call my contacts at the federal office? Tell them he crossed state lines? Try to convince them to raid the tunnels?"

"You wouldn't find him," Annbeth said with certainty. "You have no idea how extensive the tunnels are. The temple knows them better than anyone, and maps would be useless. You need Ceit. Play their game. Make this public. Call anyone you can think of, and get this story out to as many places as you can. They think they can catch and control her. The temple has no idea what that girl is. She will burn them down."

# 66

THERE WAS A KNOCK ON THE FRONT DOOR OF THE
ranch on the night of a full moon. The alien sound made Ceit sit
straight up in bed, her heart about beating its way out of her chest.
Across the room, Chooli followed suit.

"What the hell?" Chooli muttered, and then swung out of bed.
"Must be looking for Noni. She'll be pissed they didn't follow the
rules."

As Yani had warned Ceit so many months before, there was a
steady stream of visitors for Noni at the ranch; however, Ceit and
the others never saw the women who hiked down the canyon and
across the rough land to seek Noni's help. There was a protocol.
They were to tie a red piece of cloth to the Russian olive tree on the
edge of the property. That indicated to Noni that the visitor would
be waiting by the creek bed, around the bend from the ranch, as
night fell. Ceit never asked Noni what she did for the women who
sought her help. The only reason she knew women came to look
for Noni was from the little Chooli had revealed.

"She's an adiłgąshii," Chooli had said simply.

"What does that mean?" Ceit had asked, afraid to press for too much information.

"A medicine man, or woman, if you will. She knows the old ways." Chooli had laughed at Ceit's serious expression. "Relax, kid. It's not Satan, if that's what you're thinking. That bullshit is all bullshit. No, this is the real deal, women come to her for help, always have. She has the sight. It's a rez thing. Hard to explain if you didn't grow up here."

And that was all the explanation Ceit had received or even needed. No one needed to explain the power of women's magic to her. The women continued to tie the red cloth on the Russian olive, and Noni continued to mix foul-smelling herbs and leave them by the creek bed. But they never, ever knocked on the door.

"Wait," Ceit said abruptly as Chooli stepped to the door of their room. "I don't think they're looking for Noni."

Chooli stopped and turned. "Okay," she said quietly. "Make the bed, neat as you can. Make it look like no one sleeps there. Do it quickly. Then get in the closet. If it comes to it, there's a trapdoor on the bottom, leads to a crawl space. Do it now." Her voice was even and strong.

Ceit nodded and stood, quickly and concisely making the bed. By the time she was ducking into the closet, Chooli was closing the door behind her. Ceit could hear that Noni beat Chooli to the front door. The sound of muffled male voices bled through the thin walls. She heard Chooli's voice chime in. Ceit pressed her ear to the wood and strained to hear what was happening. She clutched the pendant that bore Amon's name. To summon him, she needed to reflect the light of the moon or sun off the mirror. Inside the closet, she was rendered defenseless. She did, however, find the trapdoor. No more than two feet tall and wide, it was nearly invisible. Ceit pulled on the door, holding her breath lest it creak or groan. It swung open noiselessly, revealing pitch darkness beyond. For the second time in her life, Ceit felt fear, not of the darkness but the coffin-like feel of the walls. She stared into the blackness of the crawl space, and her body went numb with shock. *I'll wait until they enter the room,* she thought. *As soon as the handle of the bedroom door turns, I'll go in.* Her arms tingled, and her legs felt unable to move. The blackness of the crawl space seemed to swirl, and she doubted whether anything could make her enter the claustrophobic darkness.

Just then, the handle of the bedroom door turned, and Chooli's voice called in.

"It's me—chill."

Ceit breathed a sigh of relief and slammed the trapdoor shut. Chooli opened the closet door. Welcome moonlight flooded the closet.

"C'mon out. Noni is making tea," she said.

At the table, Laurie sat on the long wooden bench next to Benny, whose face looked stricken. A clay teapot was on the table. Five cups sat ready. Noni stood at the stove, watching the kettle boil atop the low blue flame. Chooli and Ceit sat opposite Laurie, whose black hair was ruffled. He looked even more handsome like this, and Ceit could feel a bit of what Chooli had been suffering with for years. When the whistle started, Noni crossed over and poured hot water into the kettle, filling the room with the scent of peach leaves and mint.

"Give it a minute. The peaches are young yet. Takes a bit to steep," she said quietly.

The five of them sat silently, staring at the clay teapot. Finally, Noni poured the steaming water into the matching clay cups.

"We have a bit of a problem," she said simply.

*67*

"YOUR BROTHER HAS GONE MISSING," BENNY SAID
directly.

Ceit felt her blood turn to ice. She stuttered, but no intelligible
words emerged.

"It was on the news. He disappeared from his school yesterday
afternoon. They don't have any leads, but he was talking to someone in a uniform who looked like he worked for the city. No notes,
at least not that the news people are talking about. Weird that a
story like this is on our news. He disappeared from Los Angeles.
We never hear about that part of the country out here..." Benny
trailed off.

"I have to go," Ceit said suddenly. "I know who has him. I know
where he is."

Noni nodded. "I suspected as much. Benny will take you back
up in the morning. Nothing much you can do tonight. Where are
you going?"

"Salt Lake City," Ceit said softly. "I don't know how I'll get
there, but I have to go."

"I'll take her," Chooli said suddenly, and then glanced around at the surprised looks from everyone at the table. "What? I know how to drive. I even have a license. I want to."

"Chooli..." Noni began hesitantly.

"No, it's okay," Chooli said, turning her head to look at Ceit. "It's what? Eight hours to Salt Lake? We'll ride out at dawn, and then Benny can loan us his truck or some other hunk of junk he keeps lying around."

Benny looked around at the table incredulously. "You can't just go on your own. You're a child. I'll go with you. I'll take care of—"

Noni cut him off and took his rough hand in hers. "Yiska, you were shown this álchíní in a vision. You saw her for what she was on that first night. She is no ordinary child, and you cannot protect her in this. She does not need our protection any longer. You know I am right."

Noni turned to Ceit. "You can always come home to this place. But something tells me you will not."

"At least let me drive her," Benny said firmly, but Chooli waved her hands in protest.

"I'll take her. I need to get out of this place. I can't hide down here in the canyon for the rest of my life. I want to do this." Chooli sounded almost excited.

Noni turned to Ceit. "What will you do there?"

"What I must," Ceit answered. "I know the ones who took Alan. They are trying to find me. I have to make them remember how to fear me."

*68*

THE STORY OF ALAN ROBERTSON'S DISAPPEARANCE
had broken the day before, and it was still dominating the special
interest sections of every news report. In the end, Karen hadn't
had to use her connections much at all. Annbeth's suspicion had
been right. The temple wanted this to be public. They wanted Ceit,
wherever she was, to see it. Annbeth knew they had people in all
different fields all over the country; media was no exception. So
the story of a little boy gone missing following his sister's already
mysterious disappearance was suddenly the subject of special
interviews with specialists on the nightly news. Larry King was
even running a story on corruption in the LA foster care system.
Alan Robertson's story was everywhere.

Annbeth had been on the first flight to Salt Lake, courtesy of
Karen, who had given her an uncharacteristic hug at the airport
drop-off that made Annbeth's heart stop for a moment. She had
never told Karen how she felt—and she expected she never would.
She had no idea how it would be received and had nothing to offer

KATHLEEN KAUFMAN

even if it were reciprocated. Annbeth had spent the bulk of her life alone and would continue to do so. Even the temple family was gone now. She waved as Karen's car pulled away from the curb, took a deep breath, and headed toward what was to come.

69

TECHNICALLY, CHOOLI COULD DRIVE, BUT CEIT KEPT her hand locked on the door of the old pickup. Chooli would alternately slow to a crawl and speed up until the vehicle was shaking and rattling. She was oddly cheerful.

Despite being her roommate for the last year, Ceit hadn't really gotten to know Chooli much. She was quiet, drew in her sketchbook, listened to her music. She knew Ceit had been spending time with Noni over the last months, but she hadn't asked about it, hadn't acted as though it were odd at all.

After hours on the road, they had just passed Moab. Ceit's eyes had grown wide at the configurations of the red rock.

"It looks like Mars," she had breathed.

Chooli laughed. "Yep, that it does. Well, I guess—I don't know what Mars looks like. But it's like you're on another planet. Lot of rez kids come up here to camp. Not all the time, but a lot."

"Have you been there?" Ceit asked.

"Yep. There's a hostel over on the other side. Costs like five dollars to stay, and it's better than sleeping on the ground. I remember there were all these stray cats. They swarmed the door of the bunkhouse. We spent all night feeding them bits of lunch meat." Chooli smiled as she abruptly swerved around a Toyota whose bumper she'd been riding for over a mile. Ceit held her breath and then tried to unclench her grip on the door.

"Why were you hiding at Noni's?" Ceit asked quietly, not sure the girl would answer.

Chooli sighed. "I get it. Long drive…time to talk about the big stuff." She cast a sideways glance at Ceit and then laughed. "I'm kidding, sorta. No one likes to talk about why they are at Noni's when they're there. Feels like you'll break the spell or some shit, right?"

Ceit smiled. It was true. There was an unspoken rule that everyone minded their own business at Noni's ranch. While Ceit had been grateful for it, she was also curious why Chooli was willing to drive her eight hours away when she hadn't left the bottom of the canyon in over a year.

"I wasn't hiding so much as I was, I don't know…I don't have anywhere else to go," Chooli said bluntly. "My dad died three years ago, fucking cancer. My mom passed when I was a baby. I didn't have anyone to go to. The BIA—that's the silaó, our word for the white cops on the rez—they would have dropped me in foster care or a group home or some shit. I rode down to see Noni, left the signal on the olive tree, and she met me by the river that night. I told her what was going on. She said I had a sadness in me and I needed to heal. Pretty psychic, right?" Chooli coughed a sad sort of laugh. "But she told me that she'd seen me in a vision, all that jazz. Said I could come stay with her."

Ceit considered this. "No one ever looked for you?"

Chooli glanced at her. "You think anyone really cares what happens to a rez kid? I'm sure someone knocked on a couple doors, then the silaó forgot all about it. That was three years ago. I've known I need to leave for a while now. This is a good chance. Course, I have to go give Benny his truck back, but I might detour through Vegas first..." She gave Ceit a wide-eyed stare.

"Road! Watch the road!" Ceit laughed as Chooli swerved out of her lane and back in again.

"My turn," Chooli said. "What was it you and Noni did out in the orchard all the damn time?"

Ceit sighed. "You want to know for real?"

"Sure. Hit me," Chooli said.

Ceit took a deep breath. "I'm the Bandia Marbh, the reborn incarnation of the goddess of the dead. Noni was teaching me to harness my power and control my anger. She taught me how to lead and how to destroy anyone who crosses me."

She paused and glanced at Chooli, who gave her a sideways glance before straightening the truck out on the flat road again.

"Fine, don't tell me. None of my business, really. I figured you murdered someone. White people are always murdering people and then hiding out. It's the plot of every crime book ever. Or maybe you were one of those devil worshippers. That shit cracks me up."

"No. I'm not one of those," Ceit said with a smile. "I'm the one they think to worship."

*70*

ANNBETH HAD TOLD CEIT OF THE TEMPLE BACK WHEN they were together at MacLaren Hall, but she wondered if the girl would know where to go. The taxi had dropped Annbeth at the Crown Burgers at the periphery of the neighborhood where she had grown up. Despite everything, she felt a flood of nostalgia. She hadn't been home since she was eighteen, not since the temple had sent her to Los Angeles and set her to the tasks they demanded of her. At the time she'd always assumed they would ask her to come home again eventually. She had assumed so much.

The news reports were now talking Satanic worship and child sacrifices. Annbeth shivered. They weren't entirely wrong. The temple would have no qualms about hurting Alan if they thought it would subdue the one they really wanted; however, Annbeth knew that Ceit, even as she saw her last, was beyond their imagining.

Annbeth held an irreversible weight of guilt for her role with Ceit Robertson. She had once had a bond with the girl. Ceit had trusted her. So she sat near the window and reached out with her mind, knowing full well it would be only a matter of time before someone found her. She was sending out a beacon, and hopefully Ceit would find it before the temple did. It was the only way she knew to guide Ceit to where Alan was being kept. She visualized the dark stone walls of the worship hall, she conjured the scent of the sulfur resin that burned day and night at the altar. She called to Ceit, hoping she would listen and trust her one last time.

*71*

"HERE?" CHOOLI ASKED. "YOU'RE TOTALLY SURE?"

Ceit nodded. She needed to walk the rest of the way to where Alan was being kept. She could feel him. And even stronger than that, she could feel a humming that was growing louder and louder as Chooli approached the area. There was something else too, a static sort of conversation. She couldn't make out the words. It sounded the same as the telephone lines in a storm. It was familiar, though, and Ceit had an idea who was sending the message, whatever it was meant to tell her.

"Look, I'm going to hang over there," Chooli said, pointing to a little diner on the corner. "I'm going to eat and wait. I'll leave the truck parked here. Even if I leave the diner, go to the truck, and I'll come back. You sure I can't come in there with you?"

Ceit nodded. "I'm sure. I have all the help I need." She lightly rubbed Amon's locket, knowing the time was coming when she was going to test his promise.

Chooli was hesitant. "Okay. Hágoónee', ak'is. Nik'eh hojidlį̈į̈ doo."

Impulsively, Ceit hugged Chooli. The girl hesitated and then wrapped her arms around Ceit.

"Thank you for the blessings, Chooli, but God has no part in this," Ceit murmured in her ear.

Chooli pulled back and grinned. "Okay then, nizhóní, burn that shit down."

*72*

ANNBETH RECOGNIZED THE TWO WOMEN STANDING in the doorway of the Crown Burger. It hadn't taken them long to find her. Mayellen was Annbeth's age. They had grown up together, walked to school together, been in the same classes, often reading the same books and studying together. Mayellen had never been a real friend though. She was pious in a way that had always made Annbeth uncomfortable, even when she was a kid. The other woman was older. Annbeth recognized her as a senior priestess. Laurali was her given name, but the priestesses took temple names that were used in the community. Hers was Adria. The priestess smiled, the same expression one might give a misbehaving child, and motioned for Mayellen to follow her to Annbeth's booth.

"Hello, sister," Adria said softly.

"Adria, Mayellen." Annbeth nodded her greeting.

"It's Charna now," the girl formerly known as Mayellen said, straightening her back with pride.

"You got your temple name. Good job," Annbeth said with

sincerity. It had been one of the things denied her when she was sent to Los Angeles, and one of the most painful to give up. Having a temple name meant you were forever tied to the temple, the Maga and the priestesses were your family, and you were never left aside or forgotten, like Annbeth had been.

"We owe you a thank you," Adria said. "We felt your signal from the worship hall. The girl will certainly feel it too. You are helping her find us. The Maga will thank you."

Annbeth felt a twinge of deeply repressed emotion. Maybe she could take her place back in the community. Maybe they would forgive her actions. Maybe if Ceit showed, maybe she would see... She shook herself out of the reverie. Ceit would never serve these people; she was going to destroy everyone who got in her way. Annbeth knew that if Ceit could sense her, the path she was laying was to the temple's destruction.

"Is the boy okay?" Annbeth asked.

Charna looked uncomfortable, and Adria gave Annbeth a pursed-lip smile. "So far, he's fine. Considering who his sister is, I think we all expected a bit more. Fussy little thing, really."

"You think Ceit Robertson is going to want to lead the temple now that you did this? Think this will bring her around?" Annbeth asked flatly.

Adria cocked her head and considered Annbeth's words. "We wanted her to come here willingly. We wanted her to trust us, believe in us. That was your job, and you failed. Because of you, Director Carabus was arrested in Los Angeles. The rest of the LA team is still in hiding. More importantly, you helped the girl escape. You betrayed the temple. You fed her lies about us."

Annbeth laughed. "I didn't feed her anything. You should hope she never shows up at your door. That girl is beyond all of you. It's comical you think you could ever control her. Your parlor tricks, the missionaries, the games, all that bullshit—she is ten times where you are, and she's still a child."

Adria held out a hand. "It's time for you to come with us. Don't make me call the others. We have a couple cops in our fold. We could take you in that way, but I think it's nicer for you to just come along."

"No need to call out the troops," Annbeth said, standing. "Why do you think I came here? I hope Ceit does hear me, and I hope she finds you all. If you were smart, you'd set the boy out on the road and let her find him and then leave before you have to face her. You have no idea what you are dealing with."

"I think we do," Adria said, and held the door open for Annbeth as they walked her to their car. "The Maga is waiting for you."

73

THE STATIC CALL WAS GETTING LOUDER THE FARTHER
Ceit walked into the neat little enclave of houses. It was Annbeth—
she knew this with certainty now—but it was a different woman
than she had known at Mac.

"*Caution. He is here. They wait for you. Destroy it all, destroy it
all...*"

Ceit realized that Annbeth had been as much a prisoner as she
had in those years at Mac. This group was far beyond the Society.
The old women on Sinder Avenue lived in superstition and fear
but never harmed another. They clung to their ancient, useless
ways but bowed to the forces of the ocean and land. This place
stunk of dead things and rotten wood. This place felt as though the
very streets might collapse beneath her to reveal a teeming den of
pus and mold.

Alan was somewhere below her; Ceit knew this. She was looking for the entrance to the worship hall and the underground.
As the pulse in her ears grew to an almost unbearable pitch, Ceit

stopped and looked around. No one was watching. No curious heads were peeking out windows, even though these houses were most certainly temple members'. No, they would all be underground, waiting for her, holding their bait, thinking she would acquiesce and obey them when caught. Ceit smiled. They had no idea who she had become.

It was time—time to call her demons. With a deep breath, she took the locket from around her neck and opened the reflective glass to the sun, catching the light.

"Amon. It is time," she whispered.

*74*

THE MAGA SAT ON HER THRONE AT THE HEAD OF THE worship hall. The temple members huddled together on the floor, candles burning in their wall sconces and battery-powered lamps encircling the room. The whole congregation was there. Families lined the hallway and spread down into the darkness of the tunnels beyond. The people looked scared. *As well they should be*, the Maga thought as she nodded at Adria and Charna and stood, her arms reaching toward Annbeth.

"There she is," the Maga said, her voice silky and deep, like the rumble of thunder in the distance. "Come, my sister. We have missed you."

Annbeth stumbled forward, stepping over women and children who looked up at her, wide-eyed and uncertain. Behind the Maga in the dark corner of the worship hall, a little boy was huddled, a blanket around his shoulders. His face was pale, and Annbeth could tell he was crying. A sniffling sob shook from his form. She stopped, staring at the boy.

"Alan?" she said quietly, and the boy looked up, trying to figure out where the voice came from.

The Maga stepped forward and wrapped her arms around Annbeth. Her hands were like ice, chilling Annbeth's skin even through her clothes. "See, he's fine," she whispered. Then the Maga stepped back, placing her hands on Annbeth's shoulders, inspecting her at arm's length. "But you look not so good, hon. That hair is doing nothing for you, and there is evidently lots to eat in LA." She laughed at her own joke.

Annbeth stared in the face of the woman who had raised her, the woman who had stood as the living incarnation of everything spiritual for as long as Annbeth could remember. Only now she saw no wisdom. She saw a tired face, lined and pale. She saw two glittering coal eyes, cold and dead.

"Alan, your sister is coming for you," Annbeth said loudly, staring into the Maga's eyes as she spoke. The boy whimpered behind her.

"I certainly hope so," the Maga said brightly. Letting go of Annbeth, she turned and retook her seat. "We owe you thanks for your help in bringing her here. It was a bit dim, but even we heard your beacon. Unfortunately, it doesn't erase your transgressions entirely. I trust you remember what our teachings tell us about traitors?"

"Let it be flung into the outer darkness, among the dead gods and other useless wreckage," Annbeth intoned. She had recited the Codex Gigas nearly every day of her childhood and taken every word for truth.

"Very good, child, very good. Do you remember any more?" the Maga hissed, her voice barely audible. Annbeth could feel the figures huddled together on the floor of the temple trembling. Their energy sent a vibration through her that was unnerving and energizing. These people were afraid, and there was great power in fear.

"The blood-splashed jaws will rend him limb from limb," Annbeth repeated, visualizing the words on the page.

"Then you know what happens next," the Maga said quietly. She waved a hand, and two priestesses in dark robes approached. Annbeth knew the athame was razor sharp and reserved for only the highest blood magic.

At Annbeth's feet, a woman wrapped her arms around two small children, hiding their eyes in her chest. All around the room, she heard a hushed exhalation. No one had been punished for treason in their lifetime. Annbeth knew of it only from stories. She could feel their fear rolling in waves across the room. It lapped at Annbeth's ankles, and she felt her arms and legs grow numb as the priestesses held the length of polished stone on which sat the athame in front of the Maga.

"Alan," Annbeth said loudly and deliberately. "Your sister will take you away from these people. She will come for you. I need you to hide your eyes now."

Behind the Maga, the boy whimpered. His face hidden in shadow, Annbeth could not tell if he obeyed her request.

The Maga stood, taking slow and deliberate steps toward Annbeth, her voice intoning the words of the Codex Gigas, the darkness pulsing with the chant.

"Blessed are the strong, for they shall possess the earth. Blessed are the powerful, for they shall possess the earth. Blessed are the bold, for they shall be masters of the world. Blessed are the victorious, for victory is the basis of right. Blessed are the iron handed, for the unfit shall flee before them. Blessed are the dead defiant, for their days shall be long in the land."

As she reached Annbeth she looked into her eyes, and then she motioned to the stone floor.

"Kneel, sister. We send you with the ultimate blessing of our people, that of the dead defiant. Do not be frightened by the shadows."

Annbeth met her gaze and stared back, unblinking. "Blessed are the mighty minded, for they shall ride the whirlwinds."

The Maga looked confused for a moment, but Annbeth could feel the pulse of the energy that was amassing at the entrance to the underground. She recognized Ceit's voice in her head.

*"Tell Alan to run."*

## 75

AMON STOOD IN FRONT OF CEIT IN ACID-WASHED jeans, a faded *ThunderCats* T-shirt with the sleeves rolled to the top of his deathly pale biceps, and a blue pinstriped suit vest. On his head sat a porkpie hat in loud yellow plaid. His Converse sneakers were dotted with cartoon ladybugs.

"Yes, my liege? Your personal Bo Brady is reporting for duty," he said sarcastically, a delighted grin hanging on his lips.

"It's time," Ceit said simply.

"I figured as much. You look different—taller than the last time we met, and your spine is stronger. You woke up, little girl," he said with a hiss.

"Where is the entrance?" Ceit demanded.

Amon pointed across a broad parking lot to a storm drain covered in a length of construction plastic. "There's one."

"I need your friends," Ceit said, looking up at the demon.

"They are here. Open your senses, my liege. They are all around you, waiting for your command." Amon knelt in front of her and stared into Ceit's pale eyes. In his eyes, she saw shadows swirling. A clawlike hand reached into the black pupils of Amon's unearthly eyes, pulling the darkness out to the edges, until the sclera was stained with midnight.

"*Welcome, daughter.*"

Ceit jumped at the Matrarc's voice as it whispered in her ear.

"*You need only to bring the veil down between this world and the next, and the dark ones will follow.*"

Ceit nodded at Amon, and they set off to the storm tunnel, the world behind them lost to the swirling blackness of a spiraling storm. Ceit paused at the entrance, a moment of doubt appearing and then leaving just as quickly. She could feel the frightened energy of hundreds of souls. She could feel the weight of the blood magic as it stained the walls of this place. She took a deep breath, the voice of the Matrarc in her ear, and stepped into the darkness.

$$76$$

ANNBETH SANK TO HER KNEES, HER BODY OBEYING against her will. She felt the shock of the metal against the skin of her neck. Her breath stuck in her throat.

"Alan," she called out, "run!"

The Maga pulled the athame back in confusion as the crowd of people huddled on the floor began moving toward the door en masse. Annbeth's command had sparked a wave of panic. Annbeth felt the little boy streak past her, his energy waving like a flag. The Maga was jostled to the side as a woman stumbled in the dark and lost her balance, shoving through the dim light and running toward the tunnels that led to the surface.

"You push too hard, Maga," Annbeth hissed. "People cannot live in fear indefinitely."

The Maga called out to her priestesses, who struggled to move through the shifting bodies to get to the altar. A wave of icy air swept into the worship hall, knocking the candles from the sconces and sending the leather-bound copy of the Codex Gigas to the ground. The darkness intensified.

Annbeth felt the silky hum of bodies all around her, no more substantial than air. A mass of icy-black serpents rushed past Annbeth toward the Maga. When they reached her, they started racing up her legs, winding their way up her chest and neck. The woman opened her mouth to scream, and the serpents flooded in the open cavern. Annbeth fell back, clutching at her own throat, the image from her dream playing out in front of her.

The priestesses ran back, stumbling over the blankets and cushions that lined the floor. Around the corners of the room a presence was forming, tapping at the dark volcanic rock walls, waiting to strike. As quickly as they had appeared, the thousand serpents dissipated into smoke. The Maga fell back, gasping for air.

Ceit Robertson stepped into the temple. The extinguished candles lit themselves again. The lanterns shone impossibly bright. The pale-haired girl with the odd pale eyes was beginning to resemble the woman she was going to become. Annbeth involuntarily croaked a sound that was neither greeting or surprise, but a sort of hail.

## 77

"SO THIS IS WHAT ALL THE HOOPLA WAS ABOUT?" Ceit said coolly. "Think you talked it up a bit much, Annbeth."

A woman in dark robes, the leader of this place—who had just felt the Rabharta slithering through her lungs and choking the life from her body—struggled to stand. *She thinks she still has power here*, Ceit realized, and smiled.

"You are home...we welcome you...we worship you," the woman stuttered madly. "We always have...We welco—"

"I'm sure you do. You have no idea what it is you worship. You read from the inconsistent words of a madman and call it truth," Ceit said, indicating the Codex Gigas that lay open on the temple floor. "You run your congregation in fear. You spill the blood of innocents. You hurt my brother."

"No, no—we never hurt him. We needed you to come to us. Please forgive us...my..." the woman stuttered.

"Amon?" Ceit called behind her. The demon stepped into the space. Gone were the ridiculous clothes and hat. He had risen to fill the room. He looked like a shadow, from which a dozen rows of razor-sharp teeth caught the light. "Are you hungry?"

"Alwayyssssss..." he hissed, all the sharpness of his voice replaced with the smooth hum of a serpent's hiss.

"You called the Sluagh that killed my mother. You drove my father mad. You took my brother. Your time here is over. You will now be a meal for Amon," Ceit said softly.

The woman's face contorted, and then she fell to her knees.

"No! Not your mother! We never called the Sluagh. We cannot. We are... I'm not... I can't. The ancient magic doesn't... Our magic is illusion, tricks. The Sluagh are older than our world. We can't call them," the woman sobbed.

Ceit considered this. "You weren't responsible for my mother?" she repeated back. The hysterical woman's reaction was entirely sincere. "Is she telling the truth, Amon?"

"She cannnottt lie to youuuu. Not nowww..." Amon hissed.

Ceit turned to Annbeth. "You helped them. You kept me in that place."

Annbeth looked up at Ceit. "I know. I can never redeem that. I didn't know..."

"Go," Ceit commanded, indicating the door. Annbeth rose as Ceit held her arms up, palms to the sky. The demon Amon fell upon the shrieking woman in the dark robes as the Sluagh and Rabharta lapped up the blood that poured from her frame.

*78*

ANNBETH FELT THE ATHAME ON HER THROAT BEFORE she saw the figure holding it. Adria pulled it across her flesh in one solid motion.

"Bitch. You brought this to us," she whispered before she dropped the athame and ran toward the distant light at the end of the underground tunnel.

Annbeth gasped. The cut of the blade reverberated through her skin, the pain beyond imagining. She felt herself sticky, warm, and her entire body humming with a newfound numbness, like static. She gasped and found no air, the blood choking her. Ceit knelt beside her, looking her in the eyes.

"I owe you a debt," the girl whispered. "I cannot save you. I command the dead but cannot stop one from crossing into my realm, not yet."

Annbeth blinked her eyes. The girl was growing dimmer and dimmer in her vision, but she stared upward, trying to focus on Ceit's face. The pain dissipated. In its place, Annbeth felt a thousand hands holding her aloft. She felt the sun on her face and was wrapped in the embrace of a thousand arms.

# 79

USING HER FINGER, CEIT DREW THE ANCIENT SYMBOL of the eternal dead in Annbeth's blood on the dying woman's forehead. The haptic circle—never ending, never broken—would guide Annbeth into the afterworld with the strongest memories of love she retained. Ceit hoped she had some from this miserable place.

"Yá'át'ééh anoonééł, adeezhí," she whispered softly.

Ceit rose and walked toward the light of day that lay at the end of the underground temple. She did not know or care what became of these people. Their leader was dead, consumed by the same darkness she'd claimed to rule over. Their false god lay crushed under the weight of the city. With each step Ceit took, the black volcanic rock of the tunnel crumbled to dust. The worship hall, with its book of lies and illusions, folded in on itself. As Ceit emerged, the darkness of Amon swept out behind her, swirling her in a sort of goodbye before he dissipated entirely. She expected she would not need him for some time, but he was well fed and would be content to wait.

Alan stood trembling and lost feet from the entrance.

Ceit crossed to him and knelt in front of her pale-eyed little brother, with his sandy hair and freckled nose.

"It's okay. I'm here now," she said before he collapsed into her arms.

# EPILOGUE

MÁTHAIR SHONA LOOKED THINNER AND SMALLER THAN she had in Ceit's memory. Ceit realized she was a bit taller than the old woman now.

"Hello, Grandmother," Ceit said, and set her duffel bag down on the steps. "Alan, go on in. Grandma prepared your room. It's all ready for you."

Alan gave her a worried glance and then walked in the door. Máthair Shona reached over and drew the little boy near. Alan returned the hug, looking up at his grandmother.

"Are you living with us, Grandma?" he asked.

"No," Ceit answered for the old woman. "Grandma is living at her own house next door. Don't worry, you'll see her all the time. Go ahead. Get settled."

As Alan disappeared down the hall, Máthair Shona opened her mouth to speak. Ceit cut her off.

"You know what is happening here. You will leave us be. You will do all the official things you are supposed to do until I am old enough to do them. We will live in our parents' house, the house we should have been brought back to long ago. You have the contact information for the child protection officer, yes?"

Máthair Shona nodded miserably. "Yes, a Karen something."

Ceit nodded and then leaned in. "Then you know you do not have a say in the matter. She is watching you, as are others." Ceit ran a finger over the locket around her neck bearing Amon's name. "I have stopped asking for permission."

"Ceit... I just hope we can... you and Alan are all I have left." The old woman's lip shook as she spoke.

"You had your reasons for shunning me, old woman, but that is long past. I am home now—I am the Bandia Marbh, and I am your Matrarc."

With that, Ceit walked past Máthair Shona and waited for her to exit. She surveyed the family room. It had been three long years since she had stepped foot in the space, and in that time the reminders of the horrors that had occurred there had been cleansed. The home felt new and full of promise. It was hers now. With a sigh, she took a seat on her throne.

# ACKNOWLEDGMENTS

ONE THOUSAND THANK YOUS TO THE TEAM AT TURNER
Publishing Company for your belief in this project. Your hard
work, your dedication and passion have driven this book from
spark to completion. Independent publishers are the heart and
soul of the industry, I am lucky to be a part of your family. Thank
you as well to Matt Snow and Paradigm Talent for your support
and hard work on this project.

My family has spent the last year mired in stories about devils,
demons and other nasty little sprites. They haven't changed
the locks on me yet and I am forever grateful for their patience
and support. Writers and artists are not islands, we only exist at
the mercy and love of those that surround us. Thank you to my
husband, son, and all my friends and family far and wide for your
love.

The inception of the idea behind Diabhal came from a docu-
mentary titled *Belief: The Possession of Janet Moses*. The devil is

many things, and it exists perhaps most strongly in our fear. Janet Moses was the victim of just this sort of devil, may we learn from her pain and treat each other and ourselves with the patience and kindness we would like to see reflected in the world.